THE DEADLY FAVOUR

THE WOLDSHEART CHRONICLES

BOOK ONE

RUTH DANES

CHAPTER ONE

Summer Solstice 2015, Castle of the Eastern Coast, the Kingdom of the Woldsheart

Narrative opened by Lady Millabess of the House of Lothwold

I smiled at the priest who had visited my guardian with view to arranging a second marriage for me. I tried to look agreeable and unconcerned whilst my heart beat furiously and my spirit was revolted by what was unnatural to me.

"Of course. I agree with you, father. I have been widowed for over two years, and whilst I still miss Horace, I know I need to do my duty and marry again. I only ask that I get to know any prospective bridegroom well."

I need to bide my time.

The priest and my guardian nodded. The latter now spoke of his other ward.

"Hawise should enter a convent. There is no point in attempting to arrange another marriage for her. I have discussed this with her, and she said she would consider it. I think the Convent of the New Moon would be best. It is not too near. She needs a fresh start."

I need to swap places with her. This is my one chance of happiness. True, her behaviour has not always been impeccable, and she should leave local society, for a while, at least, but she has not technically done anything wrong. No. I am sure that a marriage could be arranged for her. Just not with anyone too judgmental or from the neighbourhood.

"Well, if both you ladies consent," the priest concluded, "I can start making enquiries on your behalves. I know the abbess of the Convent of the New Moon well and am often called to see her on church business. Indeed, I am due to meet her on Thursday. I can discuss the possibility of Lady Hawise entering her convent then, although I cannot imagine there will be any problems. The convent has barely half the nuns and novices it had ten years ago."

"Ah, the effects of war," my guardian sighed. He pulled himself out of his sad reverie and continued the conversation. "Regarding Bessy, I will speak with my wife about a possible match with her sister's son. When you see the abbess, can you ask about her nephew and her godson? Are they still free or have they made second marriages?"

He turned to me.

"Bessy, you know we would never force you to do anything you truly did not like, but I'm sure I don't need to tell you that you cannot remain a widow forever. We all know it is your duty to marry again and to try for children once more. Our house has been depleted by the war. We need to carry on the bloodline and raise the next generation. Assuming all three of the young men we have mentioned are still unattached, you may choose whichever one you please. Indeed, if you know of a fourth single nobleman whom you like, let me or your aunt know, and we will approach his family regarding a match."

I nodded.

It's a single noblewoman that I'm interested in. One who entered the Convent of the New Moon three weeks ago. Hawise must *swap places with me. I must be with Jennet. We are soulmates. Surely, there must be a man somewhere, someone of noble blood and either of our house or an ally of ours, who could overlook her self-indulgent behaviour? She did stay a virgin until she was married; she just made up for lost time after her wedding to Adam and in her widowhood to a greater degree than most. Besides, she is pretty, sparklingly bright, if a little lazy, and she has the biggest heart in the world.*

The priest made his farewells, and I went to find Hawise, trying to look calm and unruffled. I knew my dearest friend well. She would do anything for me, just as I would do anything for her, but my plan needed to be in her interests as much as mine.

It is in her best interests to marry rather than to become a nun. Hawise loves men like I love women, and she has a greater carnal appetite than me, a greater appetite than any other woman I know. She is also fonder of luxury and less devout than me. A convent, with Jennet, would suit me very well, but she would do better to marry again.

I saw my friend sitting alone under a tree by the lake. She had been sewing, but her hands were now empty as she contemplated the idyllic view before her. She smiled upon seeing me.

I smiled back and made my way to her, noting her looks. She was decidedly pretty; short, with a curvy figure, a round face with features that harmonised well together and clear, fair skin. As I got nearer, I could also see her bright blue eyes, shining blonde hair and pink cheeks.

Even when she was fat, people still called her good-looking. She should easily be able to attract a second husband. Besides, she is witty and fun to be around. She is only three months older than me and should easily conceive. She is not two months past her twenty-third birthday and comes from fertile stock. It was the war and bad luck that took her siblings and parents, not poor health. Just like the war took my ma and pa and Horace. Just like bad luck took Adam.

I swallowed. I had to trust in a better world to come and make the best of the one in which I lived for the present.

"What is it, Bessy? You look nervous."

I sat down beside my friend and told her what had passed and what I thought we should do about it.

"Father Gudarro has just spoken with Uncle Piers. Our guardians' suggestions that I marry again and you become a nun are turning into reality. Father Gudarro will make enquiries about possible matches for me and a place at the New Moon for you. Uncle Piers will also speak with Aunt Illustra about the possibility of me marrying Aunt Ankarette's youngest boy."

My friend blanched.

"Oh Gods! Can't we put this off for a bit longer?"

"I don't think so. I am as unsuited to marrying a man as you are to celibacy. My heart is tied to Jennet, who is already at the New Moon. What I suggest we do is swap places. I go to the convent, and you marry."

Hawise's pale face turned decidedly rosy.

"A good plan, but...well, I've rather messed things up there, haven't I? I have slept with too many men and been too brazen about it. I've acquired a reputation for being overly light-hearted and fickle. I know how I'm seen. Fun to flirt with, good to lie with and agreeable to spend time with but not the right sort of woman to settle down with. No, it's alright, Bessy. Goddess knows I've enjoyed myself, but Goddess knows I will soon be paying for it. No sensible man will propose to me, and few people take me seriously."

We sat in silence for a while, listening to the distant sound of birdsong and the nearer sounds of the breeze in the trees and our thoughts.

At length Hawise spoke again.

"I have cousins who live in the Kingdom of the Franks. I could ask them if they know any suitable men for me. My Frankish is not good, we both know how little attention I gave to my lessons, but it's worth a try. They might speak our language whilst I try to become fluent in Frankish."

"You could travel by boat, we're not five miles from Port Ness. We would be parted, however."

A lump rose in my throat.

She looked at me with sad eyes.

"Ah, my friend, we will be parted whatever we do, all in the name of duty. Duty we have both been avoiding.

I could not deny it. Duty had brought us to our guardians over a dozen years ago when we both lost our parents. Their duty to their dead friends had turned into a love for us, a love that we returned. Duty had then compelled us to marry, me at sixteen and her at seventeen. We both tried to love our husbands out of duty, and we had both failed but for different reasons. I could not feel the lust for Horace that he felt for me. I could only put myself through the motions with a fixed smile on my face and be glad that his job as a warrior often kept us apart.

I was also glad that I had never conceived because I was not in the least bit maternal, shocking though this was to admit. Either I was barren, he was infertile or we had not spent sufficient time in each other's company. I was sorry when he died in battle, an arrow pierced his lung, and guilty that I had not been the wife he needed and deserved. Yet I could not help also feeling a sense of relief, relief that I would never have to open my legs to him again, accept his slimy kisses again or try to look enthusiastic whilst my heart was sinking again. This had only added to my guilt.

Hawise had fared better with Adam. They had certainly been in lust, but I doubted they were ever a couple in love. They enjoyed each other's company in a shallow sort of way, glad to see each other providing it was not for too long and they did not have to talk of anything deep and meaningful, but the bond between them was not strong. Both he and she openly took lovers and were very civil about it. Due to his position as a diplomat, he was away almost as often as Horace was. When he died of food poisoning at a faraway castle, almost a year before I became a widow, she had grieved wholeheartedly, but she knew she had not lost the love of her life. She was able to partially distract herself with food, wine, dancing and men. Indeed, she had grieved more deeply for the baby she miscarried; she managed to conceive once during her interrupted marriage.

My grief had been less painful and more quietly expressed. I met Jennet which helped enormously. She was my opposite in both her looks and personality, but we got on extremely well together. She was now eighteen years of age, albino and tiny with hair as smooth and straight as Hawise's. Her features were a little too big for her face, but in my eyes she was perfection. I was of medium size and had been praised as classically beautiful on more than one occasion. My skin was as clear as Hawise's but the colour of a roasted coffee bean, and my black hair grew in spirals and in every direction but down.

Our personalities were the opposite of the other. I was steady, she was impulsive. I applied myself, she saw no point in flogging a dead horse. She loved to talk, and I could listen to her for hours. We *had* to be together. We had both agreed to enter the same convent in order to do so before my guardians asked me if I was ready to marry again.

Hawise looked at me with her customary optimism.

"Don't look so glum, we'll think of a nobleman who might take a chance on me and find a way to get you to your Jennet. Something will come up. And we will stay in touch. Come what may, we will never lose sight of each other."

To my surprise, she was correct. An unexpected event did occur that very night, and when we learned of it the next morning, it seemed to be the answer to our prayers.

CHAPTER TWO

A messenger arrived at the castle late that evening and requested to speak with Aunt Illustra or Uncle Piers immediately. I was on my way to bed, tired from the emotion of the day, and did not pay as much attention as I might have otherwise paid to her anxious expression and rushed words. Besides, the war was still going on, and messengers were not uncommon visitors, although the hope of peace was being whispered. Peace, that is to say, a lasting peace, which would encompass all ten kingdoms, currently fighting various wars both within and between kingdoms, seemed impossible. Wars had dragged on for decades, merging into new battles as soon as they were won and lost. Peace was never permanent on these isles. It was as impossible to imagine as eternal summer or pearls growing from trees.

Hawise grabbed me the next morning, looking animated and wide-eyed with emotion. She pulled me into her closet so we could speak freely.

"What is it?" I immediately asked. "Is it bad news?"

"No, it's very good news, in fact. Very surprising news, but it might just be the solution we are looking for."

"You have found a husband?"

"No, and I won't need to if we pull this off. The messenger who arrived last night came to discuss exchanging hostages with the House of Malwarden in the Westlands. You know how we called a truce with them earlier this month? Well, to ensure that nobody breaks it, it has been agreed that three people from our house will go to them as hostages. In return, three people from their house will stay here.

"If I offer myself as one of the hostages, I would not need to either enter a nunnery, just yet, or try for a second marriage. I would be doing something useful instead of just hanging around the castle, and by the time I return, I should stand a better chance of finding a husband. From what the messenger said, it's likely I would be there for several months to a year. People will have forgotten about my wild behaviour by then, plus I will be raised in their esteem by making a sacrifice for the good of Lothwold. You can go to the convent in my stead. You would also be doing something more worthwhile than killing time here."

I stared at her open-mouthed. When Hawise stirred herself, she could be brilliant. The trouble was, she rarely saw the need to do so. She had been the despair of our tutors when we were growing up. I had to confess to myself that I occasionally resented that she could excel whenever she chose, whereas I could only do well at my studies, and later acquire a reputation for cleverness, if I worked very hard.

"That's an inspired idea, but isn't it children who are exchanged?"

"Yes, but no-one wants to send their children some two hundred miles away, far into enemy territory, especially while fighting continues. There are other battles being fought besides our quarrel with them. I saw our aunt trying to raise the subject with more than one parent today. They were all in tears. Besides, there's no rule that only children can be exchanged. It's just tradition."

"Oh Hawise, would you really do this for me?" I was deeply moved.

"Of course I would. I would also do it for my own benefit and for the good of the House of Lothwold. I may even say for the good of us all, if it leads to a lasting peace."

"You would be living with the enemy. You would be at their mercy." My conscience compelled me to state the obvious.

"It is in the interest of my captors, or hosts, depending on how you see the situation, that I and the children who are sent be well treated. The situation will not last for ever, and what they do to us, we can do to their kin."

I admired her courage but could not help thinking of the gory tales that had met my ears, some of which I knew were true.

It was true it was in everyone's interests to ensure that hostages were treated humanely, but such treatment was only highly likely and not guaranteed. I knew of exchanges involving different houses where hostages had been beaten and shackled. The worst tale I had heard of concerned the head of a fourteen-year-old boy being sent to his godfather after a treaty was not honoured. I knew it was true. It was a famous story.

However, that happened over thirty years ago and in Doggerdale. That's a different kingdom and over fifty miles away. Those involved with the murder paid with their lives, and nobody approved of what they did. People learned from them that such cruelty does not pay. That atrocity will keep my friend safe because nobody wants it to happen again.

Hawise was in high spirits, her preferred state of mind.

"If you are in agreement, Bessy, then let's find our aunt and uncle now before they persuade people to hand over their children. The messenger said that the formal exchange of hostages must take place a fortnight yesterday and at Elf's Clearing in Basset's Wood."

She named a well-known place, said to be touched by magic, which was technically in the Woldsheart but some hundred miles away and not held by the House of Lothwold. Neither of us had been to the wood, never mind to the clearing. It was considered neutral territory and often used to hold ceremonies between different houses or kingdoms, such as the exchange of hostages.

"If you are sure that you are willing to take this risk, then yes, I agree and I thank you. I thank you from the bottom of my heart for doing this."

She nodded, now a little less joyful. The enormity of what she had suggested was beginning to sink in. However, she said no more, and we went to find our guardians.

By good luck, we found Aunt Illustra and Uncle Piers talking together in the herb garden. Nobody else was present, and we seized the opportunity. We greeted them, and Hawise told them her plan.

They stood in stunned silence for some seconds whilst they tried to digest her unexpected suggestion. Cold sweat spread under my armpits. We needed this to work, yet I feared for my friend if she put herself at the mercy of an enemy, far from all of us.

"Well," my aunt said at last, "I don't see why you should not do this. It is unusual to send an adult but kinder than sending a child. We were not specifically bidden to send only children, merely to send three souls of noble blood. You would be far away, but you would return within twelve months, at most. It would not harm your chance of joining Bessy at the nunnery. What do you think, Piers?"

"Or we could look for a husband for me," my friend suggested before he could reply. "By then, people will have forgotten my... wildness, and I will be held in higher respect for offering myself."

"Is that your primary motive for offering to go?" Our uncle tried not to smile.

"No, but I do confess it is a motive."

"We'll be lucky to get anyone to give up their children without bribery," he continued. "I need not state how bad our finances are. This castle costs a fortune to maintain in these troubled times. We need not bribe ourselves to give up Hawise, much as we will miss her, and it sets an example to everyone else."

He turned to Hawise.

"You and Bessy are both of age, and really, your aunt and I are guardians in name alone. We will help you in whatever way we can, be it finding husbands or speaking to abbesses, but you must both do what you believe is right. We only insist that you follow the dictates of the law and propriety, and put the interests of Lothwold first."

"I believe it is right for me to go to the Convent of the New Moon," I said. "I do not feel inclined to marry again. Instead, I feel drawn to the religious life. I believe I could do more good for our house there, through good works and prayers, than I could by taking a second husband and trying for children again. I did not conceive once with Horace. Who is to say I am not barren? My parents only had me after years of marriage, and they were both only children. Nobody could say I come from fertile stock."

"And I believe I am not suited to becoming a nun," my friend cut in before I could run on any further and make our argument look weak. "I should like to marry again, and briefly sacrificing myself as a hostage will raise my value in everyone's eyes."

After exchanging a long look, they gave us their blessing.

Arrangements were made at a startling speed after that conversation. Uncle Piers contacted the priest to tell him that Lady Millabess would no longer require a husband because she intended to become a nun. Aunt Illustra and I wrote to the abbess of the Convent of the New Moon with my intention. We received her reply within three days, and I was invited to stay for six months. If I still believed that I had a vocation at the end of that time, I could begin my novitiate.

Two sets of parents were persuaded to give up their children. A boy of nine and a girl of seven, both of Lothwold and highborn but not related to each other, were prepared for their fate. My uncle was right in saying that Hawise's leaving set an example. It was doubtful if anyone would have volunteered without her offering herself first. She was also correct in that it raised her value in people's eyes. I saw her being looked at and overheard her name in conversation. Usually, she was occasionally noted for her looks and only ever mentioned either as a loose woman or as an amiable companion. Now, people gazed at her in surprise and respect and constantly talked about her in the most admiring terms.

The messenger left our castle the second morning after her arrival, promising to return when the details of the handover had been finalised. We bade her farewell before my aunt turned to Hawise and me, advising us on what we should pack for our new lives.

Hawise's blue eyes met my black ones. I knew my expression was identical to hers.

My Gods, this is all becoming very real!

The following days flew by at a frightening speed. We settled our affairs. I received a list of what I needed to pack for the convent. I smiled as I read it. Few convents were particularly strict these days. By reading through the lines, I could see I would not be giving up every comfort I had become accustomed to. Besides, rank was considered in the monastic world as well as in the secular, albeit not to the same extent.

Hawise and the two children, Lord Drogo and Lady Rosamund, were told to pack what they might need for the next six months, in terms of considering winter as well as summer clothing. Everyone knew how to read between the lines and to ensure that nothing was to be taken that was shabby or unbefitting for a noble. It was every hostage's duty to dress and behave in a manner that reflected well upon them and their house.

We said goodbye to our friends and adoptive family. They were grateful for what Hawise was doing, and they also approved of my decision. We accepted their praise with increasingly tight smiles as the enormity of what we had agreed to do became harder to ignore.

Finally the day arrived. On 5th July Hawise set off for the Westlands with Lady Rosamund, Lord Drogo and a party of servants, guards and diplomats. They would reach Elf's Clearing the following day, by which time I would be in the convent and reunited with my Jennet.

She looked at her most beautiful as she stood in the bright sunlight. The sun turned her hair to gold under a fine veil, and it made the rubies on the pins that held it and her hair blaze. She wore a girdle decorated with the same stones and a silk kirtle to match the jewels. Underneath, she wore a pale blue shift which made her eyes look bluer than ever.

The only thing to mar this pretty picture was the terror in her eyes. Her posture was as erect as a lady's should be, and she smiled serenely, yet her eyes revealed what she really felt.

Gulping back tears, I pulled her into my arms for a last farewell. The whole castle had gathered outside to see the party off. Many were openly weeping.

"Adieu, and I will write as soon as you confirm that you may receive letters from me. You know the convent's address."

"I *will* write. If I cannot write to you, I will send a message via our guardians. Farewell, Bessy."

She released me before we could both break down. Uncle Piers made a speech that I could not follow, I felt too sick, and they boarded their dragons. With a blast of trumpets, the party headed west.

Hawise was sensible and did not turn back to wave. I and many others waited until they had flown out of sight before turning round and slowly heading inside.

"Well, Hawise has surpassed my expectations of her," one elderly matron remarked to her friend. "I always thought she was a good-natured sort of young lady, but not one who would put herself out like this."

"Maybe this will be the making of her?" her companion suggested.

"I wonder what the House of Malwarden will make of *her*."

They linked arms and moved out of my hearing.

CHAPTER THREE

Narrative continued by Lady Marjory of the House of Malwarden

I awoke on the morning of 4th July to my son's coughing and my hammering heart. Bran, born with near-useless legs some thirteen years ago, thanks to my futile attempts to get rid of him. He was a source of much of my pride and joy, and the source of most of my guilt. His constitution was not bad, apart from his disability, but he could not go east to Elf's Clearing, let alone go to the Castle of the Eastern Coast, a place I had not heard of a fortnight ago.

No. He must not. He is too ill, and how will he cope without me? He is far too vulnerable.

I immediately got up and fetched him a drink to soothe his throat. He took it with shaking hands, and it eased his cough.

"Thank you, Mumma," he whispered. "If I take the herbs with me, I will be quite well in the Woldsheart."

I shook my head vigorously.

"No, my son, you must not go. You are barely well enough to leave this room, let alone to offer yourself as a hostage. It does not have anything to do with your legs," I cut him off before he could make his familiar protest about being overprotected. "It has everything to do with your cough, your sore throat, your fever and your tiredness."

"But I must go! The council struggled to come up with three hostages. It took days to agree upon me, Lord Ness and Lady Lithuise. Nobody else is suitable. There are so few of us. Besides, they are only nine years old. I will be fourteen in October. I should be setting them an example and be there to guide them as best I can."

This was true. War and its children, famine, disease and lawlessness, had cut many lives short. No family was untouched, although some had been affected far more severely than others.

I was relatively lucky. (I had to remind myself of this frequently.) I was thirty-one years old, and I still had my mother, a cousin and my parent's ward, both of whom were like brothers to me, Cerys who was like a sister to me, my son and my two girls, as well as wider family and friends. I was healthy, albeit prone to bitterness and dwelling on the past. I was a noble-woman and lived in Castle Malwarden, paradise compared to the cottages of the peasantry and as secure as anywhere might be in wartime.

Things could be worse. Chin up. Keep going. There is no alternative, Marjory.

Bran handed the empty cup to me, and I looked at him tenderly. Without a loving eye, he was not much to look at, being of average height, skinny and sallow-skinned with a large nose, a prominent chin and straight, dull blond hair. However, his eyes were the colour of melted chocolate, framed with long lashes, and they revealed more than a hint of his intelligence and determination.

My son not only had a disability dragon, Desdemona, like anyone would in his situation, but he expertly trained hawks, and he also trained cats, as far as anyone can train such capricious creatures. Magdalena was his favourite hawk, and she obeyed him almost as perfectly as Desdemona did. He wanted to train hawks as a profession, he did not wish to inherit my business, and so I had apprenticed him to Master Evan, whose expertise was legendary.

I could feel confident of his future there, but I wondered about his domestic future. His many friends overlooked his disability, but would a wife?

Can he even father children? Or did my brews destroy that as well as his movement?

Trying not to cry, I bit my lip and wondered where Eluned and Isabeau were.

As if on cue, they rushed into the room, chatting and giggling as was their way. They made a beeline for their brother and made me smile.

Strangers always noticed how alike the girls looked. They both took after their father; quite tall, decidedly slender, and undeniably good-looking with curly, almost black hair, the darkest brown eyes and lighter brown skin. The three had dimples when they smiled, and the girls had rosy lips and pink cheeks. Now Isabeau had celebrated her ninth birthday almost a month ago, and Eluned would follow suit at the end of November, people who did not know us assumed they were twins, rather than the half-sisters they actually were. People also incorrectly assumed that Bran was their brother, I was the mother of all three children, and they all shared a father.

The fact that they were all so close and loving contributed to the impression I was happy to leave uncorrected, unless asked directly.

"Mumma, Bran cannot go to the Woldsheart and be a hostage!" Isabeau exclaimed. "He is far too ill." She turned to the boy she called her brother. "You should stay here and rest. Maybe Eluned and I could go in your place. It would be an adventure. We would have to be together for it to be a proper adventure and not just scary," she hastily added.

Her sister did not look too sure of this. As a rule, Eluned was generally the more timid of the pair. At times like this, she might also be considered the most sensible.

"What does Pa say?" she now asked. "Does he think any of us should go? He will be here soon, later this morning. I heard Granny say so."

Gethin. Their father. The man who should have been Bran's father. The man who should have been my husband and who was now a monk, which prevented him from being anyone's husband. However, it had not made him celibate. The Fornicating Friar was one of the milder nicknames attributed to him.

"I will speak with your pa, and we shall see what he says." I included Bran in calling Gethin his pa because his father had died before his birth, and all his family had ever done for us was to have provided sufficient funds for me to start trading in cloth. In contrast, Gethin visited us as often as he decently could and had encouraged Bran's love of animals. It was he who suggested that I apprentice him to Master Evan. The bond between the pair was strong, although only his daughters called him Pa in public.

"I will leave the three of you to amuse yourselves. Bran, don't overexert yourself. Girls, don't torment your brother, and leave him alone if he tells you he wants to rest."

With that, I left the chamber and headed to either find Gethin or to learn when he might arrive. I did not bother to look in the mirror, but I unconsciously fiddled with my hair and clothing whilst I walked. I did not need a looking glass to tell me that my nose would have only looked well on a hawk or that my skin was sallow. I also knew that I was too thin for my medium height, and I looked older than my years. Gethin was one of the few people to see beauty in me, but even I liked my hair. It was a glossy dark auburn and hung thick and curling to my waist. Gethin had also once compared my eyes to liquid silver.

You'll have to do. You are dressed neatly and appropriately for your rank. Do not ask for anything more.

I swallowed. Asking for more had set my life down its bizarre and painful path some fifteen years ago.

I soon saw Gethin. He stood in the Great Hall, talking to a couple of young men in his usual cheerful manner. My heart leapt. He was still handsome at thirty-seven; women still flocked to him. The monk's undyed robe did little to hide his dark good looks, for dark he certainly was. His skin was a deeper brown than his daughters', whose mothers had both been milky-skinned.

What would Eluned and Isabeau have looked like if I had borne them? My complexion is dark for a redhead but much fairer than his. Would they both be as pretty as they are? Both their mothers were praised for their looks, but they do take after him.

I pulled myself back into the present. Asking 'What if' never helped any situation.

Gethin saw me approaching him and said a few words to the other men. The three of them turned to me and bowed. I curtseyed. I was not on intimate terms with the other two men, so this greeting with a 'Good day' would have to suffice. I had no official reason to touch them any more than I had Gethin.

The man I thought about hourly smiled at me broadly. I had to remind myself that he smiled at everyone: men, women and children.

"I am pleased to see you again, my lady." His voice was as deep and rich as ever with the lilt of the south from where he came. "Are you and the children well? I hear that Lord Bran is not."

We could not be on first-name terms in public any more than I could have my heart's desire, although we always spoke freely in private.

"Isabeau and Eluned are as well as ever, merry and enjoying excellent health. Bran is still suffering from the illness my mother told you about in her last letter."

His expression became grave.

"Pray take me to him, my lady. Please excuse us, my lords."

I took him to the chamber where Bran lay in bed, looking wan and exhausted, whilst his sisters were perched on its edge, chattering away. When they saw Gethin, the girls squealed and threw themselves at him. Bran half-rose and smiled.

He greeted them all like a father after a lengthy absence. He asked Bran how he did before declaring solemnly:

"You are in no fit state to go out with your hawks, let alone to go as hostage to an enemy castle some two hundred miles away."

"What can we do?" Bran demanded hoarsely. "If we do not offer three hostages, we provoke further bloodshed by not honouring our word."

"We can go," Isabeau suggested.

"Gethin is your birth father and, as the daughters of a monk, you may not be considered," I explained.

"However, there is no rule that a man of the cloth may not be a hostage in these circumstances." Gethin turned to me. "I am of noble blood, and although I was born into the House of Pendroch, I entered the church in the House of Malwarden, therefore I am of both houses. I will take Bran's place, keep an eye on Lithuise and Ness and ensure that the truce is kept."

We all stared at him open-mouthed. Such a solution had not occurred to me because it was tradition, but not law, that children were exchanged as hostages. I had never heard of an adult being used in such a way. If I had, I would have taken my son's place in a heartbeat.

"I've been thinking about this since I received your mother's letter. My mind is made up. I will inform everyone of my decision and go with Ness and Lithuise to Elf's Clearing tomorrow morning. I see no objections. No other suitable children are at hand, and it makes sense to have an adult there."

I need not describe what I felt nor how many tears I shed. My gratitude filled my heart and my eyes. Later on, it was also gratifying to notice how the Fornicating Friar's offer raised him in the eyes of all those seated in the Great Hall. My mother's ward, the man I called my brother, Owen, was not present, and I wondered how *he* would consider Gethin's actions. His wife, Cerys, was present, along with four of their children. They seemed as relieved and appreciative as anyone else.

I wonder what Owen told her about what he, Matthew and Bernard did fifteen years ago.

I inwardly shook myself. Bernard had been dead these past

twelve years, and both his wife and unborn child followed him less than a year later. Matthew died, childless and already a widower, in the same battle as Bernard. We had made it up, as far as I could forgive, by the time they died, and that must suffice.

That evening Gethin pulled me to one side so we could have one last private conversation before he left. We spoke of the children, and I thanked him once more for what he was doing. He looked a little sheepish.

"I confess I have another motive, my Marjory."

"Oh?"

"Yes...To save Bran is my main motive and is sufficient reason for me to go. To support the two children is another, but there is a third reason which makes me glad to have the opportunity to get far away from here."

He discreetly glanced about us before continuing in a whisper.

"I have made the Westlands too hot to hold me. I need to flee to save my life."

"Eh?"

He blushed. A rare occurrence but an endearing one.

"I know what my nicknames are. We both know how I have been indulging myself over the years. You, may the Gods bless you, took in the two most delightful outcomes of my...my lack of respect for my vows of celibacy. Now I am paying for it."

"You have the pox?"

"No, I had one dose of something milder a dozen years ago, got physic and learned to be more careful, just as I learned to be more careful after Gwenllian and Megan of Merendysh conceived. The problem is that the church authorities are clamping down on the behaviour of its clergy. I was spoken to discreetly a fortnight ago. My activities over the years have been noted. No more blind eyes will be turned. The old penalty of castration for fornication by a celibate will be enforced. It isn't just fornication that they'll be cracking down on; it's everything indulgent, be it food, wine, clothing or pastimes. All the rules we have happily ignored for nigh on a century will soon be strictly enforced."

I was too shocked to speak for some moments.

"But you are not a rapist, you do not force yourself on anyone. Your partners are willing and not young girls. Oh, I never like to hear about it, but you do no harm. Why is the church taking such a hard line on this when they have been willing to look the other way for decades? And not just regarding sex but regarding how austere monasteries and convents are. Everyone knows that the rules are bent to make clerical life bearable. Who would take religious vows if they were not?"

"That gentleman's agreement will very soon become void. I and, from what I understood from Abbott Morgan's hints, many others, will suffer the severest penalties if we continue to behave as we have."

"Why?"

He shrugged.

"I don't know. These puritanical fancies take over public and private life at times. Generally, whenever society undergoes a massive change, people become more moralistic, and the talk of lasting peace might lead to a massive change. Would you not say that people are more judgmental than they were even a year ago?"

"Yes, I agree, but that doesn't explain why you need to run away. Why didn't you just promise to Abbott Morgan that you will behave better in future? Will the rules apply retrospectively?"

"He thinks not, but I might still be investigated, and if I am found wanting... He advised me to leave the Westlands, if at all possible. He suggested a trip to the Emerald Kingdom, then I received your mother's letter."

"You must go. You must go tomorrow. I could not bear it if anything happened to you."

"Oh, my Marjory, when I think how forgiving you have been over these years! All you have done for my daughters, me and their mothers."

"I broke our vow first. I had less to forgive. They are now our daughters, just as Bran is our son."

"Bran was the result of your breaking your vow. Such a happy outcome. What was there for me to forgive?"

His voice cracked. I heard people talking in the distance. We would not be alone for much longer. He knew this too.

"Farewell," I whispered fiercely. "You are the best of men, and we *will* meet again one day. Even if I have to walk to the East Coast of the Woldsheart."

"Do not put yourself in danger by following me, my angel. Abbott Morgan thought I should leave for a year or so, not for eternity. I will come back. In the meantime, I will do something more productive and noble than swiving, and you will continue to be the excellent woman that you are, mother to our three, comfort and help to your family and the head of a successful business. As I tell you every time we part, one day I will come for you, Marjory. As soon as I can, I will. Adieu."

With that he quickly bowed, kissed my fingers and left me. I spun on my heel, away from him and from the approaching talkers. We both knew he would come to me, to the children, whenever he could, but he could never come frequently nor stay for as long as we wished.

The next morning we said our public farewells along with every inhabitant of Castle Malwarden. It felt as though people were stealing sly glances at us, but that may have been my fancy. Officially it was all so long ago. At any rate, almost everyone wept, and we sent them off with as much pomp as we could muster. The parents, nurses and siblings of the two child hostages wept the most. My heart broke for them.

Thank the Gods Bran is safe here, and his fever is not so serious as to endanger his life. Give it a week, and he will be back to normal, flying on Desdemona, training his animals and laughing with his friends. Oh, let Gethin come back as soon as possible, and let it be safe for him to do so!

We expected the hostages from the Woldsheart to arrive either late in the afternoon or in the evening of the following day. All we knew was to expect three people of noble blood and from the House of Lothwold. As was usual in these circumstances, we had not been told the names or ages of those involved. I could only assume they would be children and wondered how they would react when they saw that we were exchanging Gethin for them. I smiled inwardly when I imagined their surprise and hoped that sending an adult would not cause any difficulties.

We were surprised when we saw the hostages from Lothwold. Scouts had spotted their party, and everyone who could gather to greet them did. At that time, the Westlands were under an interregnum and ruled by a council. The House of Malwarden was headed by Owen. He had come to my parents as a ward when he was ten after both his parents, the Lord and Lady of Malwarden, died. The house was governed by my parents and other adults on the understanding that Owen would take over upon turning twenty-one, which he did. He and Cerys stood a little away from the rest of us, to be the first to speak with the hostages as the Lord and Lady of Malwarden. I stood slightly further back with my nieces and nephews and the rest of my family.

We heard the procession before we saw it. First we saw the guards, then the diplomats and finally the three hostages. They consisted of a boy who looked about the same age as my girls and a slightly younger girl. Both children were quiet and still, but they looked terrified. I felt for them. The third hostage, to everyone's amazement, was a woman who appeared to be in her early twenties. She was as richly dressed as the children and seemed to be comforting them.

"Is the blonde woman in red a hostage?" my mother whispered to me. "She does not look like a diplomat or a servant, she is as well dressed as the children. She cannot be their nurse."

"She must be. Look at the sheen on her clothes and the jewels on her girdle. She has to be a noblewoman. They must have sent an adult, just like we did. What a coincidence!"

"I wonder why she has been sent, or why she volunteered.

Surely, a woman of her age and position should be married with children? I cannot see if she is wearing a necklace or not. She is clearly no nun, being dressed in civilian clothes like that."

There was no time for me to reply. Silence quickly fell as my brother and my sister-in-law stepped forward.

The three hostages were led to them by the most senior Lothwold diplomat. Everyone bowed or curtseyed, almost as one body. I was pleased to notice how elegant Owen and Cerys looked. It was so important to make the right impression.

"Sir, I bid you welcome to Castle Malwarden. I am Lord Owen, and this is my wife, Lady Cerys."

"My lord, my lady, I thank you. My name is Guy of Lothwold. May I present three children of Lothwold? Lady Hawise, Lord Drogo and Lady Rosamund. Gethin the Monk, Lord Ness and Lady Lithuise have been accepted into the House of Lothwold and will soon be at the Castle of the Eastern Coast, if they have not already arrived."

The hostages stepped forward and either bowed or curtseyed when the diplomat said their name. I looked at Lady Hawise more closely. She was undeniably a pretty woman who held herself admirably, but I could see tension in her jaw and fear in her eyes. She was wearing a necklace, to indicate a marriage, and it was wrapped in black ribbon to show she had since been widowed.

"We accept Lady Hawise, Lord Drogo and Lady Rosamund. Pray enter our castle."

Owen offered Lady Hawise his arm, which she took with a charming smile, and led her into the castle. Cerys took the hands of the shaking children and spoke kindly to them. The welcome ceremony now over, we followed them inside.

My family and I had discussed what to do with the hostages. As was customary, they would be raised with other children the same age as them in the castle. The boy would take lessons with Isabeau and Eluned, the girl would take hers with the younger children and sleep in the same room as my girls.

All four will play together and hopefully *get on. It is unlikely that Rosamund or Drogo have been hostages before, and this castle has not received any hostages for a dozen years. We none of us know exactly what to expect, which makes us all uneasy. Poor little things. I hope they settle in soon, and thank you, Goddess, for keeping Bran by me and for easing his fever a little.*

None of us had planned what to do with an adult woman, simply because we had not imagined that one would be sent to us. Me, my mother, Cerys, Owen and our cousins Madoc, Lewis and Ambrose met whilst Hawise of Lothwold was speaking with the children before dinner.

Madoc and Lewis were brothers, aged twenty-nine and thirty-two respectively, and Ambrose was twenty-four and their half-brother from their mother's second marriage. Madoc was married to Nessa, and they had three children. Lewis was married to Clementia and had four children by her.

Madoc, Lewis and Nessa were as thick as thieves. They were not especially fond parents to their children, they left them to their nurses or their tutors, and they left Clementia to her own devices and to care for her children, nieces and nephew as best she could. Clementia's heart was kind but hidden by her quietness. I always felt sorry for her. She was dull and mousy, but it was clear to see why. Nessa was as bright, dynamic and charismatic as the men, as well as being beautiful. I found Clementia good company when on her own and when she was not in a depressed mood, yet I did not like the other three. They were entertaining and witty, but I never did fully trust them. I had seen too many signs of a cold nature and a lack of respect for others over the years.

Ambrose stood apart from us, literally and metaphorically. This was typical. He was a good man, but nobody dared to go near him. In contrast to his half-brothers, he was a widower with no children.

"Well, we have quite an unexpected problem on our hands," Lewis stated. He ran a blue hand through his hair. "How do we occupy Lady Hawise? Where should she sleep at night? Who should accompany her by day?"

"We can easily resolve where she should sleep, for we have empty chambers. Let her things be taken to the Yellow Room. It is not far from our apartments or the nurseries. I expect the Lothwold children will feel safer with her close by," Cerys suggested. Her voice was as melodic as Gethin's, which was not surprising because they came from the same region, as well as the same house.

We agreed with her suggestion. After some further discussion, my mother suggested that Lady Hawise act as a demoiselle d'honneur to Cerys and help me with the business.

"She would not officially be a demoiselle. However, she can still perform the tasks that such a lady-in-waiting performs. She might also be of some use to you in your business, Marjory. Giving her two roles will keep her busy and introduce her to many people. The burden of watching her will not fall on one person."

My sister-in-law and I agreed, and I suggested that the three of us sit with her at dinner to find out more about her and to tell her what we had decided.

"We should also ask her about herself," I concluded. "We need to find out what her talents and experiences are so we can use them to our advantage."

That settled, I went to check on Bran before heading to eat. He was much recovered but not quite up to joining us in the Great Hall. He was very curious about the hostages.

"We must all make them feel welcome whilst keeping an eye on them," I told him. "The children, in particular, must be feeling disorientated and shy. Maybe you could show them and Lady Hawise your animals? Remember, although they are of an enemy house, those of our blood are at the mercy of their kin."

Bran nodded, I kissed his forehead and promised to come back later to say good night.

Lady Hawise and the children had washed and changed their clothes before entering the Great Hall for dinner. Little Lord Drogo and Lady Rosamund sat on the children's table, and I was pleased to see my girls chatting to them. One less thing to worry about.

My mother escorted Hawise to a place opposite her and between me and Cerys at the high table.

At first, I was interested in this unexpected visitor from an enemy land, and I was determined to be pleasant to her. I even felt sympathetic towards her. To be a hostage was a nerve-racking experience and one I could only be thankful not to have suffered.

By the end of the meal, Cerys and my mother liked her. I was less interested in her and struggled to maintain a calm demeanour.

I could console myself that I did not dislike her for being pretty. No. Cerys and Nessa were downright beautiful, and I loved Cerys for her cheerful personality and kind heart. I only disliked Nessa because I knew her to be two-faced and ill-natured.

I did not dislike her for being from the Woldsheart. This was a source of pride for me. I was being more noble-minded than most and refused to judge someone for their birth. Were Gethin and Cerys not from a house that had once been our enemy? Ambrose was highly unusual in that he had blood in him from all six houses of the Westlands, yet I admired him for his excellent qualities, despite not being able to make myself interact with him much.

I could even say I did not dislike her for being quick-witted and a good conversationalist. I enjoyed being around such people.

No, I disliked Hawise of Lothwold because less than an hour in her company revealed her to be a lazy woman of loose morals, who always put herself first.

I can say this without prejudice, I thought as I lay in bed that night, digesting the events of the day in order to ready myself for sleep. *She talked too much about herself, given her position, but it was as well that she did because I have the measure of her, even if the others don't. She confessed to coming here because it was that or a nunnery, then she became coy when Mumma asked why she did not make a second marriage. She said she could not be bothered to hunt for husbands. When Cerys asked if it were not necessary for the good of her house, she confessed to indolence before changing the subject.*

However, several of the men present would not call her indolent! Whispers soon went round the tables of how she is a notorious whore; she even laid with half a dozen of the men present when they were in enemy lands. To think her only response was, "I am no whore, for they are paid." And to think that Mumma, *of all people, laughed! Young Adam, who cannot be more than nineteen, actually approached her after we had finished dining, to thank her for preparing him for marriage whilst he was a prisoner in Lothwold lands three years back.*

She would even sleep with a prisoner of war, who would have been fifteen or sixteen at the time, and betrothed. He was not much older than Bran is now. If she even thinks of trying it on with him, I swear it will be the last thing she does this side of Hell.

Hot tears of outrage ran down my cheeks and made me glad to be alone. It would be a long time before I could admit to myself that I, too, had not obeyed society's rules of propriety, but I would never have had the nerve to brazen it out in front of an enemy court. I had also paid far more dearly for my sins than she appeared to have suffered.

I awoke the next day feeling calmer than I had upon going to bed, yet I still felt cold towards Lady Hawise.

Cerys grabbed me before we went in for breakfast. Her bright blue eyes were especially bright with interest.

"How do you find Lady Hawise?" she asked.

I tried to be polite because I did not want to look petty. Nobody else appeared to object to our unexpected hostage.

"Well, she certainly made an impression last night. Nobody would call her shy. Providing she doesn't seduce anyone, I don't think she'll give us any trouble."

"Aye, I agree. I will see what she is like as a demoiselle today."

We parted and did not get the chance to speak confidentially until the following morning.

I felt rather vindicated after our second meeting. Cerys reported Lady Hawise to be good-humoured and willing to get along with everyone, but rather lazy when it came to tasks that she did not like, although she had not refused to do anything asked of her.

"She rattled on about some trivia concerning fashion for a full five minutes before I changed the subject," my sister-in-law concluded. "Some of my ladies were interested, others looked bored. I believe I can say her worst faults are lechery, laziness and a shallow mind. If we can keep her from getting too close to the men, she should give us no headaches. In any case, she will hopefully be back home by the new year."

"Likely she will be too lazy to try and escape first, and I doubt she will dare flirt with Ambrose," was the only catty comment I permitted myself. Cerys laughed.

"Yes, she is unlikely to do harm, and she seems as contented as any soul could be expected to be in such a situation. The children appear to be settling in, although we had a few tears at bedtime last night. Will you talk to her about your business tomorrow, Marjory? At least she is interested in clothes, so she may be of some small use to you."

I consented, then wondered aloud at how our hostages were faring in the Woldsheart. I did not wonder what Lady Hawise thought of us, for I considered her too superficial and idle to consider anything that was not male or a new gown and right in front of her.

Chapter Four

Letter from Lady Hawise of the House of Lothwold to Lady Millabess of the House of Lothwold

11th July, Castle Malwarden

My darling friend,

I hope I find you well and that you may receive this letter. I know that Guy the Messenger will have returned to the Castle of the Eastern Coast by now, so everyone knows we are safe, but I want to write to you so we can communicate as we always did and to tell you what an official announcement may not.

I may send and receive letters. Lady Cerys and Lord Owen, the heads of this castle, have confirmed this. I trust this will reach you before you go to the convent, so I am sending it with my letter to our guardians. Lord Owen assured me that my letters will not be checked, but you will see that I am writing in the code we devised when we were girls. If I am to open my heart, I need privacy. If they do confront me, I will show them the code and your letters to me to prove we do no more harm than gossip. They have shown themselves to be decent, sensible people so far. I have to trust that my impressions are correct.

I can confirm I have lots of gossip to tell you, my dearest friend. I cannot quite believe how much my life has changed in less than a week, but I have no regrets. I truly believe I did the right thing in coming here, what is right for me, right for you and right for our house.

I am as happy as can be expected. Not as happy as I was when I was with you at the Castle of the Eastern Coast, but that situation was never going to last for ever, and I am happier here than I would have been as a nun.

I will try to describe what it is like here, the people, the place and what it is like to be a hostage. It's all so bizarre that I feel like I am dreaming at times.

To begin, our journey from home to Castle Malwarden went smoothly enough. We were all a bit dazed with shock at first, it just felt so unreal, then the children became frightened. We were all frightened, I know the tale of the Doggerdale beheading oh so well, but the adults managed to keep it together, and I distracted the children with stories. Stories which did not involve beheadings or other forms of murder.

It was so odd, so unnerving, to leave Lothwold land and to enter Sharman territory, and they are our allies. As we headed west, we passed through Ishelmer dominions, and our diplomats had to present papers to their border guard. This was even more unnerving, downright terrifying, in fact. I was never gladder that we were accompanied by an experienced guard than I was then. Luckily, the border guards permitted us to pass to Elf's Clearing on the condition we were escorted by a band of their warriors. All to be expected, although there is something very daunting about being surrounded by enemy troops, even if they are from a house of the Woldsheart. I can assure that nothing worse occurred than our dragons pulling faces at theirs and vice versa, yet such behaviour is to be expected from such childlike, capricious beasts.

We arrived in Elf's Clearing in good time, and the Ishelmer men insisted on waiting with us until the party from the Westlands came. This scared me because I did not expect them to stay, and I dreaded what they might do when united with their ally. However, I remained calm in order to keep the children calm and whispered to Guy. He reassured me that this was quite typical when hostages are exchanged.

Soon the party from Malwarden arrived. As it happened, they were also escorted by foreign troops. To my amazement, the House of Malwarden had also sent a man, as well as a little boy and a slightly younger girl. The man gave his name as Gethin, not a name I ever heard before, and to cap it all, he is a monk. He looked as astonished to see me there as I was to see him. He stared at me, and I could not help staring back, for he was a handsome man. Quite wasted in a celibate life, I'm sure.

The diplomats talked whilst the various guards loomed about ominously, and the servants tended to the dragons and children. Gethin and I gravitated towards the diplomats. They signed and sealed various pieces of parchment and took details about us and the other hostages. They all looked surprised that adults were being exchanged yet said very little, beyond that there was no rule against it, and it was a damn difficult thing to recruit hostages at this stage of a war. They all nodded and turned the subject to the likelihood of the promised permanent peace. It was interesting, almost heartening, to see how the diplomats from two warring sides regarded each other as being the same. It was clear they considered themselves to have a lot in common. I suppose they must have met each other at various times. This can hardly be the first time that their services have been called upon. To a lesser extent, the various guards seemed to be easy with each other. By the time we left, me, Rosamund and Drogo with our diplomats and their guards, servants and dragons, they seemed to be almost on friendly terms.

This would have given me food for thought were it not for the fact that we entered the Westlands very soon after, and I was acutely aware of being both in enemy territory and that I must stay calm for the sake of the children. Of course, they speak also Suvvern in the Westlands but not our dialect. I could understand people, but I had to listen carefully, and I wondered what other names I would hear for the first time. I saw mountains for the first time, and very impressive they were.

Castle Malwarden is on a larger scale than our castle, and it uses the mountains as part of its considerable defences. Inside, it is at least as comfortable as home, but things are a little different here, not only in terms of speech and some names but also clothes and attitudes.

To be frank, I felt like I had landed on another planet. I still do at times.

Somehow, we all held it together, the introduction ceremony went perfectly, and the three of us are now detained at the mercy of a lord and lady we did not know a week ago. I try not to think about that and try to concentrate on what is good.

One does not need to look far to see much that is good. Rosamund and Drogo are settling in better than I had hoped and fit in well with the other children at the castle. Lady Cerys took great pains there, Gods bless her. I am her unofficial demoiselle, and she is a pleasant, easy woman to serve. The other demoiselles are rather guarded, which is to be expected, I suppose, yet I believe they are beginning to thaw towards me. I manage to chat to them about safe topics such as dress, I don't want to appear overly proud or cold. I know I need to ingratiate myself with these people.

Lady Isolde, Lady Cerys's mother-in-law, is a quiet sort of woman but still a very charming person. One gets the impression that she has seen difficult times and plays her cards close to her chest. Given recent history, it is not only unsurprising but admirable.

I do not deal with Lady Isolde so much as I deal with her daughter Lady Marjory, who is a puzzle. This woman must be in her mid-thirties and has three children yet wears no necklace to show her being married at any time. Instead, she always wears a scarf around her neck. Fashions differ from back home, were I to describe them, my letter would be twice as long, so I will only say that I have not seen any other lady wear a scarf. She is referred to as a lady and treated like one, yet she has acquired three children without marriage. They may be adopted, but I never heard of a single woman adopting children like that. One might also ask how a woman stays single for so long without entering a convent.

Naturally, I cannot ask anyone here, and I certainly can't ask Lady Marjory. She is clever, I may say that in her favour, she runs a successful business in these difficult times, yet her manner is cool, reserved and rather proud at times. To do her justice, she does not behave unpleasantly to anyone. Indeed, she is warmth itself to her nearest connections. However, she is chilly and reserved to not only me but to some of her wider family.

Lady Marjory has cousins. Two more handsome men! They are brothers, Madoc and Lewis, and they are clearly descended from Fairy Folk, for they both have blue shimmering skin, and they are made like gods. Their tongues are gifts from the gods; they know how to converse with and charm anyone. I like them. I also like Lord Madoc's wife, a lady several years older than us, called Nessa, who also promises to be fun. Lord Lewis is married to a mouse whose name I cannot recall, and who has scarcely spoken two words to me. Indeed, I rarely see her speak to anyone.

The final person I will describe is a man I was warned about by Lord Owen. Lord Ambrose is the half-brother of Lords Madoc and Lewis and nothing like either of them. Nobody dares to go near him. Not because he is violent or lecherous. Oh, no. Nothing half as interesting as that.

Lord Ambrose is a widower of about four years. Since he lost his wife, he has not washed himself beyond his face and hands. He changes his clothes, which I assume the servants wash, but he reeks. I remember giving alms to beggars back home, but none of them smelled so bad. To save your dinner, I will not describe it beyond saying it is like a brick wall that surrounds him. One cannot get near him, which may well be the point of it.

For the rest of him, he is a quiet man, but he appears to have more about him than Lord Lewis's wife. He is said to be very clever. Having barely exchanged a dozen words with him, I can neither confirm nor refute this. He is plain next to his half-brothers and looks nothing like them. The half-brothers run some sort of business and appear to bring in the bulk of the family's wealth, while I do not quite know what Lord Ambrose does. I also do not know why someone has not insisted that he wash himself before now, but I do not despair of finding out.

I am running out of paper, dearest friend, and dare not ask for more for fear of raising suspicions. However, do not think I am being badly treated, and be assured I will write again soon.

Your partner in crime,

Hawise

Chapter Five

Narrative continued by Lady Hawise of Lothwold

I put down my pen, my hand aching from writing such a long letter, and thought hard. I honestly had run out of paper, but I had also not told my oldest friend everything. I had tried to be honest but positive, and therefore I wrote nothing that might distress her.

That is why I had not mentioned my first meal at Castle Malwarden. On entering the Great Hall, I recognised some half dozen men I had slept with when they were at the Castle of the Eastern Coast, on diplomatic missions or the like. Gods knew it had been consensual, Gods knew we had all enjoyed ourselves, and Gods knew I was not the only woman to do such a thing, yet my heart sunk to my bowels when I recognised them. I had brazened it out as best I could, it *appeared* to have worked, for nobody harassed me or mistreated me. The men and their wives were as content as I was to leave the past in the past, where it belonged. Lady Marjory was the only person to be cold towards me, yet she did not harm me.

I was relieved to see Adam and to experience gratitude and

friendly conversation from him. He well remembered the advice I had given him whilst he was being held captive at our castle. He was then betrothed and bragging about what he planned to do on his wedding night. What I heard appalled me. He had no idea of female anatomy or that it is wrong to force oneself on someone. I had pulled him to one side and gently but firmly explained the facts of life and basic courtesy. At the time, he had been wide-eyed with wonder, so I had assumed that my words had sunk in. It was clear from his behaviour to me now that they had.

That is good. You have at least one ally in him. Maybe two if he ever said anything to his wife, whose name I did not catch and whom I have yet to meet.

I was not sure what anyone else made of me. I had fended off questions about why I had not made another marriage as best I could. Time would tell if I had been successful or not.

At any rate, only Lady Marjory is cold to you. Even she is not hostile. You are a hostage from an enemy land. You cannot expect to be treated like you were back home.

The thought of home made a tear run down my cheek before I was aware of it. I had once had another home, with my parents and siblings, further along the coast, before fate took them and delivered me to Uncle Piers and Aunt Illustra. Later, another Adam and I made a home. We had been contented enough with each other, and I conceived a child off him before he suddenly died, and I miscarried. My later losses had hit me as hard as my earlier ones, albeit differently.

Castle Malwarden is not my home. Therefore, I will not feel the pain I once felt and still feel, should anyone die here or I be sent elsewhere.

This was only partly true. If Rosamund or Drogo died, it would stab me in the heart, and I knew I would feel guilty, no matter what the cause. I also knew that being sent elsewhere might involve being sent to a dungeon or a scaffold. It was a tiny possibility, yet it could not be dismissed.

I dragged myself away from this gloomy train of thought.

Be cheerful and agreeable. Go along with whatever they say. Talk only of safe topics, and take an interest in what interests them, providing it is not politics or history. That is your best route to getting through this unscathed. Do well here, impress everyone back home, and within a twelvemonth, you might be engaged to a pleasant man who suits you well. This is a little short-term pain to avoid the long-term misery of the rest of your years in a convent. You might well be better matched with your second husband than you were with your first.

You might even experience love.

With a calmer mind, I handed my sealed letters to a servant and headed outside. It was a glorious day, and I wanted to enjoy it.

Neither Lady Marjory nor Lady Cerys needed me that morning, so the time was my own. I made my way outside to where the hawks were being exercised, aware that someone, somewhere was likely to be watching me.

Being under near-constant observation was wearing and unnerving. It was also new to me. I could only truly relax in my chamber at night because I could bolt the door, yet I wondered if I could still be spied upon through small holes or by someone listening through hidden tubes. At any rate, I strongly suspected that someone had rifled through my belongings more than once.

I reacted by holding my head higher and smiling more charmingly. I must look both above suspicion and noble, the perfect lady hostage. Thus, I reached a small crowd which consisted of those dealing with the hawks and onlookers. The party included Rosamund, Drogo and Lady Marjory's children. I was pleased to note that the children appeared to be getting on well and approached them.

Lord Bran, the eldest, was sitting on his dark disability dragon and showing a fine-looking hawk to the other four. A grey and white cat stood by the dragon, also interested in what was going on. I stifled a laugh. I was no lover of cats, but I knew they were aloof creatures, so it amused me to see one showing so much interest in a group of humans.

The young party turned to me and either bowed or curtseyed. Lord Bran could only bow slightly due to his hawk and his disability. I gave a small curtsey in response and a broad smile.

"Lady Hawise," Rosamund announced in her usual enthusiastic way, "Lord Bran has got an army of animals. That hawk and that cat are only two of them. Did you ever hear the like?"

I swallowed a second laugh, but not quickly enough. The teenager turned to me.

"I assure you, it is true, madam. Magdalena here is my oldest hawk, and I own, my favourite. I have half a dozen other birds. The cat at your feet is called Gremlin. She is harder to train than any bird, aren't you, my wilful little devil? I only have three cats in all. They are part of the larger pride which live at the castle."

"What are you training the cats to do?"

"To fly and walk where I want them to. To hunt what I tell them to. To alert me to danger."

Gremlin shook her soft grey wings whilst looking at him coolly, as if to say 'Good luck with that.'

"Have you had much success there? Why do you want an army of animals?"

He smiled ruefully.

"You see my legs. I have my faithful Desdemona, of course." He patted the dragon's smooth head. "However, I would like more. I may one day need to defend myself, and I am not like other boys. Besides, I like animals. I want to get the best out of them, just like Master Evan does. One day, I hope to be able to supply people with useful cats, as well as birds and dogs."

"You aim high," was all I would say. "Rosamund and Drogo, are you also interested in birds?"

Drogo affirmed he was, and the four of us chattered for another minute or two before the younger children were called away to their lessons.

"I see you know Lord Drogo and Lady Rosamund well, to forgo their titles," Lord Bran noted.

"I do. I have known them both since their infancy."

He is an observant boy. I wonder if he has been asked to spy on me.

Before we could exchange another word, Master Evan called the apprentices to order. They obeyed and went to him. Gremlin sauntered off. The other onlookers wandered away. Having nothing better to do, I stayed.

After having sent his apprentices and animals off in different directions, Master Evan approached me. He smiled at me, and I smiled back.

Taking the opportunity to ingratiate myself, I remarked on Lord Bran's skill.

"Do you think his sisters will follow in his footsteps? It is clear that a love of animals is in their blood."

The Westlander laughed, revealing decidedly yellow teeth.

"In their blood? It is certainly in Lord Bran's blood, but I don't know about theirs."

"What do you mean?"

"Nobody told you?"

"Told me what?"

He looked around discreetly before explaining in a low voice.

"Lord Bran is the son of Lady Marjory and a fearsome, now dead warrior, from the Woldsheart. He wasn't from Lothwold or Ishelmer, he must have been from one of the other two houses of your homeland, and we were fighting against them."

"I am surprised to learn that her ladyship was allowed to marry an enemy."

My face flushed at my stupidity. Master Evan had not mentioned marriage. What if she had been raped? Luckily, he threw back his pock-marked head and laughed.

"Oh, no, she has never married. Some fifteen years ago, at the time of the millennium, she was sixteen and the beloved daughter of this castle. The family was wealthier in those days, and she was Lady Isolde and the late Lord Oliver's only girl. They had two sons, Bernard and Matthew, both older than her and a ward, now Lord Owen. The family were living in such a fine castle due to Lord Owen's inheritance.

"Lady Marjory was the pet of her family and a most delightful and favoured maiden. She had everything going for her but looks, and I will say she was so merry in those days that a man never noticed her plain face or scrawny body for more than a moment. All the castle expected her to make a great match.

"When she was sixteen, she met a man of twenty-two, who was widowed after a brief marriage which produced no surviving children. That man was Gethin of Pendroch, now Gethin the Monk and the Fornicating Friar...amongst other names. You have met him, my lady. He was exchanged as a hostage, you would have seen him in Elf's Clearing."

I was surprised to hear this and eager to hear more.

"Yes, I remember him well. I was taken aback to see another adult."

"Well, we're firm allies with the House of Pendroch these days, but back then we were on much cooler terms. We were no longer enemies, but after a few conflicts, we were not quite ready to trust our nearest neighbour. Gethin came here as a physician, he was of noble blood but of an impoverished line. He did not just catch the eye of Lady Marjory, but of almost every female in the castle, for you will grant that he is a handsome fellow, and he has always been clever, charismatic and kind.

"However, he only had eyes for Lady Marjory, and within weeks the pair were deeply in love and wished to marry. Her family thought she could make a better match, especially considering her age, but her parents were beginning to be won over by Gethin's charm and sincere feelings for their daughter. They knew his family and had met him before, so it would not have been a great leap into the unknown for her."

"Why did they not marry, then?"

He shook his ugly head, and tears came into his eyes.

"Ah, it's a sad tale, lady, and there's not a soul here who does not regret it. Lady Marjory's brothers, amongst whom I include Lord Owen, took it upon themselves to get rid of Gethin."

"Why? What right did they have to do that when their parents did not actually forbid the match?"

"They had no right, only a sense of their own self-righteousness and the belief that their sister should make a grander match. They were overly proud and too keen to prove their manhood. They chased Gethin out of the castle, far away, at sword point. They swore a terrible revenge on him and his kin if he dared to return or contact their sister. Gethin obeyed the first command, for he then had many family and friends living in our lands, but not the second. He smuggled a letter to Lady Marjory to explain that he was leaving her and why, despite loving her. He could never willingly endanger the lives of his loved ones. Instead, he would become a monk. If could not have her, he would not have anyone.

"Lady Marjory was heartbroken and furious in equal measures. Her parents were angry at their sons, but what was done was done. Besides, they still hoped that their daughter would make a brilliant match. Time appeared to be on her side. Gethin soon took his vows, and he got a message to the castle to let them know that he had bonded his eternal soul and mortal body to the church.

"You may imagine how the young lords rejoiced and believed they had done the right thing, for Gethin had obeyed them. However, Lady Marjory, still distressed beyond reason, got a message to him to say that she would never marry nor lay with a man, as she could not have him. When her parents began to talk of a possible match with another young man, shortly after Gethin's vows, she took matters into her own hands."

"What did she do?" I could scarcely credit what I was hearing.

"At that time, several warriors from the Woldsheart were at

the castle. They had come to negotiate the release of some prisoners. Lady Marjory threw herself at their leader, she flirted with him shamelessly when she could get away from her family, and he enthusiastically responded. She was then still an alluring maid with a will of iron. To cut a long story short, by the time the prisoners had been exchanged, Lady Marjory knew herself to be with child.

"You may imagine the commotion *that* caused. The pride and joy of Malwarden had deliberately ruined herself in a moment of madness. Now she knew she was carrying a baby, reality hit her. This time her brothers knew they could not bully or threaten. The warrior had as formidable a reputation as he was wealthy and well connected. Instead, one of our captains, his opposite number, went to find him to deal with this formally. There was no way to hide the scandal, so we believed he should pay too. He needed to provide for his child.

"The warrior had died in battle by the time his son, Lord Bran, was born. Our captain was hurried to Castle Malwarden by a large party of his brother warriors and his kin. Our young lords were as meek as mice, as I'm sure you can imagine. However, the Woldsheart men had only come in such a fashion to intimidate us into accepting decidedly reasonable terms. They handed over an enormous sum of money on the condition that we never contacted them again about the matter.

"Lord Oliver and Lady Isolde accepted this on their daughter's behalf, for she was still lying in. The men from the Woldsheart kept their word and departed without making any trouble. We kept ours, and Lady Marjory set up her business."

We stood for some time in the warm sunshine whilst I tried to digest what I had heard. Master Evan noted my amazement.

"It's a well-known story, my lady, so I do no harm in telling it to you, but pray be discreet. You know what I mean. Everyone involved has more or less been forgiven, and the past is very much the past. Everybody wants to keep it that way."

"Of course, I will say nothing. Would you be so kind as to answer just a few more questions?"

This amiable gossip might be my only chance to satisfy my curiosity and give me all the information I needed to survive at Castle Malwarden. He cheerfully consented.

"If a man of the House of Pendroch was not good enough for Lady Marjory in the year 2000, why did Lord Owen marry Lady Cerys a few years later? He must have married her by the end of 2004 because their eldest child is nearly ten. Also, who are the parents of Lady Eluned and Lady Isabeau, and why do they call Lady Marjory Mumma if she is not their mother?"

"I'll answer your second question first. Eluned and Isabeau have no title because none of their parents held one. Yes, I say none, not neither, because the girls share a father but not a mother. They are half-sisters, and there is scarcely half a year between them. They are no blood kin of either Lord Bran or Lady Marjory. Brother Gethin got two lowborn women pregnant at around the same time. After he learned about Lord Bran's birth, he broke his vows of celibacy and...enthusiastically made up for lost time, shall we say. However, he and Lady Marjory have never stopped loving each other.

"Time passed. Lady Marjory made peace with her family, everyone loved her son, and she set up her business to support herself. Lords Bernard and Matthew died in battle. Lord Oliver died in his bed four years later. Brother Gethin and Lady Marjory got in contact somehow and built some sort of relationship, but he cannot leave his monastery to marry her. I think he is even on reasonable terms with Lord Owen these days. At any rate, he has been a father to Lord Bran as far as his vocation permits him to be.

"Nearly a decade ago, Brother Gethin learned he had got two women pregnant within months of each other. One was newlywed with no children and a husband away at sea. The other was betrothed to a man who lived far away. By great good luck, they managed to conceal their pregnancies from their families and their community, and they both went on a retreat to a convent before they started to show. Brother Gethin was remorseful and wanted to help them. Lady Marjory immediately took charge of the situation by offering to adopt the babies. She even helped the mothers to hide what was going on by lying to their families. It worked, and Lady Marjory, Brother Gethin, Lord Bran, Isabeau and Eluned are a happy family, albeit an unconventional one. They all love each other dearly."

I thought hard. Never in a thousand years could I have imagined this was the explanation for the puzzling domestic setup.

Mistress Prim should not look down her nose at me like she does. Her behaviour has been far worse than mine. No, Hawise, that is unkind. She was sixteen or seventeen when it all happened. It must have felt like her world was collapsing, and she could turn to no-one.

How lucky they have been, and how well they have managed to make that family work. I am amazed nobody sent her to a convent or sent the children away to be fostered, but they are a loving family. Not all families are, especially ones that are blended. Bessy and I always felt accepted by Uncle Piers, Aunt Illustra and their children, yet we also always felt separate. It may have been what pushed us together, and I suspect the gap of six years between me and their youngest child did not help.

Master Evan continued his tale.

"Regarding Lady Cerys, she married Lord Owen in the summer of 2005. She gave birth to their eldest, Lord Oliver for his grandfather, at the beginning of September 2005."

He watched me to see how I took this revelation. I clapped a hand over my mouth before I could think about it.

"Aye," he continued, "she waddled down the aisle with an enormous belly, tiny creature that she is, she looked ready to topple over, and aye, the baby was Lord Owen's."

"I don't know what to say. Is that sort of thing common here?" I dared to ask.

"Oh no. Absolutely not, but nor is it *completely* unheard of. Relations between our house and hers were beginning to improve, and she came here with some other ladies to pay a diplomatic visit. She and Lord Owen fell in love and, well...a wedding was hastily arranged. Everyone loved Lady Cerys by then, she was always such a lively, friendly person and so willing to fit in with our ways, but nobody anticipated a marriage. However, her family only shrugged their shoulders and insisted that they were wed before the baby was born. We were the more powerful of the two families, and I think they thought it a good match for her.

"Lord Oliver and Lady Isolde were not pleased with her behaviour or their son's, and Lady Marjory was *furious* at her brother for his hypocrisy. He was certainly aware of his good fortune and bad behaviour and felt appalled at his past actions. I believe he has never regretted marrying Lady Cerys, but a blind man can see how deeply he regrets parting his sister from her true love. However, Lords Matthew and Bernard were killed in 2003, and it pushed the family together. They did not want to fall apart, so Lady Cerys became part of the family, and life moved on."

I drank in this head-spinning tale, trying to digest it all. So far, I had had little to do with Lady Isolde and less still with Lord Owen. I spent much of my waking hours with Lady Cerys. I could never have believed that such a seemingly perfect chatelaine had had such a shameful start to her marriage.

Why am I judged so harshly when I was a virgin when I married? Nor have I ever forced or tricked anyone into doing anything. All my partners were willing adults. Yet Lady Cerys is so admired. One only needs to see her with her family, her demoiselles or the servants to see this. The Westlands is a different kingdom, not a different world. The situation at this castle cannot be considered normal.

A noise in the distance pulled me out of my thoughts and caught Master Evan's attention. His apprentices were returning. I had stayed long enough, any further questions might make him wonder what my purpose was.

He is an unusually loose-tongued fellow. Has someone sent him to spy on me? Did he expect me to confide in him, in return for such unexpected gossip? Have I been fed bait to see what I do with it?

"I'll bid you good day, sir, and not detain you from your work any longer. I will hold my tongue, you may be assured of that."

He could not say much more in return because the apprentices would soon be within earshot. We said farewell, and I thought I should return to Lady Cerys. It was nearly noon. I could not afford to offend anyone by being late.

When I entered her rooms, she was with two of her demoiselles, Lady Isolde, a servant and Lady Nessa. They were all talking rapidly with worried faces.

"I'm just repeating what I heard, madam," the servant was saying. "I thought you should know as the Lady of Malwarden. I thought my niece was repeating the fairy tale of the Deadly Favour at first, but no. I misunderstood her. It has actually happened."

Nessa saw me and called out a greeting, causing the rest of the group to turn away from the servant. The servant stopped talking and also looked at me.

Feeling as conspicuous as I always did when I entered her ladyship's rooms, I dropped my gaze respectfully and curtseyed deeply. The other women also rose and curtseyed. The servant was already standing and made to leave.

"No, pray don't go," I said, aware that I must cause no inconvenience and also glad to have an excuse to leave. "If you have confidential matters to discuss, I can return another time." I turned to Lady Cerys. "Would it be better for your ladyship if I joined you in the Great Hall when we eat our midday meal?" I had to remember they said 'midday meal' even though they did not eat exactly at noon, whereas we said 'lunch'.

"No, it is alright, Lady Hawise, you may stay." Lady Cerys turned to the servant. "Thank you for coming to me, Jane, and telling me what your niece has told you. I will repeat it to Lord Owen, and we will decide what to do together. It may be that we will need to speak with you or you niece. For now, you may leave us, and do not breathe a word of it until I speak to you again."

Jane nodded and curtseyed with more reverence than I had. As she left the group, she seemed to see me for the first time.

"I beg your pardon, madam, but you are Lady Hawise from the Woldsheart, aren't you?"

"Yes, Jane. I am."

The young woman looked at me. She looked about nineteen years of age at most.

"I would like to thank you, lady. My husband and I owe you so much. I will not say more, you know…but I thank you. He told me everything after we were married, and it is thanks to you that we are happily married."

Now I was truly perplexed. The other women in the room stared at us with undisguised curiosity.

"I'm sorry, Jane, but you must be mistaken. I had not seen you before today, and I have never met your husband."

"You have, lady. You have. His name is Adam, the son of Old Adam, and he was then a warrior. He was a prisoner in your lands three years ago, where he met you. He always says you practically trained him for marriage, lady, and I agree."

Lady Cerys's moon-white face flushed angrily.

"I don't think any of us need to hear this, Jane. The seduction of a boy, who would not have been quite sixteen by an older woman in whose castle he was being held, is not something I wish to have mentioned in my presence."

Jane looked at her with the horror and astonishment that I also felt.

"Seduction?" the servant gasped. "No, my lady, I beg you, but that is not true. My Adam came to me as pure as I came to him, and I can swear on anything holy that I was a virgin when we married. Lady Hawise explained the facts of life to him and the importance of treating your spouse with kindness and respect. He owns that he would otherwise not have treated me with the dignity I deserve, nor known how to consummate the marriage."

She stared at the floor, now a deeper crimson than her

mistress. Indeed, Lady Cerys's red anger had now turned to blanched amazement.

"That is what happened?" she asked me, with none of her usual cool dignity. "You never...? You merely spoke with Adam?"

"Yes, my lady. If Jane will permit me, I will say that he was something of a braggart then, and I feared he would unwittingly do a great wrong if someone did not interfere. So I took it upon myself, as someone with knowledge of marriage and who had authority over him, to gently correct him before firmer correction could be required."

Pink shame washed over Lady Cerys's face, something I had never expected to see, and over the faces of many of the others.

"Madam, what did you think I had done? What do you think of me?"

Is this one of the reasons why Lady Marjory has been so cold towards me? She is the only one with a son who is around that age, as far as I know. Would I have been treated differently if they had known the truth?

Lady Cerys recovered herself.

"Jane, I thank you for clearing this up. You may leave us. Lady Hawise, I sincerely apologise. Adam was heard thanking you for preparing him for marriage on the evening of your arrival, saying that without it he would not have known what to do. This was spread, and its meaning was quite twisted by the time it reached my ears. However, I should have spoken with you directly, rather than believing something so base. I apologise. I will only say that nobody has been gossiping behind your back about this."

Jane scurried out of the door. I felt relief but also awkwardness.

"My lady, I wholeheartedly forgive you. Indeed, I was unaware that such a rumour had spread about me. I must only beg that you spread the truth instead. I know my reputation is not unblemished, and I blame nobody but myself for that, but I do insist that there are depths to which I have never sunk."

I made myself look them in the eye. They were all looking at me with more respect than they had before.

"Of course," Lady Cerys said. The others made noises of agreement, while her mother-in-law looked at me with something like sympathy in her green eyes.

Lady Isolde bade me to sit, and we talked of more casual matters until it was time to eat. Emboldened by Lady Cerys's sudden change of heart towards me, I pushed my luck a little further as we walked towards the Great Hall.

"May I beg for your advice, my lady? If I may be so bold, you came here a decade ago from what was then an enemy house. Anyone may see how beloved and respected you are. You are now not only part of this house but one of its heads. I would never attempt to step out of my situation, I only want to know how best to fit in with the people of the castle whilst I stay here. This is different to anything I have experienced before, and I don't want to cause offence."

She smiled her charming smile at me.

"Of course. Walk with me when we take the air in the rose garden this afternoon, and we will talk then."

She kept her word and familiarised me with a few points of etiquette to which I had been oblivious.

"But you have done nothing to offend, Lady Hawise," she reassured me. "I would have spoken with you sooner, if you had. I appreciate this is a new world for you."

She smiled at me so warmly that I pushed my luck a little further.

Returning her smile with my one of own, I asked about the Deadly Favour. We were standing some distance from the other women. Nobody else was in the rose garden apart from those who had been present in her rooms that morning.

"I came in just as Jane was telling you about it. Is it something to worry about? Might I be able to help?"

Her smile changed. Although she did not frown, her expression became guarded, and she shook her head, making her smooth black hair shine in the sunlight.

"No, it will not affect you. Let us talk of other matters."

I might have been raised in another kingdom, but I still knew when I was being politely dismissed. I was a hostage from an enemy house, an enemy land, and not a demoiselle d'honneur, raised from birth to be in the service of the House of Malwarden.

It was to be expected, but it still stung. With a light-heartedness which I did not feel, I began to speak of Bessy and her decision to become a nun. Lady Cerys took an interest in my friend, and I recalled that it would soon be her birthday.

Chapter Six

Narrative continued by Lady Millabess of Lothwold

I awoke on the morning of my twenty-third birthday feeling as contented as a well-fed cat. The sun streamed through the window of my cell, and I sighed with happiness. I looked about me. Technically I was sleeping in a cell, which is what the rooms where we slept alone were called, but the word did not do justice to the spacious, richly-furnished chamber that I had decorated to my taste with belongings from my old life. I was also not alone. My beloved Jennet was sleeping beside me. There was ample room for her in the wide bed.

Life at the convent was better than I had dared hope. Abbess Richeldis was all too happy to turn a blind eye to what the thirty-three women and girls under her got up to, providing the convent ran smoothly and we turned a blind eye to her activities. She was as fond of her own way as anyone else under her roof, and she liked to read romances over a goblet of mead or to go on long walks with friends that took her away from her duties. Everyone else led a similarly relaxed life. There was another couple amongst the nuns, and several monks from a nearby monastery came to visit some of the nuns and novices.

Jennet and I were not technically novices, having yet to formally start our novitiates. Nobody insisted upon it, so we wandered about the convent, dressed in our civilian clothes, performing the duties required of us. Our clothes instantly distinguished our ranks, and we naturally split into small groups according to rank. Out of the nine soon-to-be novices, only three of us were noble, Jennet, me and Matilda, a girl from the House of Sharman, with whom I got on well.

Jennet stirred, and I kissed her awake. She smiled.

"Happy birthday, my love."

I kissed her in reply.

The bell for the first service of the day rang, and we ignored it, safe in the knowledge that almost everyone else would. We eventually disentangled ourselves, got up, washed and dressed before heading for breakfast.

I think I remember what I was wearing on that bright August morning, not because it was my birthday or I was so happy, but because of what happened next, a life-changing moment, although I would not realise it at the time. I wore a peridot green kirtle, my favourite colour, over a cream shift. The kirtle was made of heavy silk, and it was embroidered with gold and brown thread. The shift was made out of lawn so fine that it felt as soft as the silk kirtle. A costly girdle, embellished with pearls, was wrapped around my waist, and I wore a translucent veil, held in place with a pearl-studded band on my head. The mirror and Jennet's words told me I looked well, and I believed them.

A letter arrived for the abbess, which would not have excited my notice, had it not been for the effect that it produced upon her. Her usually placid, round face took on a decidedly concerned look, and she took herself off in a hurry. We all wondered what the letter might contain.

We found out at lunch. Once everyone was served and seated, Abbess Richeldis rose, looking most distressed.

"My dear daughters, I have received some news of which I should make you aware."

Silence fell, and we looked at her expectantly. She continued in the same anxious tone.

"This morning I received a letter, the same letter that has been sent to the heads of all religious houses in every kingdom. The High Priest has ordered a thorough review into the activities of his houses. For nigh on a century we have been left in peace to interpret the rules as we see fit. Now, there will be an investigation and a clampdown on any deviation from the rules that were first set out more than one thousand years ago. We may expect visitors within the next fortnight to ask questions and to insist upon changes."

A babble of discontent spread around the room. We could not quite believe our ears. I looked at my companions. Every one of us showed the same shock and disbelief.

"Reverend Mother, that is madness," one of the nuns dared to exclaim. "How can anyone live by rules which were decided upon in the tenth century? So much has changed since then. Many events have occurred which our founder could never have foreseen. Besides, how will they enforce these many rules in the many different religious houses? There are fifty convents and monasteries in the Woldsheart alone."

A murmur of approval echoed around the room. The abbess looked at us sadly.

"I am told that the original penalties, laid down in 992, will apply."

We were aghast.

"They would not dare!" I was bold enough to cry out. "Nobody here or in the civilian world would stand for it."

My sisters heartily agreed with me.

"What do we do now, Reverend Mother?" Matilda asked timidly.

She thought carefully for a moment.

"Carry on as you are for now. We do not even know when we will be visited. I will not let anyone be punished retrospectively. I see no need to change how we do things until we are ordered to change."

This news provided food for thought throughout August, but because no-one appeared by the end of the month, we thought we were safe. I visited my guardians at the Castle of the Eastern Coast and told them what I had been told. Their daughter Rowena was visiting with her family and said she had heard a rumour to this effect, but she had not credited it. Nobody else had heard anything. They advised me to try to forget it.

"After all, it may be a fuss about nothing," Aunt Illustra counselled. "Fighting is still going on, even though it is less widespread than it was, and peace treaties are being drawn up. The clergy have enough going on what with burying the dead, healing the wounded and providing spiritual guidance. The High Priest and his minions should have no time to implement reform. Besides, the Westlands is still under an interregnum. That is a concern even for us because of the instability it is generating. He should interfere there. If he must interfere at all."

She broke off uneasily, thinking of Hawise, like we all were. She was a prisoner in that unstable kingdom. She had written cheerful letters to me, but I could not be completely convinced. I admired her courage as much as I always had and could only pray it would not be tested too severely.

Gethin the Monk and the two little children from the Westlands were at the castle, and I took the opportunity to observe them. I was curious after reading Hawise's description of him.

I could not appreciate a handsome man in the way she did, but I had to admit he was good-looking. I spoke to him briefly and saw him in a group. I could only conclude that he seemed pleasant enough, and I approved of how he kept an eye on the boy and girl who had been sent over with him. The children seemed happy until one noticed the wariness in their eyes.

Like Hawise, Drogo and Rosamund, they will never truly relax until they come home. Nor will we ever truly relax until that day comes.

On the morning that I was due to return to the convent, a clear day in early September, a solemn-looking nun and two equally grave monks arrived at the castle. They spoke to my guardians and Brother Gethin separately.

"This looks ominous," Rowena whispered to me. "Could they have come from the High Priest?"

It turned out that she was right. The three also wanted to speak to me.

This came as a surprise to me. I had not even formally begun my novitiate. What influence could I have on how the Convent of the New Moon was run?

I entered the solar to find not only the three strangers but also Brother Gethin awaiting me. This was another surprise.

Trying to conceal my astonishment, I curtseyed respectfully to the party.

"Good day. I am Lady Millabess of Lothwold. I understand that you wish to speak with me."

Only Brother Gethin smiled at me. The strangers remained stony-faced as they introduced themselves as Agnes of the Convent of the Green Man, and Harold and Percy, both from the Monastery of the Parhelion. They named places far from my castle but still in Lothwold lands. Agnes and Percy were of my house, whereas Harold was of the House of Ishelmer.

Sweat dribbled down my spine. A lot of effort had been put into gathering these people together, one from an enemy house and all of them from far away.

I will not judge someone on their blood, unpopular as that line of thinking may be. Besides, once someone takes religious vows, they become a brother or sister to the world. No, I know I am nervous because this looks very serious indeed, and I don't like how they are staring at me. She is looking at me as though I were a naughty child, caught in the act of some misdeed.

"I have been told that you are visiting your guardians, Lady Millabess, and that you are a novice nun at the Convent of the New Moon. You passed through its doors in July."

"Yes, sister."

She looked puzzled.

"My eyes tell me that you are wearing cosmetics and an outfit made almost entirely out of silk, with a girdle of cloth of silver. You are also wearing jewels in your hair."

I did not reply. She waited for a moment before continuing in the same sarcastic tone.

"Not all of these statements may be true, Lady Millabess. Indeed, you should not even be using your title. Novices are supposed to shun worldly distinctions. You are not only wearing civilian clothes but civilian clothes which are as far removed from what a novice should wear as I can imagine. Finally, novices should not be making or receiving visits for the first three months of their novitiate, unless some close kin of theirs is dying. Is that the case, Lady Millabess? Is someone close to you, in this castle, dying, and does your adorning yourself ease their suffering in some way?"

I blushed but refused to apologise or gaze downwards. Instead, I raised my eyebrows at her coldly and would not speak. I was indeed *Lady* Millabess and not someone to be spoken to in such an insolent manner.

Sister Agnes regarded me coldly for a few seconds before continuing.

"Do all the novices dress so richly? Do they all make visits?"

"Not all. We are not all of noble blood, nor all so happily situated near our loved ones."

"Dare I ask if all the novices are so deliberately obtuse in their speech?"

"Sister, I am not a novice. I have yet to start my novitiate. The same goes for most of the other women and girls who are not yet nuns and are living at the convent."

Sister Agnes, Brother Percy and Brother Harold now looked horrified.

"Do you mean to tell me that you have been staying there for several weeks without making any commitment? And you are not the only one to do so?" Brother Percy could not quite believe his ears.

"It is so, brother."

They stood aghast, then Sister Agnes took charge.

"Brothers, we must away to this convent this evening as we intended. Unless the blessed founder was unpardonably indulgent, some gross mischief has occurred. Millabess, we insist on your accompanying us."

She included Brother Gethin in her speech, who did not look as enthusiastic as the other monks. I nodded. I did not bridle at her dropping my title because I had another concern. I had originally planned to travel back that afternoon because we were going to have a party that evening.

"Very well, sister. I will go and pack."

I left before they could delay me, determined to get a message to the convent before they arrived. Brother Gethin appeared just as I was handing it to a gold sprite.

"Do you go with us, brother?"

"Yes. They insist."

"But you are a hostage. Don't you have to stay here, in the castle?"

"The High Priest's command overrides everything. Besides, I am not going far. The Convent of the New Moon is a short journey away and surrounded by your guardians' lands."

I nodded, thinking he might be an ally. Hawise had told me all that she knew about him in her last letter. This was not an austere man. He could scold not us without being a hypocrite. The rest of the convent knew about him because I had related her tales to them.

I would have held my tongue, had I known he would visit there. Still, with his reputation, he might appreciate forewarned women. Some of them would love to lie with him, I'm sure.

I discreetly took another look at him. Even his baggy, undyed robe could not disguise his good looks. I noticed he also wore a scarf made out of sky blue material around his neck, which was not something I had seen before on a monk. It was half-hidden under the neckline of his robe.

"What does that scarf signify?" I asked. "I have not seen a monk wear one like that before."

He tucked the thin cloth further into his robe whilst saying that he was a physician at his monastery, and it was a sign of his position.

Rowena approached us, and I told her what was happening. She was not impressed.

"Rank is rank, Bessy. It is all very well everyone being equal behind a convent's walls, *in theory*, but no sane person would expect titles to be foregone or for you to give up your fine clothes. Not until you have become a nun, and even then I'm sure a little leeway could be applied. I'm sure your founder would have soon seen that there is a difference in the practical and the theory, had they lived long enough to see the convent grow. No, rank is rank and ho—"

"I'd better oversee my packing," I quickly interjected. "My belongings will not impress that sour group, but they are mine, and so I will take them back to the convent with me." I knew that Rowena was about to say, 'and house is house', forgetting Brother Gethin's presence. It was a favourite saying of hers. She flushed and returned to the ridiculousness of an order taking its rules literally.

I next spoke to Brother Gethin when we were about to take our leave. I needed to get him on my side.

"The thing is," I whispered, "we're having a party later on today, and I'm not sure if they will have got my note to warn them."

"Ah. What sort of party?"

"Oh, nothing too wild. Just some mead and some food, some music, and the monks and novices from the monastery down the road are bringing happy herbs for us to smoke. It won't go on all night."

His bushy black eyebrows nearly met his hairline.

"Are you mad? How do you think that three will take it?"

I was taken aback.

"Well, it's not like we knew they were coming. Sure, the abbess received a letter about the proposed reforms, but no real details were given. We were hardly going to give up all comforts until we had to."

"You are living in a nunnery and should have begun your novitiate weeks ago. You should have given up your comforts then."

"And you, brother? Have you given up *every* comfort in life?"

I was beginning to get annoyed. He had seemed so reasonable and on my side. Now he was showing himself to be quite hypocritical. Hawise had told me how he had done worse than attend parties since taking his vows.

He reddened with annoyance.

"I cannot say my behaviour has been exemplary. I'm sure you have heard—" He broke off because Sister Agnes was approaching us.

I made my farewells and wondered what was awaiting us at the convent. I also wondered when I would be allowed to visit the Castle of the Eastern Coast again.

Maybe I should have left as many of my belongings with my guardians as I could. What if that sour-faced trout and her grumpy minions decide to confiscate my things or sell them for alms? Technically they can, but I cannot believe they would dare. More importantly, can they prevent me from seeing my family? Can they prevent me from writing to Hawise?

These were terrifying thoughts. Brother Gethin noticed that I looked anxious as I got off my dragon, and he forgot our near-quarrel.

"I will try to work with you, not against you. As you know, I am a hostage here, but I have been ordered by the church to help with their investigation and reform. I was in no position to refuse. Many monks and nuns have been similarly forced. Some, like these three, have volunteered. Now, how bad do you think this party will *really* be? How can we play it down, if your note did not arrive in time?"

The sound of a hurdy-gurdy and a pipe and the noise of chatter and singing answered him. The other two monks and Sister Agnes whirled round on me in horror.

"What is going on?" Brother Harold demanded.

A loud whoop inside the convent answered him. I guessed it was Sister Ida. She was one of those quiet women who always let their hair down at a party and become loud.

Brother Gethin bit his lip and hastily looked into the distance.

"Millabess, you will take us to the source of that noise directly," Sister Agnes ordered.

What could I do but enter the convent, calling out where we were very loudly, as if I were giving guests a tour of the place? It was the one warning I could give to my sisters.

Jennet heard me and staggered out to greet me, undeniably a little worse for wear. She flung her skinny arms around me but thankfully did not kiss me.

"Bessy! Glad you could make it in time. Come in, everyone is here, and we've a small mountain of happy herbs. Brother Wilf has done us proud. Oh, hello. Are these your friends? Come in. There's plenty to go round."

She grabbed my arm to steady herself. Sister Agnes gasped in horror.

"Are you drunk, young lady?"

"No." Jennet was indignant. "I can hold my mead. Come on, Bessy." She pulled me inside. I tried to explain who the four were, but she was too drunk to properly understand, and she kept asking me the same question over and over again in a loud voice.

We made our way to where the party was being held, in the refectory and the garden just outside it. Some fifty people, monks, nuns and novices plus a couple of civilians were singing, dancing, drinking, eating, smoking and chatting. Two nuns were playing musical instruments with great enthusiasm and some skill. Several couples were kissing and cuddling. Few people wore their habits as they were supposed to be worn. Many, like me, were wearing civilian dress of one form or another. It was a merry scene but not one to make our visitors smile.

Brothers Percy and Harold and Sister Agnes tried to bring everything to a halt. Brother Gethin hung back. They clapped, shouted and called for silence for minutes before succeeding. It was too noisy and there were too many people, most of them high or drunk, spread out in a large room and a garden. It took even longer for everyone to grasp who these people were and what they wanted.

When silence had finally fallen, Sister Agnes began to castigate us. She explained who she and the three monks were and how things were soon going to be very different around here, or else. Our blessed founder would be appalled if she could see what was being done under her roof.

"Where is Abbess Richeldis?" she eventually concluded. I could not tell if she had said all she wanted to say or if she simply needed to draw breath.

The nun who had been playing the pipe put down her instrument and staggered towards her. The distinctive smell of happy herbs followed her, and her eyes were red.

"What?" she sullenly demanded. "What do you want with me and my women?"

Sister Agnes lost her temper.

"What I want, nay what I insist upon, is that your house reforms itself instantly and completely. That your convent becomes worthy of the name and becomes an example to the world. That you follow the principles of charity, chastity, obedience and poverty. At the moment, you are not worthy to call yourselves nuns!"

The abbess raised a shaking hand. For one moment I actually thought she would strike her.

"Enough. I am in no state to hear you today. Come and talk to me tomorrow, if you must." She waved her away dismissively.

Sister Agnes looked ready to combust when Brother Percy stepped in.

"Perhaps that would be for the best. Nearly everyone under this roof is under the influence of alcohol or drugs. We will get no sense out of them tonight. We should speak with them tomorrow morning."

Sister Agnes paused.

"You are right, brother. I have wasted enough time today. Millabess, you are sober. You may show us to the guest chambers. We will address the female half of this...rabble at breakfast tomorrow. Brother Percy, pray write to Brother Norbert as soon as you can. He and his party may deal with the men and boys tomorrow. They should arrive at the monastery by noon."

The party over, my companions slunk off, muttering darkly. Brother Gethin helped a young novice monk to his feet.

"I swear I'm not drunk," he slurred.

"I'm sure you're not."

He offered the youth his arm, who took it, then promptly vomited. Brother Gethin quickly spun him to face away from him.

"Is that the Fornicating Friar?" Sister Ida asked a little too loudly as one of the nuns tried to get rid of the happy herbs by setting fire to the stash. A small group immediately surrounded her, stopping her with loud pleas and calls to be discreet.

I quickly led Sister Agnes and her three monks to the guest chambers.

Brother Gethin spoke to me briefly that evening to ask if such a party was typical of my convent.

"Well, I've not been here long. It's the third party we've had since I arrived. The other two were about as well attended."

He shook his curly head.

"Is our convent *very* dissolute? I thought every convent was like ours."

"Yours is no worse than many," was his only reply. "However, I'd brace yourself for tomorrow morning. This is my first mission, but I can tell you that whatever is going to happen will not be pleasant."

He was correct. The only blessing for me was that I was not suffering from a hangover whilst the stinging reprimand and dire promises were issued.

Sister Agnes began by displaying the bull from the High Priest and finished by listing the terrible punishments which the disobedient could expect. In between, she berated us, especially our Reverend Mother, for turning a House of the Gods into a place of indulgence and indolence. She kept stating how very different things would be, starting from today.

To begin with, we were all told to dress as the nuns or novices were meant to be, and those of us who were meant to have begun their novitiate were expected to make their first steps in a ceremony that very evening.

"The novitiate will be made *properly*," she stressed. "It will take one year and a day, *as the rules state it should*, starting from this evening. Those who complete it will become nuns. Those who do not will be returned to their families. I confess that we have not set the best example."

We all looked at her with hope and surprise.

"Brother Gethin made his novitiate in nine months, and I took thirteen," she confessed. We all sighed inwardly. "However, you must not use our imperfect example as an excuse for laxness. You must all strive to make the best novitiates that you can and ask yourselves unflinchingly if you are truly worthy to enter our sisterhood."

We were to begin our new lives in earnest. Brother Gethin had been a physician at his monastery, and he also left it regularly to tend to patients. I was tasked with accompanying him to the nearest village to see what medical aid was required there. I wondered if I had been chosen because I was interested in healing and herbs and had helped at the convent's infirmary or because Sister Agnes knew I would be immune to his charms.

This isn't so bad, I thought as the pair of us walked into

Landesmar. *It's a pleasant day for a walk, Brother Gethin appears to be the best of the four, and it should be interesting.*

It was tricky to chat with him because Hawise had told me so much about him, yet I knew I was not meant to know what she had told me. He did not ask me how Sister Ida knew his nickname. Instead, he was content to talk about medicine and to ask me what I knew about it and about the health of the local population.

I could easily tell him what I had learned. I had picked up quite a lot from my aunt Illustra, who was skilled, and at the convent. I had not been trained for a profession as such because I had been expected to marry and run a household.

It was not so easy to tell him how little I knew of the lives of the peasantry and the middling sorts in Landesmar and the surrounding areas. I knew it was my duty as a noble and a religious to provide alms and care, but my conscience told me that I had only ever provided money or goods. I had taken very little interest in their lives. Instead, I had relied on others to tell me what I needed to give and to whom.

Brother Gethin should have taken one of the novices or nuns from the lower orders with him. I am a lady. How am I supposed to know what is needed?

It turned out that a lot was needed in Landesmar. The long war had caused epidemics to flourish and harvests to fail, and many villagers were suffering from poor health. Minor ailments became serious very quickly. The local physician, cunning men and wise women were overwhelmed. Far from resenting an outsider's interference, they were grateful for all the help they could get. The infirmary at my convent was too far for the majority to travel to, and only the gravely ill were willing to be taken there.

My cheeks grew hot. I had had no idea that I was failing in my duty to such an extent. I also did not like how I felt when I was around the common people. Unless they were servants or nuns and novices who politely kept to themselves, I did not know how to behave. I felt ill at ease and conspicuous. What did they think of me, and what did they expect from me? They seemed so alien to me that I did not know what to say or do.

Brother Gethin knew what he was doing and gave me tasks to do, for which I was grateful. By the time he treated a child for an infected cut, I was almost relaxed.

"You won her and her father over," I told him as we headed back to the convent. "You left them both in good spirits."

"Physic is as much to do with the mind and the spirit as it is to do with the body. I told the little girl a fairy tale from the Westlands to put her at ease and to distract her from what I was doing to her knee. Mind you," he laughed wryly, "my choice of story might have been unwise."

"Oh? I did not hear it. I was busy with the old woman who was complaining about her headaches."

"I told her the tale of the Deadly Favour. Parents tell it to their children to stop them from running off with strangers. Still, as her father did not object to me, perhaps she did not see me in that light."

I remembered Hawise's mention of Jane the servant's report to Lady Cerys and the latter's reluctance to explain anything. My curiosity was alive.

"What is the Deadly Favour?"

"It's a story about a group of evil spirits, disguised as kind humans, who approach children. They soften them up with sweet words before showing them some sort of favour, like say...hair ribbons or sweetmeats. Then they encourage the child to dance away with them, and neither they nor the child are ever seen again. The child is missing, presumed dead."

"Sounds like a useful lesson for a child who trusts too much to learn."

I was already mentally writing my next letter to Hawise. What was going on in Malwarden lands?

Chapter Seven

I was careful not only to write in our code but to include a warning of what was happening at the convent and to send the letter as soon as possible. I strongly suspected that Sister Agnes was going to clamp down on our letters. I noticed how loaded down the sprites were and how a large proportion of them were gold. The other inhabitants of the convent clearly had the same fears and were willing to pay for the fastest and most expensive courier.

An air of desperate recklessness quickly fell over the convent. We wanted to grasp every pleasure we could, for who knew when they would be taken away from us? Jennet and I grabbed every opportunity we could to be together. Up until the arrival of Sister Agnes and her minions, we had been relatively discreet, but now we became more daring. We were less cautious, and it was inevitable that we would eventually be caught by someone who cared. Looking back, I can only shake my head at our naivety.

It was lucky for us that it was Brother Gethin who caught lying in her cell, half dressed, in each other's arms. I shudder to think what the other three would have done.

There was no way we could deny what we were doing, nor did

we attempt to. Jennet blushed and looked at the floor. I managed to hold his appalled gaze, waiting for him to speak.

"I could hear you down the corridor. Anyone could have come across you. What if one of the others had heard you, instead of me?"

We could not argue with that, and so we got dressed. I got up to leave.

"Please don't tell anyone," Jennet begged.

"I won't, but surely, you can see what you're doing is wrong? You are required to hold every nun and novice as a sister of equal value, apart from the abbess, who is to be your mother. You will be required to swear a promise of lifelong chastity when you make your final vows."

He carried on lecturing me as he escorted me to the still room, where I was meant to be. It infuriated me. Hypocrisy always did. I carefully checked that nobody was around before speaking my mind.

"You have a short memory, brother."

"What do you mean?"

"Brother, I lie with *one* woman. Your reputation precedes you. Need I say any more?"

"I don't deny I have broken my vows of chastity repeatedly, but I have never taken any of those women into my heart. I cannot because someone else already holds it. Nor have I ever done anything on church property or when I was meant to be at my duty."

"I will not give up my Jennet." I could state no more than that.

"Lady Millabess, do you know what penalty you will suffer if you are caught lying with your Jennet by anyone other than me? I was sent to the Woldsheart out of fear of castration. Aye, castration. The old punishment for a fornicating monk. It's not been carried out for over two hundred years, but I was reliably informed by a very well-placed source that all this will soon change. I can only trust his hope that punishments will not be applied retrospectively. It would be impossible to castrate you, but you know what the female equivalent involves."

Images of hot irons flashed up in my mind's eye. I gasped before I could stop myself. The expression in his eyes softened.

"Like I said on the day we met, I want to work with you, not against you. Let me warn you. Change your ways and obey every rule that a novice nun should obey or leave the convent. You are far from taking your final vows. You will have the opportunity to leave."

"I came here because it was preferable to making a second marriage." I did not see the point in lying in the face of his honesty. I also felt it would be disrespectful.

"You might think differently now you can see how things will be. I suspect many will leave because convent life is not what they expected. Some novices might even be pulled out by their families, for fear of the harsh penalties that they may incur if they disobey."

Brother Gethin was right. Life at the New Moon completely changed within a week. Abbess Richeldis was pensioned off to a place far away. She was above sixty but in excellent health and more than capable of running the convent until the new regime hit it. We all wept to see her go. Sister Agnes installed herself as a temporary abbess until a suitable permanent candidate could be appointed. The three monks remained to help her.

My civilian clothes, my jewels, my books, my lute, all of my possessions which I had taken for granted were sent back to my guardians, with a generic explanation. The rules were now being properly applied, and a novice nun had no use for such worldly goods. I was now indeed a novice nun. My hair was still long, but I covered all of it with a plain kerchief, and my body was covered with a robe of coarse, undyed linen. What I wore under the robe, my shift, drawers, stockings, kirtle, petticoat and boots, were identical to what every other novice wore and of poorer quality than what I was used to.

I had taken my first vows, the vows that showed I was beginning the novitiate, along with the other girls and women who were not nuns at the convent. My days were spent in worship, in the infirmary, visiting the needy in Landesmar and in contemplation. I also had long talks with the senior nuns about my spiritual journey and what it meant to be a nun. Sister Agnes, Brother Percy or Brother Harold were almost always present, watching us with beady eyes and listening intently. Brother Gethin was rarely alone with any of us, apart from me and two other nuns who loved each other. I wondered if that was to preserve us or to preserve him.

As novices, we were not meant to visit anyone or receive visitors for the first three months of our novitiate, but even Sister Agnes had to make concessions to appease angry families. Many parents, siblings and aunts turned up at her door, demanding to see their relations who were unexpectedly being kept from them. She permitted visits to the convent at the beginning of October.

"We made our first vows on 10th September," I said to Jennet during the afternoon of the 28th of that month. We had had few opportunities to be alone since Brother Gethin caught us, and we would have not dared do anything if we had been presented with more. "So much has changed since then. I can't wait to see my guardians. Did I tell you they will visit at the weekend? Will you see your father and stepmother?"

"Yes."

She continued to polish the brass in front of her. Since Sister Agnes had taken over, we had begun to do menial work, much to my distaste. However, this was not the reason for my unhappiness. On the rare occasions when we could speak, Jennet was monosyllabic, and she avoided looking at me. I had asked her more than once what I had done to hurt her, but she merely shrugged and said nothing was wrong.

I did not repeat the question that afternoon. Instead, I took a different approach.

"Jennet, we are quite safe chatting, providing we say nothing that inflammatory. I promise again that I will never do anything again which could endanger either of us. I will not touch you anymore than I would touch someone else. I will not call you by a pet name. We will be lovers in spirit alone. Nothing will part us."

"Yes. You've said so before."

I bit my lip as my throat constricted and tried to focus on rubbing my section of the brass. I tried to tell myself that she was just scared of any punishment we might receive for past offences.

"When are your folks coming?" she suddenly asked.

"They told me that they will get here for around two o'clock on Saturday afternoon."

Silence fell again. Emboldened by her unexpected curiosity, I asked her the same question.

"I don't know yet." Her garnet eyes focused on the shining metal in front of her. She would not look at me, and she held her head awkwardly. I knew her too well to not know when she was lying.

To save myself from more pain, I left her as soon as I could. She barely seemed to notice I was gone.

I vowed to avoid her as much as possible, in the vain hope that she would miss me, come and find me, apologise and explain. She did not. Matilda received a letter the following day from her mother, ordering her to leave the convent. Lady Mariynn stated that she did not want her highborn daughter to work like a peasant. As Matilda was under twenty-one and not yet a nun, she could be withdrawn if her parents ordered it, without her consent. This did not come as a surprise to Matilda, nor was she disappointed. She was happy to leave us at the weekend. Jennet was present when she told us. Matilda and the other novices left us alone. I expected her to speak, but she did not. Instead, she quickly followed the others out of the room, looking decidedly embarrassed.

She next spoke to me at eleven o'clock on Saturday morning. I saw her in the garden with her father and stepmother, both of whom were talking to Sister Agnes. Many other visitors mingled with the nuns and novices.

"I give you permission to leave this very hour," the new abbess stated. "You may travel in your convent garb, if you send it back to us as soon as you can. Likewise, only take whatever you need that you do not have at home, such as a comb, and send it back if you can."

"No, we have sufficient for our daughter," her father proudly declared. "She need not take anything with her. Jennet, do you want to bid anyone farewell before we leave? You will permit this small indulgence, Reverend Mother?"

Before either woman could reply, I stepped forward so they had to see me. They all turned to face me. Jennet looked both guilty and defiant, Sister Agnes looked suspicious, whereas Jennet's father and stepmother looked neutral. I could feel my face turning cold and my jaw dropping. I can only guess how I looked.

Jennet took charge of the situation.

"Let me speak with Millabess for one moment." She took my arm and pulled me away, trying to screen us from notice by moving behind a large party.

"Bessy, I am leaving. I didn't tell you because I didn't want to hurt you. I don't like the convent's new regime. It's too harsh, and the penalties we can suffer are too cruel. I wrote to my father. He is looking to arrange a marriage for me with Oswin, a distant kinsman of ours."

I staggered back as if she had stabbed me. She moved to leave me, but I quickly grabbed her arm. Despite my shock and pain, I had questions for her.

"I thought you came here to avoid marriage. I thought you were like me, you loved women, and you did not want to lie with any man. You told me that your father tried to betroth you to Oswin a year ago, and you were determined to prevent it."

"That was Godwin, not Oswin. Godwin was beneath me. His

grandparents were shepherds, and his income is two-thirds what my father's is. No, if I marry Oswin, I shall be rich and with my social equal. If not, there is still time to look for another suitable match, and I will be more comfortable in the meantime than I would be here."

"Don't you love me? Was this...everything between us...just a lie to avoid a marriage to someone you did not care for?"

She shook her head as if to get rid of a tormenting fly.

"Look, I like women as well as men. You know you're beautiful. I didn't fake anything there...but I need to look to my future. We have to look after ourselves in this world. When we made our pact, I thought I'd be living an easier life without the threat of hot irons and Goddess knows what else hovering over me. Obviously, all that's changed so..."

She moved away. I tried to grab her arm again, but she possessed a wiry strength and fast feet.

"Farewell, Bessy," she called cheerfully over her shoulder. "Thank you for your good wishes, and I wish you luck with your spiritual path."

Suddenly, a hand grabbed *my* arm and pulled me away. I spun round in surprise. It was Brother Gethin. He was pulling me towards the infirmary, telling me loudly that he needed my help with preparing tinctures.

"Come with me," he hissed, dropping my arm. "You look ready to collapse. Sister Agnes is already looking at you very shrewdly. It is as well that Brother Percy has distracted her."

I obeyed and silently followed him to the empty infirmary.

"I thought she loved me," I whimpered. "I thought what we had was real. I thought we could have a special friendship without the physical side of things. Did she just use me? Was it all just a lie?"

He looked at me with sympathetic eyes. I recalled that he was also parted from the woman he loved.

Yet according to Hawise, the love between him and Lady Marjory is reciprocal and real. It is a strong, passionate bond which has withstood much trauma. What is worse? To love like they do or to be deceived as I was?

"Here." He broke through my thoughts and thrust a pestle and mortar at me. "Stand next to me and grind the herbs I will chop. Keep your voice to a whisper if you must talk. I don't think you are in danger because she has left the convent. Sister Agnes must have guessed what passed between you, but it is in the past. For the love of God, do not write to her or try to visit her. She, I hate to say, will never contact you. That should keep you safe."

"Thank you," I whispered, now grateful for he had done.

He nodded and began to speak in a louder tone of the value of tinctures and the many ailments they could heal. I barely took in anything he told me. My thoughts were a whirlwind. I could not digest how Jennet had dropped me and had only agreed to be with me in the first place because her father's first choice was a relatively poor man with humble roots. How much of our relationship had been based on lies? She had said she found me attractive, but could I even believe her there? I ran over every touch and word we had exchanged, trying in vain to find some sign of her deception.

By the time my guardians arrived, I could appear calm and clear eyed. I was able to talk and act in a way that might only be attributed to living under a harsh regime. They certainly thought so.

"Do you want to stay?" Uncle Piers asked me. "This is not what any of us expected."

I found myself answering immediately and truthfully.

"Yes."

"If you left, you could stay with us before marrying again," Aunt Illustra offered.

This was my reason for staying. I could not face a second marriage, especially after Jennet's betrayal. How could I ever trust someone like that again or lie with a man?

"No, I will stay here, thank you."

They told me how there would be other opportunities for me

to visit them or for them to come to the convent before I took my final and irreversible vows. I nodded, still sure I was making the right decision. The lesser of the two evils.

Sister Agnes did not approach me. I stared at the ceiling of my cell that night, wondering if I dared write everything that I wanted to write to Hawise.

Chapter Eight

Narrative continued by Lord Ambrose of the many houses of the Westlands

The autumn of 2015 began with distant rumblings of trouble which turned into hurricanes that threatened us all. My profession as a watcher meant that I did not only see what was going on in the other world, that strange place of the internet, democracies and aeroplanes, but that I saw almost everything which was happening in my world. I knew more than most people did because I talked to many different people about the other world, our world and the void between them.

They braved the smell of my unwashed skin to speak to me, a lord who might have some influence over events. My decision not to wash was paying off in an unexpected way. If someone approached me, they had something important to tell me. Nobody bothered me with trivia.

The interregnum of the Westlands had begun in the summer of 2012, when all possible candidates for its throne were finally dead, and the council which governed my homeland was failing to keep a grip on the country without the authority of a monarch. More Westlanders were now more worried about their unstable government than they were about the ongoing war with their neighbour. It was not enemy troops that looted, raped and slaughtered but homegrown criminal gangs, grown bold by a lack of effective deterrents. The militia mostly did their best, but they were sent here, there and everywhere by their commanders, unable to stay in one place long enough to enforce order. Some had even defected to the Woldsheart, or even worse, to criminal gangs. Poverty and its siblings, famine, disease and despair, were rife.

Many earnest discussions took place as to what was to be done, but any relief was temporary in the face of such poor government.

One fine day in mid-October, I was back at Castle Malwarden when Marjory brought me fresh news of plague in a nearby village.

"Owen and Cerys have, of course, ordered its isolation for forty days and nights, and they have sent relief. Almost all the harvest has been gathered, which makes the situation slightly easier."

I nodded approvingly.

"Any news?" she asked me.

"All of the inhabitants of the other world, with the exception of a select few, remain ignorant of our world, long may it continue. No evil creatures from the void between the worlds have escaped since the last one was caught and shot in the spring."

"Good."

"However, I have heard two more reports of missing people. One is an adult, this time, a man of twenty. The other is a girl of ten. Both are of the House of Malwarden and living in our lands, although they do not live near each other. The council, some watchers and the militia are investigating, and they do not think the pair knew each other."

"Do they think these were so-called Deadly Favour disappearances? Were there signs of it?"

"We don't know in the case of the man. He appears to have

vanished without warning last Thursday afternoon. However, the girl's friends reported that she had a fine necklace of glass beads, which her family say they did not give her, and she spoke of a kind lady who gave her sweetmeats in return for trying to look for her lost cat. Her friends say the girl spoke as if she was proud of seeing this mysterious lady who gave her presents, when her friends never saw her nor received anything."

"Did she describe the lady to her friends? Could anyone else have seen her?"

"All the children could say was that she was a lady, who was nice to their friend and able to provide a costly-looking necklace. Three girls saw the necklace and said it looked of higher quality than anything they or their mothers possessed. Nobody saw the lady, the cat or the sweetmeats. It's just what the missing girl told her friends."

"Did the girl suddenly vanish too?"

"Yes, sometime between noon and early afternoon on Monday."

"Were any strangers seen near the man who disappeared?"

"None were mentioned."

We walked around the quiet orchard, deep in thought for some time. This was more worrying news after years of uncertainty that promised nothing good.

"I will remind my three to be careful and not to go off with strangers," she eventually said. "Cerys and Owen will do the same. As for Nessa, Madoc and Lewis..." Her voice trailed off.

"Clementia will do her best," I offered. "Besides, you, Owen and Cerys always show your love and care for them."

"It's as well that we do because Gods know the other three fail in their duty as parents. They leave everything to Clementia, tutors and servants."

"How do the little hostages get on?"

"They have both settled in, as far as I can tell. Eluned and Isabeau get on well with them, especially Rosamund. I am proud to say that Bran keeps an eye out for them. He is quite a big brother to them."

"Good. They will go home in January, won't they?"

Marjory's face fell.

"Between you and me, I don't think that's too likely. It's too dangerous to travel far. It's not so much the war as the criminal gangs. Our best hope is to persuade the Lothwold government to not exchange the hostages until things improve."

"It is in their interests as much as ours to do so," I soothed. "Nobody wants their kin to come to harm, especially when it was done on an unnecessary journey."

Besides, Gethin is unlikely to return to the Westlands anytime soon. He needs to behave himself in another kingdom and be seen to be behaving himself in order to stay intact.

Marjory's face told me she was thinking the same thought, so I tried to distract her.

"How do you get on with Lady Hawise these days? I have not seen her for some weeks, what with being called hither and thither on business."

"She improves on closer acquaintance, I'll give her that. She's not a complete flibbertigibbet or absolutely self-centred. I have heard her talk in very concerned tones about her family and friends. She is capable of caring, and she serves Cerys well. I think she has mastered the art of getting on with people, and I have managed to use her in my business. She is personable and has shown moments of shrewdness. However, we will never be close friends. Her situation as a hostage will always be a bar, and our characters are completely dissimilar."

How do you find her?"

"Pleasant enough. I don't speak with her much."

Marjory was too kind to tell me that I rarely spoke to anyone much, and my smell kept people away. I knew we were only having a long conversation because we were outside and walking in a stiff breeze.

I was particularly happy to keep Lady Hawise away. Quite

frankly, the woman terrified me. I could only agree with most of the castle's inhabitants in that she had charming manners, an easy-going nature and a pretty face, but she still scared me.

It was her sexual appetite and her licentious behaviour that filled me with fear. I had seen hints of it in how she looked at certain men and how she flirted. Nothing could convince me it was paranoia. I dreaded her turning her beautiful blue eyes my way. Sex, in general, unnerved me, although I would never admit it.

When I was a young man of eighteen, I had very much looked forward to marrying Sophie. Lady Sophie of Malwarden, who lived by the coast. However, her scars soon became mine, and sex quickly terrified us both. We managed to consummate the marriage, but only three times, and sex rapidly became a taboo subject and something to avoid at all costs.

Only Owen knew what had passed between us, and only later did I learn what had happened to Sophie before we were bound together. She died just after our second wedding anniversary due to complications caused by years of self-inflicted starvation. I was left guilt-ridden, resentful, determined never to marry again and without much idea of how to be a husband or how to be intimate with a woman.

Not washing my body worked. Nobody approached me, unless they had to, and I was no heir under pressure to marry and continue a great lineage. I was left in lonely peace.

Lady Hawise's robust health and appearance, her confidence, her extroversion, and her reputation both fascinated and repelled me. Her hearty appetite and general strength of body and mind made me shudder. The rumours about her, which did not make her blush, were merely the icing on the cake. She was the opposite of Sophie in every way possible. I was never gladder to have avoided soap and water than when I was in her presence.

By the end of the month, events had occurred that pushed Lady Hawise and my late wife, and even politics and missing children, far from my mind.

Due to the war and the interregnum, those living in my country had become familiar with violence, famine, disease and poverty to varying degrees. The poor suffered the most, but nobody was immune. Chaos and uncertainty were part of everyone's daily life. However, there were limits. Protests sometimes occurred, but no-one expected the flag to be violated. Similarly, dogs were occasionally used as weapons, but nobody ever imagined that dragons could be thus employed.

To violate the flag meant to take the bright and familiar flag of one's nation and to deface it with paint, before setting it on fire. It signalled a protest to end all protests, a riot in which all rules of society would be ignored. The aim was to overturn not only the current government but the very system under which government operates.

This had not happened anywhere in living memory, nor for the past thousand years in the Westlands. It did take place a century ago in Doggerdale, and the effects were still being felt one hundred years later. The act of violating the flag was taboo because of its consequences. It went against the natural order of things, yet it was not unimaginable because people had done it.

The use of dragons as a weapon *was* unimaginable until it happened. It had never been done before. Disability dragons were loyal helpmeets who would defend their owners, but only if life or limb were in danger. Regular dragons were like chariot-sized children or cats. Docile towards us, contrary at times and prone to squabbling with each other. The idea that one could be trained to aim its fire at people was unthinkable. The idea that someone would train it to do so sent shivers down any sane person's spine.

It was the sabbat of Samhain, and we celebrated it enthusiastically at Castle Malwarden. That is to say, most people did. I, as always, kept my distance. My time with Sophie had deadened my appetite for joy. Besides, I did not want to encounter her soul at the time of year when the veil between our world and the next is at its most permeable.

Lady Hawise joined in the merriment, shrieking and laughing

as the traditional raucous games were played. Marjory looked happier than I had seen her in weeks, and her children were as excited as any other child in the noisy, crowded castle. Owen, Cerys and my Aunt Isolde were joining in with as much gusto as anyone else. Even meek Clementia was animated.

I slipped away and fetched my telescope. It was a fine night for stargazing, and I had not had the opportunity to gaze out onto a clear sky for a long time.

I made my way to the tallest tower, relishing the peace and cold air after the noise and heat of the Great Hall.

Something that was not celestial caught my eye. Something which looked like bright lava, something I once saw on my travels, was blazing brightly in the distance. I put my telescope to my eye and adjusted it before gasping with horror, unwilling to believe what my senses were telling me.

Our nearest village, Mendoc, was ablaze. I could make out burning buildings, leaping orange flames and tiny people milling about.

I ran back to the Great Hall and interrupted the game of Guess Who I'm Thinking Of. It took half a minute of precious time to get everyone's attention.

"Mendoc is on fire! The entire village has gone up. I was stargazing and saw it through my telescope. We must go there immediately."

After the expected cries of disbelief and demands that I repeat myself, I made myself sufficiently understood to gather a party to go there directly. We flew on the fastest dragons we had, but by the time we got there, the village was an unbearable wall of heat.

A woman staggered towards us and recognised Cerys. She fell to her knees.

"Lady, save us! They violated the flag, then they used a dragon to burn down the church. It laughed to see the holy building burn before setting fire to several cottages, and it's spreading. Help us. If you cannot help us, madam, who can?"

This news was more appalling than the flames. At first we

thought we had misunderstood her, but our eyes confirmed it. An emerald green dragon wandered about, breathing fire at random. People fled, screaming.

"Saints and holy souls preserve us," I whispered, making the sign of the circle.

"Human, I'm scared," my dragon Herbert whimpered. "That's a bad dragon. They shouldn't be using their fire like that."

I tried to soothe him, but he was becoming dangerously fractious, which set the other dragons off. We had to dismount for our safety.

The green dragon saw us and lumbered over, but luckily we were prepared with bolts and crossbows. Guards shot it dead, which turned our dragons hysterical.

We all did the best we could on that dreadful night. A human chain, which I headed, carried water from the river to extinguish the flames. The most experienced dragon trainer amongst us calmed our beasts. People went to help others.

Finding out exactly what had occurred was not our first priority, and in any case, it proved to be harder than we had anticipated.

We eventually learned what had happened.

Late in the afternoon of 31st October, just as it was getting dark, three men and a woman rode into the village on a bright green dragon. With them, they carried the flag of the Westlands, which attracted attention but not concern.

They made their way to the marketplace, by the church, which was busy with people. There, the woman gave a barnstorming speech, damning the corrupt Council of the Interregnum and the nobility who oversaw a dying state. It was time to turn the failed world on its head and forge a new one through fire.

Incendiary speeches were not rare in these troubled times, so nobody was too disturbed by the young woman's fiery words. That changed when two of the men held the flag taut whilst the third threw black paint on it. The dragon then set it alight.

This shocked everyone present. Like me, they struggled to believe their eyes. The protesters were not shocked at what they had done. Instead, they cheered, patted the dragon and led it to the church, whereupon it drew breath and set the ancient building on fire.

Panic ensued. The group of four seemed to vanish, nobody knew who they were nor where they went. The villagers' only concern was for their own lives. It seemed a blessing from the Gods that none of them died or was severely injured, yet the devastation to homes and livelihoods was enormous. The damage to everyone's peace of mind was incalculable.

I met Owen two days after the attack. My shock and fear was mirrored in his freckled face.

"My God, cousin," I whispered. "What do we do now?"

CHAPTER NINE

Narrative continued by Lord Owen of Malwarden

I had no answer to Ambrose's terrified question, yet I hoped to have one soon. The Council of the Interregnum, men and women from all over the Westlands, would meet that afternoon. With their help, Cerys and I hoped to work miracles and decide what to do next.

The violation of the flag and the use of a dragon to commit arson were so terrible that nearly all of the council gathered at our castle with very little notice. Only those who pleaded sickness stayed away. Cerys and I attended, but nobody else from my family was part of it. Unusually, a foreign ambassador was present, Fulk of Lothwold. His lord had heard what had passed and had sent his spokesman west to issue dire threats.

"His lordship insists that order is restored or the Westlands will be invaded in order to bring it about," he stated smoothly.

I stared at him, quite aghast yet not entirely surprised. Fulk was a man in his fifties who had been an ambassador for more than twenty years. His manner was cool and confident to the point of arrogance. The Lord of Lothwold was not known for either his diplomacy or his wise words.

"Of course, his lordship may not invade another sovereign land without his sovereign's permission, something Queen Elixabeth will never grant. Naturally, I must obey my lord and master and come here to repeat his words, despite being disgusted at their stupidity. However, I do agree that order must be restored and maintained. It is in the Woldsheart's interests as much as it is in the Westlands'. Nobody wants an out-of-control state on their border. Violence spills over borders, followed by refugees when we have enough poor of our own, we cannot trade with such a state and homegrown ne'er-do-wells are inspired to launch their own violent campaigns. No, order has to be restored and maintained."

As the head of the House of Malwarden, I felt obliged to speak.

"I can assure you, sir, that we are tackling this. The miscreants are being hunted down, the dragon was shot, the militia have increased their support, and we are providing alms to those affected."

He shook his head.

"That's a temporary solution, and we both know it. The interregnum must end. It generates political instability and its many woes."

This was something we could all agree on. The problem was we had no suitable candidate. If we had, he or she would have been crowned years ago.

"Why has no monarch been anointed?" Fulk asked.

"The last of the line died out three years ago, and we could not choose anyone else without sparking a civil war," Magnus replied. He had married Cerys's sister and once led the warriors of Ishelmer. Upon his marriage to the head of the House of Pendroch, he resigned and acted as his wife's consort. He did not give away national secrets. This problem occurred all over the civilised world. There was as much rivalry between houses as between kingdoms. "Whoever we choose, someone will object. They will produce someone with a better claim ad infinitum, but we all need a figure to get behind."

I nodded. The beauty of our system was that the quality of the actual monarch did not matter too much. A child, an idiot, a despot or a madman could sit on the throne. Any or all, and courtiers could ensure that a good image was maintained in public, whilst the council ensured that business ran smoothly behind the scenes. However, a wise, humane adult with experience of life was to be preferred.

"What we need is someone who has links to every house in the Westlands and is likely to produce healthy offspring. Someone who will listen to advice and who sees the world clearly. Old enough to have experience and young enough for the demands of the job. Such a person does not exist," my wife stated with sad simplicity.

It hit me like cold water.

"Ambrose," I whispered.

"What?" many voices demanded.

"My guardian's nephew. Ambrose. He has blood from every house in the Westlands in his veins. It has gone against him in the past, but now it is decidedly in his favour. He turned twenty-five about a month ago. He has years of experience as a watcher. He is noble. His health has been good the whole time I have known him."

Cerys shook her head.

"That is true, but you do not add that he reeks to high heaven. He literally has not washed for years. Not since his wife died. That is not the act of a sane man, and to be perfectly frank, I wonder at his state of mind. He keeps to himself to a ridiculous degree, it cannot make him happy, yet he seems to wilfully live in a lonely prison of his own making.

"However, his marriage was enough to drive anyone out of their wits, poor soul. Gods rest Sophie, poor soul." She quickly made the sign of the circle.

Not everyone was familiar with the story, so she was obliged to explain. I was annoyed. This was family business, and I did not see the need for her to talk about it any further than necessary to make it clear why Ambrose could never be king. However, I had to admit that I could now see why we had not approached him earlier.

She told the sorry story, one that always made me sigh inwardly. Ambrose had not always been a gloomy man, nor a smelly one. In his youth he had been a cheerful, friendly man, always in the shadow of his elder half-brothers, but a better man than both of them put together. He did have many good qualities. His intelligence and determination showed. In those days he was even called handsome. Again, he was overshadowed by Lewis and Madoc, but many girls and women gave him a second look.

Sophie arrived at Castle Malwarden when he was eighteen and she was seventeen, in the late autumn of 2008. We knew little about her, only what her parents had reported to my aunt and uncle, both then still living. I could only curse their naivety.

Marjory's pain is down to me and our brothers interfering too much and where it was not warranted. Goddess knows how my conscience still kicks me, and deservedly. I am amazed that she and Gethin have anything to do with me at all. However, it can go too far the other way. My aunt and uncle were phenomenally lax in not meeting their prospective daughter-in-law and merely relying on the word of their old friends, her parents. They should also have let Ambrose meet her before the betrothal was finalised, like he kept begging to.

They met shortly before their wedding. It was clear that something was not quite right, but my aunt and uncle would not listen to their son's calls for a delay. However, it was only after the wedding that the real problems were revealed.

Sophie was a plain girl with a skull-like face the colour of a raw mushroom, coarse dark brown hair, a surprising amount of hair on her arms and bulging eyes with a haunted look. Her appearance suggested much mental and physical suffering and years of insufficient food. This was all true.

Sophie had suffered physical violence from a family friend soon after she turned thirteen. When her parents discovered their daughter's torments, after more than three years of vicious assaults, they arranged for the perpetrator to meet an accidental death, and they looked for a bridegroom for her. They believed that if she could have a fresh start with a nice young man, who looked and sounded nothing like her attacker, she would heal.

Naturally, this failed miserably. Sophie could deal with her pain by severely limiting her food and had done so for years. This was not enough in the face of the physical and emotional intimacy of marriage. Ambrose had no idea of what she had suffered, none of us did until several months after her arrival. In the meantime, she became hysterical, seemingly without reason, lashed out at anyone, especially her husband, and suffered night terrors which also terrified him.

Ambrose was patient. We all were. He tried to help her, but she could not speak. We only learned the truth after her mother eventually confessed. The news hit Ambrose like a castle wall. He was consumed with the guilt of not realising what she had endured, doubly so because his attempts to comfort her through touch had only caused her further pain.

We tried to help her, we sought medical advice, but to no avail. Her pain consumed her, she sickened, and eventually, her heart gave out.

Consumed by grief, guilt and rage, Ambrose vowed never to marry again. Nobody challenged him. It then became apparent that he had also pledged never to wash again, but again nobody tackled him.

That was unwise. We were right not to push for a second marriage, but we should have made him wash and dragged him back into the world of the living long before now. Bad habits have become entrenched. How do we make a functioning man out of him, let alone a husband, a father and a king?

Cerys concluded her tale, and the rest of the council nodded soberly or looked appalled, depending on whether or not they had heard the story before.

"It sounds like Ambrose is not the right man for the job,"

Magnus sighed. "Besides, what would we do for a consort? We cannot choose a woman from the Westlands, it would cause too much infighting, but which foreign bride would be suitable? From what country should she hail?"

We considered the House of Ishelmer in the Woldsheart and the House of Tinvaal in the Kingdom of the Isles, both our allies at one time or another, and not currently our enemies. It was useless. We could only think of young girls, too young to wed for years that we did not have, or women past the age of childbirth.

"There is Morwennat of Tinvaal," someone suggested. "She is fifteen and as well grown as one might expect such a girl to be, but she is more like a girl of eleven or twelve in mind. She is not slow, just so childish. However, she is of good family and appeared healthy enough when I saw her at the last equinox. Her parents are reasonable people. We could do worse."

It was not enough. We needed an adult consort. Someone who understood the weight of their responsibilities yet would still undertake them.

"Then who?" someone else demanded. "Who else is there to approach after years of fighting? So many branches have been snapped off so many noble houses. There is nobody else."

"There is." Cerys's eyes lit up with a sudden idea. "Our eldest hostage. Hawise of Lothwold. She is the right age, she enjoys good health and good spirits, and she is bright and amiable. We know all this because we have observed her in trying conditions for months. I would also add that she has a kind heart. I have seen how she looks out for people, like the other hostages. She is noble and not from the Westlands. Lothwold is our enemy, but this marriage might secure a lasting peace."

"All that is true," I conceded. "Yet you do not add her faults. She is promiscuous, she has merely had no opportunity to indulge herself whilst under our protection, she is lazy, and I don't think she takes life at all seriously. These are lethal faults for a consort."

"I think she hides a lot of what she feels," Cerys stated. "She has served me since she arrived in July. From the odd escaped sigh and pensive expression, I am convinced she thinks and feels far more deeply than she lets on. In addition, the ability to hide one's emotions is invaluable in a public figure. You cannot deny that she knows how to charm and her knowledge of etiquette is perfect, even if she does not always put it into practice. Let her past remain in the past. There are many in high positions who have done worse and are still accepted." She hastily looked down at the table.

We sat in silence for some time. Ambrose and Lady Hawise were not the ideal choices, but there was literally nobody else to choose from. Any other monarch would cause a civil war. Any other consort was either a child or someone unlikely to bear children. Fulk was right. The interregnum had to end before the kingdom collapsed.

I addressed the room.

"Let us vote on it. Those in favour of Ambrose becoming king, stand."

I stood, and everyone followed suit, except Fulk, who was not permitted to vote.

"Those in favour of Hawise of Lothwold becoming his consort, remain standing."

Nobody moved.

It was as if a great cloud had finally been lifted, yet I was now very nervous. Neither man nor woman was what anyone would have voluntarily chosen, yet a choice had been made. A choice that might just move our country forwards to peace, prosperity and better relations with our neighbours.

"That settles it. With your permission, I will approach Ambrose right away."

They gave me their permission.

"And I will find Lady Hawise," Cerys declared. "If she consents, we can write to the Queen of the Woldsheart to ask her to permit the marriage. There is no point in approaching her majesty if she refuses."

"Why should she refuse?" Magnus was incredulous. "It's a

great honour and a damn sight better than being a hostage."

CHAPTER TEN

B y unusual good luck, Ambrose was still at the castle, and I quickly found out exactly where he was. He was reading one of his beloved books with evident pleasure in the library, thus ensuring that nobody else came into the room. I instinctively began to breathe through my mouth and looked at him more closely than I usually did.

He was a wiry man of about medium height, a little taller than me but much shorter than his brothers. His golden brown skin only appeared pale against his curly blue-black hair, while his eyes were a deep purple-grey. The more romantic women had compared them to a sky just before a storm, as well as praising his long eyelashes and bushy eyebrows. His face was striking rather than classically handsome, but again, he had attracted female notice before he renounced soap and water. Today he was as plainly dressed as ever. One would only realise he was noble because the fabric of his clothes was clearly of high quality.

What would he look like if he were better dressed, freshly scrubbed, and if he had a crown on his head?

"Ambrose," I called. He looked up, startled. "Sorry to disturb you, but I need to speak with you about something important. We need to go to my closet. We must not be disturbed."

Looking slightly anxious, he complied. As he rose, a smell of onions and armpits hit me. I turned my face away from him, silently vowing that even if he refused to become king, he was not getting away without washing for much longer.

It's disgusting. We should have pulled him up on this years ago. It cannot be doing him any good, either to his body or his mind. If I have to personally pin him down, then so be it!

We reached my closet, and I bolted not only its door but the door to the outer chamber. Privacy was vital.

"What is it, cousin?" he asked. "Has somebody died?"

"No, and what I am going to propose will save many lives."

I took a deep breath before giving the speech I had mentally been preparing since I left the council.

"The council met this morning, Ambrose. I need not tell you what we discussed. The current situation is dangerous. We are even at risk of the Woldsheart invading us. Yes, one of their diplomats was present. The root cause of our political instability is the interregnum. We need a monarch, and we need one now. We discussed this, and we agreed, agreed unanimously, that we need someone who is young but experienced in the ways of the world, noble and linked to every house, intelligent and determined."

I sank to my knees. He stared at me with wide eyes and a slack jaw.

"Ambrose, my dear cousin, I beg you as the Lord of Malwarden, as a member of the council and as your kinsman, to accept the throne of the Westlands. Take it, and take us out of a situation which is ruining not only our country but also our neighbour's. This will end so much suffering. It will even end the war if you take Lady Hawise of Lothwold as your consort."

I looked up. He looked ready to faint. I got up and sat down. He likewise sank into a chair, still silent. This was not going as I had hoped.

I waited, and he eventually spoke.

"Cousin, I cannot."

"Why?"

"Look at me. I can barely cope with my life as it is. I cannot begin to contemplate how I would manage being king. How would I even cope as a husband and a father? Marriage to Sophie nearly killed me. Besides, Lady Hawise terrifies me."

His last sentence puzzled me.

"How does she terrify you?"

"She is so...so confident, so loud and so healthy. She is frank about her appetite for men and for life in general. Look at me. I am a shadow beside her. She would eat me for breakfast, then wander off for a mid-morning snack. I could never marry again, but if I had to, such a wife would be the end of me. No, pray let someone else take power."

"They will. Ambrose, if you do not take power, those who violated the flag will. Should we capture them, others will still be inspired by their actions and emulate them. Someone, someday soon, will bring down the nation. I need not list the consequences."

He sat in silence, and I took the opportunity to continue.

"Take power, start washing and start interacting more with the world, and take Hawise of Lothwold as your bride. You would feel much better if you were clean and talked more, we all would, and Lady Hawise is the perfect consort."

He laughed bitterly.

"No, she is." I insisted. "Marrying her ends the war with her house. It gives us a good position in the Woldsheart and boosts our standing amongst our other neighbours. It signals a change towards stability and strong rule. People like someone to get behind and cheer. She is pretty, charming and knows how to make herself agreeable. I believe she also has a sharp brain and a sound understanding, when she chooses to use them. You are both young and healthy, you should be able to have children and secure the succession."

He looked at me, and I could see my words were sinking in.

"You would both have to change," I concluded. "She will have to stay faithful to you for the rest of your life, like any consort must. She will also have to stir herself and take life more seriously. You will have to wash, re-join the world, be sociable and be a faithful husband. But honestly, are these such hardships that you will sacrifice the very future of our nation for them? She likes men, and she has a good heart. She might even make you happy."

"Is there truly no other way out of this? Nobody else could take the throne?"

"No. We discussed this as a council, and you are the only person who has all of the qualities that would be necessary for a monarch to be accepted. Hawise of Lothwold is the only consort that you could take who would not present diplomatic problems and who is likely to bear children."

He sighed so deeply that I feared a refusal.

"Owen, if there is no other way to bring peace and prosperity to our kingdom, then I will go now and wash. I will then present my acceptance to the council and every inhabitant of the castle. Will someone speak with Lady Hawise in the meantime?"

Had he not stood up, I would not have dared believe my ears.

"Yes. Cerys should be with her now."

CHAPTER ELEVEN

Narrative continued by Lady Hawise of Lothwold

I little suspected what lay in store for me when Lady Cerys hurried back from her council meeting one chilly afternoon in early November. I was working with her demoiselles, organising relief for those who had suffered in Mendoc. We talked only of recent events and worried over what the future held.

At least neither I, Rosamund nor Drogo can be blamed for this. From what little we know about the perpetrators, they were not from our house or our kingdom. This castle has a new, more interesting enemy.

Lady Cerys bustled into the Great Hall where we were working and made straight for me. I could not help but see the determination and anxiety on her face.

"Lady Hawise, please come with me."

I put down the parcel I had just wrapped and nodded.

Hold yourself well, Hawise. Whatever happens next, let nobody says you acted in an undignified manner. Hysteria will help nobody. A quick curtsey to her ladyship and another to the other women to excuse yourself, then follow her with your head held high. Resist asking her any questions. You will soon find out what is going on, and she would likely fob you off. Nobody ever told anyone important secrets as they walked through busy corridors.

Lady Cerys led me to her chamber, bade me to go through it to her closet before locking the chamber door. She closed the closet door firmly after her. I was now more puzzled than petrified.

"My lady, what is happening?"

She bade me to sit and looked at me with apprehension.

"Lady Hawise, I must tell you what passed in the council today, what will happen and the great favour I must beg of you."

I was now thoroughly mystified. What power or influence did she imagine I possessed?

"Madam, I will gladly do whatever I can to help you, but I am a foreigner and a hostage. I cannot see how I can help you with council matters."

"You being of foreign blood is one of the reasons why you can help not only me but hundreds of thousands of people neither of us has ever met."

She then told me what had taken place in the council meeting, the news that Fulk of Lothwold had brought and the necessity of ending the interregnum now. She explained why Lord Ambrose was the only suitable monarch, she told me about his unhappy marriage, and she explained why I should be his queen.

"Lady Hawise, you have many good qualities, as well as being unlinked to any house of the Westlands and being likely to bear children. You have been in my service for almost four months and under the most trying conditions. During this time I have seen evidence of your intelligence, your fortitude and your compassion. If you applied these qualities to being queen consort and Ambrose's wife, you would save so many lives, the lives of those living and of those yet to be born."

I stared at her, aware I was quite slack-jawed and goggle-eyed with amazement. Any thoughts of dignity had long been forgotten.

"Owen is with Ambrose now," she continued. "If you give me

your consent, your queen will be applied to. I very much doubt she will refuse. It is an honour to have a daughter of her kingdom sit on a throne, and she must want a lasting peace as much as we both do."

"I don't know what to say." That was true enough. Out of anything Lady Cerys might have had to say, I could never have guessed this. Peace, a second marriage, and to be released from being a hostage were my dreams, but I never thought all three would be achieved so quickly and in such a dramatic way.

The idea of living in the Westlands for the rest of my life, at the centre of power and as the wife of Lord Ambrose made every nerve in my body shrink. I wanted to go home, but once again, home had changed irreversibly. Bessy was now a novice nun, living under very strict conditions. We could not resume our old friendship. As Queen Consort, I would enjoy power, but the responsibility and scrutiny terrified me. Besides, how could a man as scarred as Ambrose make a responsive husband or father, let alone a king?

All this weighed against a lasting peace and exchanging one trying situation for a less trying one. I would also enable the exchange of the other hostages. Brother Gethin would have to remain in his exile, but no-one could change that.

I knew my duty, but I doubted my abilities. I knew my disposition and my faults. God knows they had been pointed out to me often enough. I craved lovers, luxury, freedom and fun. Being Queen Consort would only guarantee the second. I could certainly wave farewell to the first and the third.

Lord Ambrose was not a husband I could stomach. I found myself telling this to his cousin by marriage in politer terms.

"Let me frank, madam. We both know that Lord Ambrose does not wash. We both know how he smells. How is he to lead the nation in such a state? How am I to go anywhere near him?"

Lady Cerys insisted that he would be made to wash and regularly. I thought that made him sound like a stubborn little boy. She then explained why he had given up soap and water.

"He was not always like this," she concluded sadly. "Before his marriage, he was a good-looking young man with winning manners and a sincere heart. People valued his company. You might be able to bring some of that back. He would benefit from your liveliness and your good nature. In turn, he would support you."

"He sounds damaged. Can a man with such mental scars become king? It's not his fault, but he has years of bad habits to overcome. Has this lack of washing even harmed him physically?"

"Scars can heal. Besides, we have no choice. There is literally no other candidate who would not provoke a civil war. He is not cruel, I can promise you that. He will not harm you or any child you may bear. You and he will have to undertake a medical exam and a spiritual exam before it is announced, so we can check his health then. Gods know what we will do if he is found wanting..."

Her voice trailed off. She was right. This was our one chance of peace.

"If Lord Ambrose and I pass these exams, and if Queen Elixabeth consents to my marriage, then I will do it. I will marry Lord Ambrose and be the best wife and consort I can be."

She fell back in relief. I realised she had been holding her breath. To my surprise and discomfort, she kissed my hand.

"Thank you. You have saved so many."

The rest of the day fled by at a terrifying speed. Neither Lord Ambrose nor I were permitted to breathe a word about what had happened. A priest and a physician would examine us the next day. Lady Cerys had sent a messenger to fetch them.

Lord Owen spoke to me privately and made his pleasure and gratitude clear. I did not know what to say. Whilst under his power and protection, he had always treated me well enough, yet my situation was going to rapidly change. I would join his family and be a rank above him. I did not know what to feel.

I won't be a hostage for much longer, but I won't really be free again. I wish my family were still here. I wish I could go back to being a little girl again, when everyone was still alive, yet also have

Bessy in my life. My God, what would they all say? What will Bessy say? I need her. I need to see her now.

I bit my lip and looked about me as we ate in the Great Hall. To everyone's surprise, Lord Ambrose was present, looking clean and smelling fresh. People nudged each other and whispered. Supposing this change was brought about because of me or his change in situation, I looked at him with more interest than before.

He was sitting near me and talking to Lady Marjory. It was amazing what a good wash had done for him. He looked so much healthier and held himself so much straighter. I had to admit he was handsome. Not as handsome as Brother Gethin, Lord Madoc or Lord Lewis but definitely worth looking at and such an improvement compared to his previous appearance.

Lord Lewis was neighbour at dinner, and he was charming towards me, yet he did not succeed in charming me. My opinion of him, Lady Nessa and Lord Madoc had dwindled since we were introduced. At first I was taken in and captivated by their immaculate manners and apparent concern for me, a captive in a strange land. I also enjoyed their company, for they were lively, witty and knew how to make themselves agreeable. However, I once saw Lord Lewis tell his son off. The reason seemed justified, the boy had been playing about with a knife and could have cut himself, but the five minutes of ferocity directed at the seven-year-old was not. The father did not stop shouting and swearing, getting right up in his son's face, until the boy cried. He then let him go, but the look of triumph and pleasure in his eyes turned my stomach and my opinion of him. I had seen less dramatic examples of such malicious behaviour from Lord Madoc and Lady Nessa, which led me to form a very different view of them compared to my first impression.

I was careful to keep my thoughts to myself and to keep my countenance pleasant and my conversation light. Whether I was a queen or a hostage, a wife or a widow, I did not want to let my guard down around either of those three.

Lady Marjory and I will never see eye to eye, but I feel safer around her than I do around them. She may be a cold woman, possibly also a judgmental one, but she is a decent person. This pleasure in cruelty is simply not something she indulges in.

Lord Ambrose turned the conversation to a subject which was not light-hearted. The so-called Deadly Favour. No more children had been reported missing, but a young man called Bryn had suddenly vanished.

"Were those responsible for taking the children also responsible for taking Bryn of Lower Warden?" I named a village that was relatively near Castle Malwarden. I had been told about the disappearances some weeks ago but only felt able to discuss them in public now my position was changing. As Queen Consort, I needed to know this. As a hostage, it might look like a desire for gossip or to gloat at my enemy's misfortune.

"We believe so," Lady Marjory said. "However, so little is known about Bryn's disappearance. It is still being investigated, and people are still looking for him."

"His poor family," Lady Nessa sighed. "How they must be suffering." Her sister-in-law, Lady Clementia, agreed.

We talked of the matter for some minutes. I found myself observing Lord Ambrose more than anyone else. This man was to be my husband and rule a nation, what was technically still an enemy nation to me. Through him, I would take Westlander nationality and royal status.

He is not bad looking at all. He has such a charming smile, such good teeth, and the sort of looks that grow on you. Washing has done him good. Surely, we will both pass both examinations tomorrow?

The Bishop of the Westlands examined Lord Ambrose's spirit whilst Gytha of Merendysh, a renowned physician, examined my body. She got me to strip, checked various parts of me and asked me dozens of questions.

"You have excellent health. You have no venereal diseases from your previous partners. I would just say that your spirits have been a little affected by your months as a prisoner, which is not surprising. There is no reason why you should not marry Lord Ambrose and become queen, my lady."

I thanked her heartily and re-pinned my hair and veil. What she said was a great relief to me because I had worried that my previous indulgences had given me a disease of some sort. I had always taken precautions and had never had any symptoms which might not be attributed to worry, yet the fear that I might be infected with something nasty sometimes kept me awake at night.

Nobody can say I should not marry Lord Ambrose. I won't remain a hostage or return to the Woldsheart and end up in a nunnery. At least I can prove myself to be a fit wife here through my Lothwold blood, my high birth and my good health. Back home my reputation could never be bleached and those qualities meant nothing. I just need to pass the bishop's examination.

His Excellency was harder to please than the physician. He was concerned that I was flighty and quite aghast at the sheer number of men I had slept with. In turn, I became flippant, despite knowing that such a defence was likely to backfire. He raised his neat eyebrows on more than one occasion, lectured me on the need to think on serious matters before announcing that he was satisfied with me, providing I followed his advice regarding my future conduct.

Giddy with relief, I nodded. I could not have expected a more lenient outcome.

I wonder if he is under pressure to pass me? Lady Cerys said that there is no other possible consort who would not cause more problems than she resolves. I wonder how Lord Ambrose has fared. The bishop and the physician might also be under pressure to pass him.

Gytha of Merendysh re-entered where room where the bishop and I sat, looking distressed. My heart sank.

"What is it?" the bishop asked. "I found little wrong with his lordship's soul. What have you found on his body?"

She paused and looked at us both.

"He is well apart from...Come see for yourselves. He has a terrible skin condition from years of not washing. If he had not changed his linen regularly, I dread to think in what state he might be."

I hurried after her, wondering what was wrong with him. It was hardly surprisingly that some five years of not washing had harmed his skin, although I had not seen any sign of it on what was visible at dinner, namely his face, neck and hands.

Ambrose was dressed in just his shirt and breeches. The rest of his clothes were in a neat pile on a chair. He stood looking at us like some sort of frightened animal. My heart became tender towards him.

"Sir, would you prefer for me and His Excellency to leave the room?"

"You should stay, you will see all of me soon enough."

The bishop made his excuses and left us, assuring us of his silence as he left.

How vulnerable he must be feeling. It sounds like he's only ever slept with his wife, and that was a disaster for both of them. How many people have seen his body since he became an adult?

With a look that quite melted my heart, he took off his shirt, paused, turned his back then removed his breeches and underwear. I did not know quite what to expect. From the front, he looked like a naturally thin young man who lived an active lifestyle. His build was slight, and he had well-defined muscles with black hair on his limbs and chest. There was nothing odd there. When he showed us his back view, I had to clamp my hand over my mouth to stop my scream of horror.

From his shoulders to his backside, he was covered in what looked like tiny tubes and holes, some green, some yellow, some white. It was almost as if he had rolled in something.

"Good Goddess, Ambrose, are you not in pain? Did you not know that you had this?"

He turned slightly towards me, still covering his groin with his hands.

"I feel something, especially when I sit, but I never liked looking at myself, and I could hardly see my back view. Gytha has shown me using that mirror. It must have spread over time. I first felt something in between my shoulder blades about a year ago then the feeling, a sort of bumpiness, spread. I suppose if I had not agreed to this, it would have spread all over my body. Would it have killed me?" He turned to Gytha.

"Well, yes. If you had left it long enough to cover your entire body, then yes, yes it would. However, it can be cured." She rummaged around in her bag and produced a large jar of cream.

"Rub this on morning and night. Keep using it until the jar is empty. It will have gone by then, and you will suffer no lasting effects."

He thanked her.

"I am happy to say that you have both passed both examinations."

"Even with this condition?" He sounded incredulous.

"Yes, because it is curable, if you want to cure it, and I can see that you do. The bishop and I will inform the council via Lord Owen and Lady Cerys that we see no impediment to you becoming king and queen. I will leave you now." She curtseyed and left, shutting the door before I could hurry after her.

Lord Ambrose had pulled his breeches back up and looked awkwardly at me. I wanted to leave but saw an opportunity that I had to take.

"Shall I do your back?" I made myself smile as if unconcerned.

"Thank you." He handed me the jar and turned away.

I opened the jar and noticed a smell of something fresh and medicinal. Gytha had not said what was in it. It felt cold on my fingers.

"Brace yourself. It's freezing."

He flinched slightly as my fingers made contact with his shoulders. I instinctively grabbed his other shoulder to steady him. The tubes felt hard and squelched under my fingertips. I repressed a shudder.

I must not let him think I am repulsed by him. Poor man.

*When was the last time someone touched him apart from Gytha,
who only did it to perform a duty? Was it a loving touch?*

I kept smoothing the white ointment over his back, spreading
it thinly over the tubes and holes. I came to the waistband of his
breeches and paused.

"Do you want me to continue?" I asked, sensing that to go
further might be to go too far.

He turned around and took the jar out of my hand.

"I will be alright now. Thank you, Lady Hawise."

I nodded, curtseyed and left the room, aware of his eyes
following me.

The next few days passed in a strange atmosphere. The
council had sent a messenger to Queen Elixabeth to ask that I
might marry Lord Ambrose, soon to be King Ambrose III, and
become Queen of the Westlands. Everyone else at the castle knew
something was up but not what. Those who knew did not
breathe a word. Rosamund approached me, asking what was
happening and if it was to do with me, her or Drogo.

"Has something bad happened with the war?" she whispered
with frightened eyes. "Will we be punished?"

Heartily wishing I could tell her and Drogo the truth and put
their minds at ease, I smiled and lied.

"No. I asked someone and was told that what has happened is
not serious and will not affect us. They could not tell me anything
more."

She left, not completely satisfied.

*Poor girl and poor boy. I can only hope that we will soon be able
to put their minds at ease. They should be able to go home soon, and
the children from the Westlands will come back here. How good that
will be!*

I was not present when the messenger returned to Castle
Malwarden. I was sewing for the poor with the demoiselles. It was
early in the afternoon of 14th November, a Saturday. A servant
called Lady Cerys out of the room, a common occurrence,

someone always needed something from her, before returning to fetch me.

Then I knew.

I put down my sewing, excused myself and left the room, very aware of the growing whispers behind me.

Let there be no whispers tonight, only shouts of joy. Let this work.

The servant led me to Lord Owen's closet, where he was waiting with his wife and Lord Ambrose. Their faces spoke for them.

"Queen Elixabeth has granted her permission, Lady Hawise," Lord Ambrose declared. "Will you do me the honour of becoming my wife and consort?"

"Yes, sir. Yes, I will. I would be honoured."

It felt like a dream.

Lady Cerys and Lord Owen seemed to exhale.

"Welcome to the family, Hawise." She kissed me on both cheeks.

"Thank you, Cerys." I returned the gesture.

Lord Owen did likewise, then Lord Ambrose looked at me. He kissed me so quickly on one cheek that I did not realise he had done it until it was over. He took my hand and held it whilst we talked about what had to happen next.

He and I would return to what we were doing before we were called away and sidestep any questions. Lord Owen would write to Queen Elixabeth to tell her I had accepted. Lady Cerys would brief the council, who were still at the castle.

At dinner that night, Lord Owen would rise and the rest of the council would follow. Lord Owen would then ask Lord Ambrose to become King of the Westlands. Lord Ambrose would accept on the condition that I would be his consort. I would rise, walk over to him and give my consent. He would then embrace me, and the council would cheer and hope that everyone would join in.

A dozen curious eyes greeted me on my return to my sewing, but nobody asked me any questions, and I kept quiet.

Will these women accept me as their queen? Hawise the slut. Hawise the hostage. Hawise of Lothwold. Can I really be transformed into a regal consort?

By the time I entered the Great Hall for dinner, I was shaking and aware that I was pale, for my face felt cold. I had changed into my second best gown of deep blue velvet, aware that to change into my first would attract too much attention too early, yet people would remember this moment. I wanted to look my best for it.

The room swam. Grace was said. We sat down. People began to pile up their plates and fill their goblets. I touched nothing. Instead, I kept my eyes on Lord Owen. After a few minutes, he looked at me significantly, nodded, then rose.

The members of the council rose seconds later, almost as one body. Everybody turned to stare, clearly on edge and not sure what was going to happen next. I tried to breathe deeply.

Owen spoke in a clear voice which rang out across the large room.

"Lord Ambrose of the many houses of the Westlands, on behalf of the Council of the Interregnum, I beg you to accept the throne of our noble country and become King of the Westlands. Take the crown and bring peace and justice to our land."

The whole room held its breath. Nobody spoke, but everybody seemed to look at each other.

Lord Ambrose answered. I noticed how confident he sounded and that his voice had a pleasing quality to my ears.

"Council of the Interregnum, I accept the throne with gratitude and swear by all that is holy to be worthy of it and your faith in me, on one condition."

"Name it," Lord Owen replied.

"I wish to choose my consort."

"Name her, and we will accept her."

This is it. Don't move yet.

"I wish for Lady Hawise of Lothwold of the Woldsheart to be my bride, thus ending the conflict between our land and hers."

I rose, so conscious of the gaze of dozens of people, and walked as gracefully as I could towards him. I curtseyed as deeply as a subject should to her monarch.

"My lord, I am honoured, and I accept."

He raised me and pulled me into his arms, clumsily kissing me on the ear. I threw my arms around his waist, hoping it was not narrower than mine.

The council cheered, and I felt both Lord Ambrose and I hold our breath but only for a second. The rest of the hall stood up and began to cheer and applaud, calling out their good wishes for us. Some of the children were too young to appreciate what was happening, let alone the enormity of the situation, but they were still caught up in the charged atmosphere.

I looked about me, barely daring to believe my eyes and ears. People were overjoyed. They not only accepted our decision, they embraced it.

"I can't believe it," my betrothed whispered in my ear. "We've done it."

I nodded, trying not to cry and failing. I did not let go him, nor he of me. I was even more grateful that he had begun to wash again. Standing close to him, the crown of my head near his lips, I was far from repulsed by him. I did not feel overwhelming lust but something was there.

Maybe this won't be so bad. In any case, few people marry for love. Many happy marriages have begun under worse circumstances. He is nothing like Adam, but in time, I might be as happy with him as I was with my first husband. We will make this work. The people are behind us. We cannot fail.

The rest of the meal passed smoothly, yet after I got up from the table, I felt panic rising within me. What I had felt when I offered to become a hostage the previous summer was nothing to the enormity of my current feelings of dread.

I was sitting with Lord Ambrose in the solar, we had been left alone, when the panic overwhelmed me. Out of nowhere, I felt engulfed in the most dreadful sensation. My breathing became rapid, I simply could not get enough air, and it felt as though I were drowning. My body became numb and clammy. I honestly thought I was about to die, yet I did not want to attract any attention to myself.

Lord Ambrose was with me in an instant. He sat beside me, put an arm around my shoulders and put a clean cloth loosely over my nose and mouth.

"Breathe slowly and deeply, in and out. Don't move the cloth. It will help you."

I stopped trying to push him away and followed his directions. After some time, I do not know how long, I was able to speak.

"I am alright now. Oh Gods, that was awful! How did you know what to do? What was it?"

"I don't know what it's called, but I have experienced the same for several years. I was advised to hold a cloth loosely over my mouth and nose and breathe deeply and slowly when it happens. It works, so I always carry a cloth on my person."

"Thank you."

We sat like that for some time. I felt calmer, but not completely calm, and utterly exhausted.

"I will go to bed," I eventually said. "It is early, but I am so tired. Good night, my lord, and thank you once again."

We both got up and stood awkwardly for a second. I wondered if he was going to kiss me. He did not, but he smiled and said:

"Call me Ambrose in private, now we are betrothed. Good night, Hawise."

"Good night, Ambrose."

I smiled and left, making my way to the yellow room where I slept. As I walked down a corridor, I overheard Lady Marjory and Lady Cerys talking to each other in earnest whispers in a room which opened onto the corridor.

I hurried along. I supposed they were Marjory and Cerys now, or even cousin, yet I guessed they were talking about me, and I did not want to listen to it.

Eavesdroppers only ever hear ill of themselves, and I do not want to hear their true opinion of me, my abilities or the situation. I especially do not want to know what Marjory thinks.

I paced about my chamber for some time before I was ready to sleep that night. I badly wanted Bessy beside me so I could talk and talk. I wondered how she was faring under the convent's new harsh regime. We still exchanged letters written in our secret code, but we both believed that her convent would put an end to our secret correspondence before long, and we would have to write blander letters in Suvvern.

Chapter Twelve

Narrative continued by Gethin the Monk

Bessy the Novice received word that her friend Lady Hawise was going to marry Ambrose and become my queen on the same day that Marjory's letter to me arrived. We were both shocked and had ample time to talk together in the infirmary. We neither of us could quite believe it.

"How does your friend feel?" I asked. Marjory had mentioned the woman in several earlier letters. She did not exactly dislike Lady Hawise, she even held a higher opinion of her than she had after their first few days together, but she still felt she was flighty and prone to taking the easiest option in life.

Lady H is very capable of kindness, she wrote, *and she has brains. I will even allow her to be loyal, after a fashion. I hear how well she speaks of her friend who you know, and I see how she will not speak badly of people. However, she is simply not fit for the office of queen or suitable to be Ambrose's wife.*

As for the latter, I do not believe any woman is capable of being a good wife to Ambrose because he is not capable of being any sort of husband. Washing himself took us all by surprise, but he has left it too late. His body may be undamaged, but his mind, his habits, his ability to be with people have been shattered beyond repair. His marriage to Sophie was the first great evil of his life. The second was us not tackling him when he gave up washing and retreated into himself. That guilt will never leave me. How is such a man to take a woman as his wife and get her pregnant, let alone hold a turbulent country in his grip as its king?

As for the former, Lady H is too lazy for the demands of public office. I have listed her good qualities, now I will list her vices: laziness, a love of luxury, and an inability to resist temptation. Ten to one any child in her belly will not have been put there by Ambrose. Her future is likely to mirror her past. She was approached today about her new wardrobe. As I saw her eyes light up, my heart sank. It's all about the sweetmeats of life with her. She will spend money the country does not have on silks, velvets and cloth of gold and let thoughts of jewels distract her when she should be a mother to the nation. At least she will be obliged to adopt our fashions and look more like we do. That might make her feel better because she will fit in more, or she might enjoy standing out as someone exotic.

For God's sake burn this once you have read it!

Bessy gave me a welcome insight into the mind of a woman I had only met briefly, yet had heard so much about and who would soon wield such influence.

"To be frank with you, brother, Hawise is terrified. She sees marrying Lord Ambrose and becoming queen as her duty, for it will bring peace and stability, as well as honour to her house and kingdom. I know she can be lazy, but she has always had a strong moral compass. She will do this because she sees it as the right thing to do.

"She has been an excellent friend to me, quite like a sister ever since we first met, when we were both orphaned at the age of ten, and our guardians took us in. Truly, she is a special person. However, I do not know how she will fare as Queen of the Westlands or as Lord Ambrose's wife. She has not told me much about him in her letters, but I know he mentally removed himself from society, and I do not know how anyone copes as queen these days. So much responsibility and so many conflicting expectations."

Bessy's mentioning a moral compass heartened me, especially because she also listed a fault. Anyone in power needed the ability to know right from wrong and the courage to act accordingly.

I cannot judge her for her past. Gods know mine is tainted, and I would still be enjoying myself today, were it not for the threat of a knife and cauterising irons.

I paused. I knew that my promiscuity was not just driven by lust but also by despair. I needed to distract myself from the pain of being apart from Marjory and our three children. It had been hard enough when I lived in the Westlands, but now in exile, it was a hundred times worse, not least because I did not know when my exile would end.

If it ever does. Marjory and I had snatched minutes and hours to ourselves every few months or so. I saw the children whenever I visited. Blind eyes were turned. That world is now gone.

Bessy started to speak again and pulled me back into the present.

"What can you tell me of Lord Ambrose? Do you think he will be a good king and husband?"

I answered her truthfully.

"He was an excellent man with good abilities and an appealing personality. He was quiet and thoughtful, but all the better for it. People knew he cared. Bran's determination reminds me of him at that age. However, he married a girl who was extremely troubled, and it scarred him. He is now unrecognisable from what he was then. Although he never became a bad man, he became withdrawn, and I'm sure Lady Hawise has told you how he kept people at bay. I do not know how much he has changed at heart, but such experiences must alter a man.

"I am confident of his intentions. I am sure he will do his utmost to be what the Westlands and what your friend needs, but as to if he will succeed..."

I could not finish my sentence.

"Hawise needs a good man who will be kind to her and speak frankly," Bessy stated. "She has her own scars which she keeps hidden. The loss of her family, coming to live with relative strangers, then losing her husband and miscarrying have marked her. She would rather die than let her cheery mask slip in public, but she needs someone who will support her in private."

"I hope Ambrose will do that. I hope she will also be able to support him. That is vital in any marriage, let alone a royal one, and at such a turbulent time."

We worked in sober silence for a few moments before I felt the need to unburden myself. A bond had grown between me and the novice nun. We had confided in each other over the months we spent working together, side by side, in the infirmary. I had grown to like and respect her. We trusted each other.

"I fear for my son and my daughters. I consider all three of them my children, and I have the usual parent's worries, but recent events in the Westlands have made them worse. The violation of the flag and the arson in Mendoc were bad enough, but they will send ripples throughout the land, unless the perpetrators are caught and severely punished. I never thought such things would happen. Never.

"I also fear the girls, at least, will fall victim to the Deadly Favour. Bran is old and sharp enough not to be tricked, whilst they are young and trusting. I never thought that would happen either. It was just a fairy story that we all grew up with."

Bessy looked at me sympathetically. Relieved to be able to unburden my mind, I continued.

"If only I had been able to marry Marjory all those years ago! She would not have had to shoulder every care of the children alone, and I would have been with them constantly. Every time we part, I tell her I will come for her one day, I will come for her as soon as I can. Yet who knows when I will see any of them again?"

"If only Lord Owen and his brothers had not interfered."

"Aye. If he was not tormented with guilt to this day, I would not have been able to forgive him. His adoptive mother feels similar pangs, and she should. He was a lad of fifteen then, and his brothers were also in their teens. Lady Isolde and Lord Oliver could have intervened, but they chose not to. I think they believed Marjory was suffering from calf love and should grow out of it and make a better match. I even believe they were proud of their boys for defending their sister's honour."

I laughed bitterly, and Bessy interjected.

"Yet Lord Owen got Lady Cerys pregnant before they were wed."

I nodded.

"Marjory was furious at both him and her parents because they accepted the situation, albeit reluctantly. However, we all get on now."

"Do you mind if I ask you something?"

"Ask whatever you like."

"How does Lady Marjory take your swiving? It would have broken my heart if Jennet had done that."

"She does not mind because she knows it is a physical release. It's lust, not love. She has my heart. Other women just have my attention from time to time. Or had, rather. I would not risk anything now."

She was thoughtful for a moment then said:

"You remind me of Hawise in that way. Not because she also lay with many, but she has used food and wine when she was in great pain. When she first came to the Castle of the Eastern Coast, shortly after losing her remaining family, our guardians had to steer her away from the sweetmeats. When she miscarried, she overate and drank to numb herself. It was the same when her husband died. She gorged herself and threw herself into any man's arms that would have her. To be sure, she has always appreciated food, drink and men and had a good appetite, but this was not about greed. It was about killing pain, or at least briefly putting it to sleep."

I could not deny it. Had I taken Marjory for my wife, I would have never so much as flirted with another woman.

"Do not fall into bad habits like we have, Bessy. Be strong. Jennet was false, and she is not worth your tears."

She nodded, but I could tell the pain was still there, though whether that was the pain of the deception or of missing Jennet I could not say.

"We have indeed fallen into bad habits," she said too flippantly. She plucked at her robe, which was slightly too big for her and neatly mended. "The rules about dress are also being properly enforced. We share all clothes, except kirtles, and that's only because they shape themselves to our bodies. You monks share every item, I suppose."

This was true. Clothing was now common to all and was discreetly marked to indicate size. Whenever I needed to change my clothes, I chose what I needed from a chest which was available to every monk and novice. However, I still wore my scarf. I touched it self-consciously.

"Do you not worry that they'll take that away from you, brother? We are not meant to have any personal possessions which are not strictly necessary. I cannot see either of them realising that love is a necessity."

Bessy now knew about my scarf. Shortly after Bran's birth, I acquired a length of blue cloth from which I sewed two scarves. One for me and one for Marjory. We could not wear necklaces, for we were not married, but this was the next best thing.

I knew who Bessy meant by 'they'. Who else had turned our lives upside down, and with barely disguised glee?

"I think I'll start hiding it. It would kill me if Sister Agnes or her minion Brother Harold got hold of it."

I did not include Brother Percy in my speech because I did not think his heart was in our persecution, and he felt as sorry for us as I was starting to feel sorry for him. The short, stout man with the sandy hair and freckled face looked both watchful and miserable whenever I saw him. I had noticed how he tried to warn unsuspecting nuns of Sister Agnes's approach by talking loudly to the bloated slug whilst she tried to creep up on the nuns. She was indeed like a slug, always slithering down the corridors of the convent on some foul mission, with her scrawny sidekick never far behind. Brother Harold might encourage Sister Agnes, but Brother Percy was often heard suggesting that a lesser penalty be inflicted or a second chance be granted.

"I wonder if Brother Percy knew what he was getting into when he agreed to join Sister Agnes. Maybe, like me, he had no choice."

"I hope Hawise knows what she's getting into and she can handle it. If not, the consequences will be catastrophic."

Chapter Thirteen

Narrative continued by Lord Ambrose of the many houses of the
Westlands

Once I had accepted the throne and Hawise had accepted my offer of marriage, events moved quickly. We had to plan a wedding and a coronation on a very limited budget whilst ensuring that nobody felt snubbed. The history of the houses of the Westlands and those of the Wolds-heart were turbulent and memories were long. The recent history between the two kingdoms was even worse. Offending nobody would be a real challenge.

I also had to get to grips with the government and deal with three major problems; the poverty caused by the war, catching those who had violated the flag and finding those who had vanished due to the Deadly Favour.

I tackled this in the best way that I knew how, by being direct, unflinching and methodical. This was my one chance to save my homeland. The thought of failure terrified me.

Hawise spoke to me privately the day after I gave her the cloth. She solemnly assured me that she would do everything she could to help me as my consort.

"I want to promise this to you in private because I mean it so sincerely. I know my reputation is that of a shallow woman, but that is only part of me. I can take life seriously and apply myself to hard tasks. I will be the best wife and consort I can be. The best mother I can be, Gods permitting. I will not lie with anyone but you, and I will do nothing to harm the monarchy. You have my loyalty, Ambrose."

I was touched. Since we had begun to spend more time together, I was beginning to see her in a different light. She certainly had courage, a kind heart and a sweet nature. Her flippancy concealed a sharp mind. I was no longer intimidated by her. Indeed, I believed I might trust her. She was going to take her position seriously.

Her looks had not changed, but I was seeing them in a different way too. It was not the change to a fancier wardrobe that made me look at her more fondly, it was my better knowledge of the woman. I had always agreed that she was pretty, I could now call her attractive. If I had to take a second wife and become king, Hawise of Lothwold was a good choice of partner.

"I thank you, Hawise. I appreciate your words. In turn, you have my loyalty, and I will try my best to be what you need, as a husband and as a monarch. In time, hopefully, also as a father to your children."

She smiled, and we discussed our wedding and coronation. Both ceremonies had to take place as soon as possible to avoid any challenge to our claim. I had to stamp my authority and provide an image of steadfast stability as quickly and as firmly as I could. We had fixed upon 4th December. The wedding would take place in the morning and the coronation in the afternoon. Royalty, nobles, courtiers and diplomats from the Westlands, the Wolds-heart and a few other kingdoms had been invited. Deciding who to invite and where to place them had been a diplomatic headache. I was glad of the advice of the Council of the Interregnum.

"I will keep the council as it is but under a new name after our coronation," I told her. "Every monarch needs advisors, and they are the best people for the job."

She agreed.

"They are experienced men and women whom you can trust. Tell me, will your half-brothers ever have a place on it?"

"Have they or their wives approached you about this?"

"No, but I have noticed how much more attention they pay me since I accepted you. I do expect such a request at some point."

"I will never give Lewis, Madoc, Nessa or Clementia any power, aside from what they already have. Clementia is utterly ruled by them, so to give her power is to hand it to them. I do not trust the other three and never will do. I suggest you don't either."

She hesitated, then spoke.

"I never have. I was impressed with Nessa, Madoc and Lewis at first, whilst I scarcely noticed Clementia. However, I have seen how they act when their masks slip. I once saw Lewis getting great pleasure in reducing one of his lads to tears, and I have seen enough from Madoc and Nessa to indicate a similar spiteful nature. I agree, Clementia is under their thumbs. Gods know what she really thinks and feels because she never expresses any opinion that is not theirs."

I nodded, pleased that my betrothed was confident enough to speak thus with me and that she had not been taken in.

"We will have to keep a discreet and constant eye on them," I said. "Marjory, Owen and Cerys will help."

"Not your Aunt Isolde?"

"No. My aunt feels family loyalty so strongly that she does not see the faults of those in hers. She also believes in standing together. She would believe we are tearing the family apart."

"At least they are not often at the castle, and their profession keeps them occupied. What exactly is it that they do?"

"Nobody knows."

She looked at me in astonishment. I continued.

"They have some sort of business which involves a lot of travel and trade with foreign kingdoms. They have been able to travel at short notice throughout the war, and they bring in a lot of money. The reason why the castle is so secure and luxurious is largely due to their money. Unfortunately, that gives them influence, which I would prefer them not have. Yes, we live well and sleep soundly and yes, the poor receive alms because of it, but I wish it was Marjory's business that was the benefactor. I trust and respect Marjory more than I ever will them, and she is open about what she does."

"Do you think what they are doing is illegal? Has nobody ever questioned them about it? Oh Ambrose, if they are involved in something that breaks the law, it will reflect so badly on you as king."

I sighed heavily.

"I know. That is another burden to bear. I have suspected for a long time that they are doing something illegal because of the amount of money they have, and they can travel freely, yet they fob people off when they are asked questions. If the questioner persists, they hint that they will take themselves and their funds away from Castle Malwarden. Nobody has ever questioned them further, nor have they left us. Whatever they have been doing, they have been doing it for many years."

"Do you have any idea what it might be?"

I shook my head.

"No. My only guess is that it is something criminal and lucrative. If it did not bring in serious money, they would not bother."

Hawise paused, and I could see her mulling over my words.

"What were Lewis and Madoc like when you were growing up? Did you get on?"

"Despite what you might think, they were never cruel to me. We share a father, who was a good man but a weak one, for he turned a blind eye to anything unpleasant. He saw how his boys were turning out. It pained him, therefore he did nothing. By the time they were Bran's age, it was too late. They were beyond anyone's influence whom they did not already care for. They abused their privilege as nobles, taking whatever they fancied, whether it was theirs or not, and insulting and assaulting anyone who displeased them, and who was not more powerful than them. They got into business with a man called Eoin, a man from the Emerald Kingdom, who is now dead. Within a short space of time, they had earned a lot of money.

"They married at around the same time, Lewis was almost nineteen when he wed Clementia, then a few months later Madoc married Nessa. I believe they met them through their business, Eoin introduced them, and our parents did not object. I know for sure that Eoin died within a year of Madoc's wedding, and it devastated them both. They regarded him as a father figure and treated him with more respect than they treated our father.

"My mother was a good woman whose biggest mistake in life was to wed my father. Had he not had Lewis and Madoc, she would merely have had the challenge of being bound to a man who could never be strong for her nor stand up in the face of difficulties. As it was, she had to manage two vile stepsons. That is why I have no younger siblings.

"She could not leave, so she taught me how to survive. That's why my half-brothers were never cruel to me, they did not get the chance. From my earliest years, I learned how to read a room, be self-reliant, defuse a situation and defend myself physically. She encouraged me to study and to make allies. That's why I was able to become a watcher. I had acquired the necessary skills in childhood to analyse an alien world, whilst remaining hidden from its inhabitants."

"What happened to your parents?"

"They both died of the plague shortly after my wedding to Sophie. At first I blamed my bad marriage on their deaths, I thought grief was affecting us, but I could not do what my father did and ignore the truth forever ..."

Hawise took my hand and smiled at me sympathetically. I placed my free hand over hers, marvelling that I was comfortable with this small intimacy.

You will have to do a lot more than hold hands to consummate your marriage, and you must do it more than once. To keep her satisfied and to ensure the succession. Gods, how can you think you can keep a woman like this interested? A man like you?

"I do not envy your childhood, Ambrose, although I do envy the skills you took from it. Determination and self-discipline. You see a task and tackle it, never giving up. As for me, I am only glad that beating uncooperative children had fallen out of fashion by the time I was handed over to a tutor. I was the despair of him and everyone which came after. I do not brag, I know I have abilities, but how I envy you and my friend Bessy, who made the most of your talents. I have wasted so many opportunities, and how I regret it!"

Her face fell slightly. I squeezed her hand.

"I'm scared," she continued in a tone that, for the first time, made me feel protective of her. "So much is going to be required of us, and I have never been tested like this before. We will always be on display. We will have no settled home. Instead, we will move from castle to castle, staying with various nobles."

"We will make this work. I know why you want a home, why would you not after your childhood? However, we will make this work. The nation is behind us. Some two hundred thousand people want us to make this work. It is never too late to learn. I am learning not to hide away, to be with people and to communicate. I can no longer keep people away with a foul body. You will learn to apply yourself. I know it."

She smiled at me and might have kissed me but for a knock at the door. She was wanted to talk about wedding clothes. We said we would meet at dinner.

Now alone for the first time in hours, what a contrast to my old life, I looked in the mirror. I looked different. Larger, healthier, less scared and more determined. I might not yet look like a king, but I would not actually be one until I was crowned.

I touched my necklace. It was a twist of solid silver, a classic style for men, and what I had proudly chosen as a young man when my betrothal was announced. I had worn it every day since Sophie first fastened it around my neck. It was now wrapped in a length of white ribbon to signify that I was a widower and about to marry again. Hawise's gold and sapphire necklace had been similarly decorated.

I sighed heavily. At twenty-five, I was still a young man, but I felt ancient and worn out.

How am I, of all people, going to do this?

Chapter Fourteen

The day of our wedding and coronation was a freezing cold grey Friday. There was no breeze, but a hint of snow was in the air. This was not a great omen, either for my marriage, my reign or a cheering crowd, but I could not afford to be superstitious. I had to play the cards I had been dealt as well as I possibly could.

I woke early but not sufficiently early to justify lying in a warm bed for more than a few minutes. I needed to get up and prepare myself for the most important day of my life.

To think you thought your wedding to Sophie was going to be the most important day of your life. The first chapter of a happier age! No, there were signs that something was not right. You tried to raise your concerns but were shut down. You can trust your judgment, and now people are obliged to listen to you.

I paused in the chilly chamber. Could I trust my judgment now? I believed Hawise was the best wife and consort I could choose. I believed she might even make a good mother. Was I just telling myself this because, once again, I was obliged to wed?

I shook my head. No. Hawise was only like Sophie in being a woman. I was several years older and much wiser. The political landscape had changed. History would not repeat itself.

A servant entered with hot water, followed by another with bottles and towels. My day had begun.

I cleaned my teeth, washed, shaved and combed my hair with great care. I liberally applied cologne to my armpits. I could not afford to fall back into bad habits. It was not fair on Hawise, nor would it inspire any faith in my leadership. The clothes which I put on were not only clean but also new and made out of higher quality fabrics than anything that had ever touched my skin before. Cambric bleached as white as fresh snow. Kitten-soft velvet which felt heavy and warm. Boots made out of leather as smooth as butter.

I scarcely recognised myself in the mirror.

As was customary, I ate alone with my groomsmen and other male family members, while Hawise dined with my female relations, and the guests ate in the Great Hall. Owen was in extremely high spirits. How he laughed and chattered! It set the tone for the rest of the meal. Everyone was relieved that the interregnum was ending and ending peacefully.

After breakfast most of the men and boys left, leaving me with who should have been my closest companions; Owen, Lewis, Madoc, and Cerys's brother-in-law Magnus. It was customary that the bride and groom were kept apart until the actual ceremony, and we had some time to kill. I was always glad to be with Owen, and I got on well with Magnus whenever I saw him, but I would have paid good money for my half-brothers to be far away. I was convinced they were up to something, maybe trying to unnerve me, because they asked how I was feeling and thanked me for taking the burden of the crown. They made the expected lewd remarks about the wedding night. Owen and Magnus joined in.

I smiled blandly. This was something I had tried not to think about.

A knock on the door brought Marjory, come to take me to the church. Lewis jumped up to escort Hawise. I would have preferred to have sent Owen but felt obliged to offer the job to Lewis as my nearer relation.

My cousin looked her best in a fine gown of blue and silver brocade, and she was smiling, but I knew she did not entirely approve of my bride. She and Hawise were never less than polite to each other, yet I knew that was as far as their relationship would ever go. Hawise had said nothing to me, apart from damning Marjory with faint praise. Marjory's facial expressions and tone of voice had indicated that Hawise as a wife was better than no wife at all.

Today she looked every inch the noble lady, come to support her kinsman and his bride. The scarf she always wore was clearly hidden under her gown. I knew she would not have taken it off.

"Are you ready?" she asked.

"Yes."

We set off. Magnus, Madoc and Owen walked slightly ahead of us, talking merrily. Marjory and I did not speak. I felt too nervous, and I guessed what feelings weddings stirred within her. However, her face was serene and her posture was excellent. I could hope to match them. We were both highborn and raised to perform in public ceremonies.

As we left the castle, I was glad to see crowds of people and to hear their cheers. I found myself grinning naturally. I waved and called my thanks. They accepted me. They wished me well. Before I knew it, we were at the church.

Madoc, Owen and Magnus slipped into their seats. Marjory escorted me up the aisle.

"Every eye is upon you, little brother," Madoc whispered, as he sat down. "What a day for you. What lies ahead!"

I smiled at him blandly and turned my head towards the priest.

Several minutes later Hawise reached the church with her party. There was a collective hush as they entered the hallowed building. I turned to look at her.

She looked beautiful. The lavender-coloured gown, the silver circlet and the dark pink cloak suited her, but there was more to her good looks than that. There was more to them than her flowing, bright hair, excellent teeth and clear skin. Her personality and her character shone through her joyful smile and her expressive eyes. She looked like she could be a queen, yet she was still herself, and what she was, was attractive.

She looked up at me, and I took her hands. The priest cleared his throat, and the ceremony to bind me to Hawise of Lothwold for the rest of our lives began. The wedding ceremony, always short, was over before I was aware of it. It was almost like being in a dream.

The priest reached the end of the ancient words and smiled broadly. He declared us man and wife, woman and husband, bound together by the will of the Gods and inseparable unto death. In a ringing tone, he permitted us to kiss. Hawise, my wife, looked at me almost shyly. Still feeling like I might be dreaming, I gently pulled her towards me and kissed her on the mouth.

It was the first time we had done so. The usual liberties of courtship had not applied to us. Ours was a political alliance, our personal desires must come a distant second. However, she kissed me back, and I felt something like lust for the first time in years. Happy tears formed in her eyes.

Might happiness be within my grasp? Could I make her happy? Am I capable of it?

The congregation roared its approval, and the first part of the day was over.

"We did it, husband," Hawise breathed. She looked surprisingly shy.

I could not think of anything to say in response, so I kissed her forehead.

We made our way back to the castle at a sedate pace through a river of noisy well-wishers. Hawise grinned and waved, as though she had been born for the role. Whatever shyness she felt, she hid it well. I could only hope that I was hiding my feelings of unreality with equal success.

We would spend relatively little time together on that momentous day and almost none of it alone. Technically it was a day of celebration, yet for my wife and me it was a massive event that we had to host and make it look effortless.

After the midday meal, Hawise and I went to change into our clothes for the coronation. I washed and cleaned my teeth again before adding more cologne to my body. Our outfits would be more sumptuous than what we had worn for our wedding. Now we were about to become royalty, we could wear cloth of gold and diamonds.

Hawise looked splendid in a lapis blue cloak over a crimson gown. Like me, she wore a cloth of gold girdle around her waist. Her hair was still loose, but she now wore nothing on her head. For the first time since she could toddle, she would appear bare-headed in public.

The coronation was performed in the same church by the same priest, as it was customary for the most local priest or priestess to do the job. This time, Hawise and I waited to be summoned to the altar by the roar of the crowd. We could only be crowned by their consent.

Silence fell as we reached the altar. The priest stood between us. When he spoke, he sounded even more authoritative than he had that morning. It truly sounded as though the Gods were speaking directly through him.

Lightning shot down my spine.

The priest spoke of the sacred trust between a monarch and their people and how a consort must honour their monarch and this trust. He described the solemn, lifelong responsibilities involved.

Hawise stared at him with a transfixed gaze.

How can anyone think she won't take this seriously?

Finally he turned to me. In his hands he held a golden crown decorated with diamonds.

"Lord Ambrose of the many houses of the Westlands, you

have been invited to reign as King of the Westlands by its people. Do you accept this invitation?"

"Father, I do."

"Do you solemnly swear unto death to uphold the laws of this land, to rule wisely and justly? To be a merciful father to your subjects?"

"Father, I do."

"Do you solemnly swear to uphold the teachings of the church and to be guided by its values in all that you say and do?"

"Father, I do."

He raised the crown high above his head. I knelt and closed my eyes, then felt its weight upon my head. He ensured it was secure before booming:

"Rise, King Ambrose III. The Westlands is your domain. Rule it well!"

He turned to Hawise.

"Lady Hawise of the House of Lothwold of the Woldsheart, you are married to King Ambrose III. Do you consent to be his Queen Consort?"

"Father, I do."

"Do you swear to obey him as your sovereign lord?"

"Father, I do."

"Do you swear to support him until death does you part and raise your children as worthy princes and princesses?"

"Father, I do."

He raised another crown, also gold but smaller and plainer with no embellishments. My wife knelt and closed her eyes. When she opened them again, she was my Queen Consort and mother to her adopted nation.

He joined our hands together and urged us to do our sacred duty by guiding and guarding the nation. We nodded, and the ceremony was over.

The congregation roared its approval more enthusiastically than it had at our wedding. Its relief could be heard. Its land had a king and a queen. Two intelligent healthy adults who could rule and raise the next ruler. The years of uncertainty were over. By taking a woman from the House of Lothwold, the war was over in all but name. A peace treaty would be signed very shortly, and the child hostages could then go home.

Hawise smiled at me as if to say 'We did it', and I beamed back at her. Another part of this important day was almost over.

We processed back to Castle Malwarden under a hail of blessings and cheers. The peasantry and the middling classes were as relieved to finally have a monarch as the nobles were. I was genuinely moved and let the people see it. I needed them to see my appreciation of their approval and to have them begin to trust me.

The last public part of the day was a feast and dancing, very like any wedding, albeit on a much larger scale, and great care had to be taken so nobody felt snubbed. Everyone's place at the tables had been agonised over, and similar care had gone into deciding who would ask whom to dance.

As the merry evening wore on, I could feel myself becoming more nervous. The most private event had to be heralded by the last announcement. I glanced about me. Most of the many dishes had been eaten, and dirty plates littered the tables. The dancing had ended, and musicians provided quiet background music, over which people could talk. People stood about chatting, a goblet in hand. The youngest children had fallen asleep under the tables.

I steeled myself. I could not falter now. Taking a deep breath, I found my wife. She was talking to Owen, with whom I also needed to speak. They guessed what I was about to ask.

"Are you ready?" Hawise asked. She was flushed with dancing and merriment.

I nodded and squeezed her hand, hoping mine was not clammy with fear. She looked at me encouragingly.

Owen made his way to one of the benches and climbed onto it. Silence fell. My stomach lurched, but I reminded myself this was why I gave Lewis and Madoc the jobs that I had given them. I could give Owen this job, a job I knew they would have used to undermine me.

My cousin threw back his ginger head and bellowed the age-old words:

"Lad, it's time to do your work!"

The hall erupted. Whoops and cheers rattled through my ears. My cheeks burned, and I could only hope my smile was not too fixed. Hawise blushed a brighter pink and grinned.

We had rehearsed what to do next. Most couples did, despite it being meant to be a spontaneous moment.

I bowed to her in an overly elaborate manner, careful to keep smiling. She returned it with the deepest of curtseys and offered a hand. I flamboyantly kissed it to thunderous applause, then offered her my arm, which she took. I did not want to risk lifting her like many new husbands did. She was not exactly fat, just extremely solid, and I expected she weighed more than she looked. The fact that she was not tall would also make it hard for me to sweep her off her feet gracefully.

Instead, we made our way, arm in arm, pursued by dozens of whooping people to our chamber. I opened the door with mock ceremony and bowed. She laughed and entered before blowing a kiss to the jostling crowd. I beamed, trying not to catch anyone's eye, and closed the door.

Thus the public parts of the day were over. Everyone retreated, their footsteps and their voices faded away. Not even my half-brothers could interfere now.

I was now completely alone with my wife.

I was terrified.

Oh Goddess, how can I physically do what needs to be done? Years of suffering with Sophie has destroyed me.

Hawise sat on the giant bed. Her waist-length hair was tangled and shone gold in the candlelight. The crown which she received that afternoon had been replaced by a gold and diamond circlet for the dancing. She now removed it. Self-consciously, I removed the silver band from my head. I took her circlet and placed both mine and hers on top of a chest. I turned back around, feeling awkward. She was looking at me in a kind manner.

"Come here," she beckoned.

I obeyed, shaking. It was impossible to stop shaking. The woman who took my cold hands in hers was nothing like my late wife, yet that was no reassurance. Life had taken me to dark places which no reassurance could soothe.

"Hawise, I cannot," I breathed. "Sophie...I'm sorry, I should not have married you. I cannot...could not marry anyone. You know what happened in my first marriage. It annihilated..."

I burst into tears. Madoc and Lewis were right.

Hawise embraced me. "I know. And it's not your fault. We will rebuild ourselves. We will make our marriage work, and we will both be happy. I will be a happy wife with you."

"I do not think I can physically..."

"We do not have to do everything tonight. There is time. Come, let us prepare for bed and lie down together. It has been such a tiring day, yet nobody could deny it has also been a triumph?"

Dumbly, I nodded, scarcely able to believe my ears. Could this woman, infamous for her man-eating appetite, really be so tender, especially when it must inconvenience her? She had surely been celibate since she had left the Castle of the Eastern Coast, and she must have found it a strain.

I washed, cleaned my teeth and combed my hair, trying to avoid her eyes. I reached for my nightshirt, my new nightshirt. Now we were king and queen, everything we once possessed had been given up for alms. What jewels Hawise's guardians had lent to her had been sent back to them. Instead, we took our belongings from the royal wardrobe. Technically we now owned nothing, we merely borrowed from what had been accumulated over decades and centuries and had been fashioned to fit us and current fashions.

"Shall I put cream on your back?" Hawise asked, just as any wife might ask her husband.

I was now clad only in the shirt I had worn for the latter part of the day. The jar of cream was not yet empty. I had managed to apply it to myself with the aid of a spatula, but I had no idea what I now looked like from behind. Besides, it would be churlish to refuse.

"Yes, please." I turned my back and took off my shirt.

Hawise smoothed the cool ointment over my skin. I shivered.

"What does my back look like? And...my backside?"

"Completely clear, but I think you should use up the rest of the jar, like Gytha said."

"Yes, I agree."

Her fingers reached my waist, and she paused.

"Please carry on," I made myself say.

She rubbed more of the ointment onto my buttocks. It felt so strange to be touched somewhere so private after so long.

Less than a month ago I had not washed myself, apart from my face and hands, for years. This is progress.

I turned around and thanked her when she had done and put on my clean shirt. She was also dressed for bed.

We got under the heavy covers, and I pulled the curtains around us. Someone had lit a fire, but it was still freezing.

"Come here," Hawise whispered in the dark. I moved towards her and pulled her into my arms. She rested her head on my chest, the crown under my chin. Her hair felt like silk, and I told her so.

"Thanks, I just wish it was thicker. I envy Marjory's fat plaits."

"But your hair is not thin, and it's such a pretty colour. You always look nice. So many people admire you. I've never heard anyone say anything bad about your appearance."

"Oh, we all have our insecurities, I suppose."

We lay in the darkness for some time, our eyes becoming accustomed to the lack of light. She felt warm against me.

She turned slightly towards me, paused, then said.

"I am going to kiss you, touch you. Tell me when to stop."

I put my mouth to hers in response. I could not be passive.

This was not Sophie, someone both hysterical and aggressive from fear. This was a woman who liked men and who wanted me.

She must tell me if what I do does not please her.

"Guide me, Hawise. What do you like?"

Her teeth gleamed as she smiled. She pulled me into her arms and began to kiss me, her arms caressing my back and shoulders. She knew what she was doing, what she wanted. All I had to do was follow her lead.

I wrapped my arms around her, how Sophie would have fought to set herself free, but this bold woman from the Wolds-heart only gave a whimper of delight and moved even closer. Blood rushed to my groin, she felt it, and she liked it. She pressed herself against me, exciting me further. I had not felt so free, so much a man, so much myself and *alive* for years.

Hawise broke off to remove her nightdress. She pulled back the covers to reveal herself. What a pearl she was. Her skin was luminous, and her body curved in and out like a fertility goddess. She knew she was beautiful, and she rejoiced in it.

"Let me see you naked, Ambrose. I have only seen you from behind. Let me see all of you without your clothes."

Before I could lose my courage, I sat up and pulled off my shirt. I kicked away the covers. Hawise pulled me towards her. Her eyes were large, her pupils were dilated and her mouth was soft.

"You are a beautiful man." She pulled me on top of her and kissed me more passionately than before. I began to kiss her neck, which she liked, then she said:

"I want you inside me, Ambrose. I want to feel all of you."

"Guide me. How do you like it?"

She lay underneath me and guided me. I could not quite believe it. *I* was giving a woman pleasure. What had been disgusting to Sophie, to the point that we soon gave up, made Hawise moan with joy. I found that I stopped thinking and instead, only focused on what I was experiencing and my wife's ecstasy.

Afterwards, I held her in my arms, her head on my chest.

"Your heart is beating so fast, Ambrose." She looked up at me and smiled.

"You've done what nobody else ever could." I was blunt with amazement. "You've made a man of me, and you've made me happy."

CHAPTER FIFTEEN

Narrative continued by Queen Hawise of the Westlands

Ambrose slept well on our wedding night, soon drifting off to sleep after we had consummated our marriage. He was at ease, but I was not. I lay awake in the dark for a long time, mentally composing a letter to Bessy so I might calm my wild thoughts and be able to sleep.

My wedding, coronation and wedding night had all gone better than I had dared to hope. There were no lewd catcalls, and everyone seemed genuinely pleased that we were marrying and taking an empty throne. I felt we had both performed our parts well.

My wedding night was confusing. It had been so good to touch a man and to feel him inside me after many months of abstinence. Yet it was not just abstinence that had made the experience enjoyable. I had come to genuinely like and respect Ambrose. I enjoyed his company, and I could appreciate his deeper qualities: his astute mind, his firm sense of right and wrong and his courage to act upon it. He was also brave to push through so much pain and fear to re-join the world, take a troubled kingdom and take a wife.

I looked at him whilst he slept, just about able to make out his features in the darkness.

He is handsome. I find his willingness to please me attractive, and I enjoyed myself tonight. Considering his past and how little experience he has had, it went better than we could have dared to hope. I did not think he would be able to consummate our marriage for many weeks. I think I can teach him enough so we can have fun together. He will definitely make a willing pupil.

I rolled over, trying not to groan and wake Ambrose. What I had described was very good. It was more than what many wives had. I tried to compare it to how I felt when I first married Adam, but it was impossible. They were two very different men, and I had been at a completely different stage of my life, living in a different country and in a totally different political climate. Besides, being Queen Consort was a world away from being a diplomat's wife.

The bed was the most comfortable I had ever slept in. Whichever castle we stayed in, our apartments were guaranteed to be the most luxurious. The nightdress crumpled on the floor was made out of the highest quality cambric. The jewels I had sent back to my old guardians were a drop in the ocean compared to the sparkling mountains I might choose from.

That's just it, I realised with a jolt. *Nothing I wear or use is mine. It belongs to the kingdom. I am merely borrowing items as its queen. I will never have a home of my own. I am living in someone else's castle again and always will do. My behaviour must be directed by diplomatic needs for the rest of my life. I will rarely be able to put my own stamp on anything. I may not even take lovers because too much is at stake. Ambrose and I must only lie with each other until death does us part.*

I took deep breaths, trying to stay calm. I did not want to wake my husband and have to answer his questions. He was a good man, I could happily kiss him and lie with him. That was as much as I had ever asked for. My new status and fortune were both unexpected blessings and millstones.

Few people find true love, everything that they want in a spouse. You have a pleasant companion, someone you can respect and might well one day trust, and a man you like to go to bed with. That's what you had with Adam, and you were both content. It would be foolish to ask for more.

I wondered if we might have babies before silently sobbing myself to sleep.

When I next awoke it was daylight, and Ambrose was not lying beside me. He was standing by the window, looking out onto the day. He turned towards me and smiled. It seemed genuine.

"Good morning, Hawise. Did you sleep well?"

I made myself smile back.

"Yes. Did you?"

I got up and briefly kissed him. I did not want him to experience my morning breath nor taste his.

"Shall I call for hot water? It is probably time that we stirred ourselves."

He consented, looked troubled, then asked:

"Do you think anyone will ask if we consummated our marriage last night?"

This threw me slightly.

"Why...I don't know if anyone would, I suppose they will take it for granted that we have. If anybody should ask, I think we should say yes and leave it at that. It isn't anyone's business but ours."

"Hawise, everything to do with us is now everyone's business. We are king and queen. Public property."

The servants arrived with hot water and asked what we might like to wear. I tried not to look too disturbed. Ambrose was about to speak to me, but the servants quickly returned with armfuls of clothes. As was customary, we would dress ourselves the day after our wedding night, but in future others would do so, although someone would still come to dress my hair.

I chose a teal green gown which laced up the sides. As

Ambrose fastened the laces, I had to breathe in slightly. I loved the rich colour, but the gown was very fitted and could not be let out any further.

I cannot afford to comfort eat. Everyone will see every change in my appearance and judge me. Besides, most of my meals will be taken in public. What sort of queen stuffs her face for all to see?

My husband noticed my pale face when he fastened the second lace and took my hands in his.

"What is it, my love? You look ready to faint."

"I'm terrified," I whispered. "Everything we do and say will be noted and possibly twisted. We will live splendidly but entirely in public. We will enjoy great wealth and power yet own nothing and carry enormous responsibilities. I *must* give you children..."

He embraced me and did not feel too thin.

"We will get through this together. You helped me last night and made me realise what joy I can experience. I will do the same for you. I am not just your sovereign, I am also your husband."

I nodded. Two of my demoiselles knocked with my jewels, so no more could be said, yet I had heard enough. Ambrose was stronger than many thought him to be.

We went to breakfast in the Great Hall and took the seats of honour. Cerys and Owen had to give way to us, which made me feel uncomfortable, although they seemed to consider it the natural order of things. I looked as cheerful and contented as possible. Nobody must think I was anything less than completely confident and satisfied.

As I buttered a roll, it occurred to me that I could not pour my heart out to Bessy as freely as I had before. I might still write to her, and I might still use our code, but Ambrose had my first loyalty. It was not only fear of discovery that would halt my pen. I could not put my need to confide in my oldest friend above my vows to my husband. I could still write truthfully, just not frankly.

This was a bitter blow.

After breakfast, we took our exercise. Ambrose went off somewhere with his men, while my ladies, Cerys, Clementia, Lady Isolde and I went riding. Lady Isolde's age meant I did not feel comfortable dropping her title, even in my thoughts. Marjory was busy with her business, and I was relieved not to have to include her. We would never be close, whereas I could feel a real bond developing between me and Cerys. I would miss her when we left, which would be after those who violated the flag had been caught and punished.

Lady Isolde had never been anything other than polite and pleasant towards me, therefore I enjoyed her company. I scarcely noticed whether Clementia was present or not. She was so quiet and unobtrusive. As for my demoiselles, they would travel with me from castle to castle and support me. I got on well with them, but the barrier between royal and ruled was too large for immediate intimacy.

Be patient. Many great ladies form bonds with those who serve them. It just takes time. The youngest are young girls indeed. It will prepare you for motherhood.

After I had got off my horse and changed my clothes, I made my way with Cerys to the Great Hall where the former Council of the Interregnum, now the Royal Council, met. Ambrose might be king, but every great man still needs advisors.

Nessa saw us as we walked to the Great Hall. She curtseyed deeply.

"I saw you ride from my window, madam. I hope you had a pleasant time. It is such a fine day for it."

"Yes, we did, thank you."

"You must have got quite as far as the Forest of a Thousand Pines."

"Yes, we were in view of the forest."

I wondered what she was playing at. Her beautiful brown face was the picture of innocence, yet I did not trust her any more than I trusted her husband or his brother.

If she is angling for an invitation when I next go out, she is wasting her time. I will choose my companions where I can. I've

*taken on her eldest daughter Jane as a demoiselle, which is quite
enough for that side of the family. Gods know I now have few real
choices I can make in my life.*

"Cerys, I've been thinking," I said, as soon as Nessa had
walked off. "I have access to so many luxuries, clothes, jewels,
horses, the best of everything. However, in reality, I own
nothing."

She nodded.

"Do you think I could buy some clothes of my own? Just a
couple of simple outfits, something I could wear in the privacy of
the solar or my chamber. I want something that is *mine* and not
the monarchy's."

She looked a little taken aback. We were still by ourselves, so
she could speak openly and call me by my first name.

"Hawise, I hear what you are saying, but you cannot. Kings
and queens of the Westlands do not own personal property in
that way. You can take whatever you need and alter it, but to buy
something like you suggest would look very odd indeed. In these
troubled times, you cannot be seen to be doing anything odd. I'm
sorry. Maybe one day you will be able to introduce changes. But
now is not the time."

I nodded, we had reached the Great Hall and could talk no
longer. I straightened myself and entered the room with all the
regal grace I could muster.

Good news awaited me. The captain of the local militia gleefully reported that the four who had violated the flag had been
hunted down and captured.

"I received news of it not an hour ago. The woman and the
three men were caught trying to cross the border with the Woldsheart. It was Lothwold territory, and it was Lothwold warriors
who arrested them. Thanks to your majesty's marriage with
Queen Hawise, they are escorting them to Castle Malwarden.
They should arrive this afternoon."

A buzz of joy murmured around the room. This was good
news indeed.

Not only have they been caught, but the manner of their capture will help keep me and my marriage in people's favour.

Ambrose insisted that the four be handed over at the castle with maximum discretion.

"We must keep this to ourselves for as long as possible. They must be handed over as quietly as possible and be taken directly to separate cells. I don't want a mob turning up any more than I want them to have the chance to confer with each other. They can say what they have to say at a trial tomorrow. Once the trial is underway, it will be impossible to keep it secret. The news will spread after a judgment has been made, for I do not imagine the trial will last long."

He looked at Owen, as though he might be treading on the Lord of Malwarden's toes, but Owen only nodded in agreement. Everyone agreed this was the best solution.

He isn't a charismatic man or a loud one, but he has the correct air of authority, and he makes wise decisions. A woman can be proud of such a husband, and a queen can stand beside such a king without blushing.

We managed to get the four prisoners into their cells without alerting anyone unnecessarily. I did not see them, my role was to distract the court by leading a riding party, but Ambrose was present, and he told me about them that night.

How different this is from last night. So much has happened in a day. We have something more pressing to deal with than the marriage bed, and I feel that I know my husband a little better. I respect him more than I did twenty-four hours ago.

"What are they like?" I asked as soon as we were alone in our chamber. "Did they confess to anything?"

He had been washing his face, and he dried it with a towel before answering.

"The militia did indeed bring us the three men and the woman who violated the flag at Samhain. Nobody has escaped en route. The woman is the youngest of the party, I would put her at nineteen or twenty. She gave her name as Isleen and had an

144

accent from somewhere to the west of here, but I cannot quite place it. The men must be in their mid to late twenties. Two of them look like they could be brothers. They gave their names as Oliver and Rodnap, and they sounded local. The third man was the oldest of the group, and I could scarcely make out what he was saying, let alone say where he might be from. He gave his name as Ness. I never heard such a garbled way of speaking before.

"They were muddy from days on the road but did not appear to have been roughed up by the warriors or the militia. It looks like they surrendered quickly. The militia tell me they had no personal property save a small bag of coins on them. Their dress would indicate they are Westlanders and lowborn but not destitute. Isleen's gown, in particular, looked quite new."

"Do you think they were trying to disguise themselves?"

"Yes. And I think that's why they had nothing on them that would identify them. Isleen and Ness looked like they had dyed their hair. His eyebrows and eyelashes were much darker than his hair, and it looked like the roots of her hair were blonde, whereas the length was auburn. However, I did not get close enough to see properly. Isleen, Rodnap and Oliver seemed surprised when Ness opened his mouth. I don't think he usually speaks that way."

"What did they have to say for themselves?"

"Not much. They looked shocked and exhausted. Isleen asked me twice if they would get a trial and when. I told her yes and tomorrow. They were examined by a physician shortly after arriving. He found nothing that might tell us more than they were willing to tell. He found no injuries or marks that were not consistent with old fights and rough living. We gave them food and water, which they attacked with gusto, but they do not look overly thin, and it was a long journey."

"It sounds like someone has been sheltering them."

"My thoughts exactly. It means they have supporters, supporters who are still out there, somewhere."

We sat in silence for a few moments before he continued.

"I received a report this afternoon of some people who are supporting them but not as in providing practical support."

"Oh?"

"They might not be dangerous, but such support could grow. There is a group of adolescent girls, about three dozen in their early teens, who think the four are freedom fighters. They are writing pamphlets and singing ballads which describe the four in the noblest terms. They have completely romanticised what happened. However, it is unlikely that they have ever met the four because the physical descriptions they give do not match those we have caught."

"Have we definitely got the right people?"

"I hope so. I hope we find out tomorrow. I should also add that the descriptions of those who violated the flag vary slightly in writing and in song. The girls do not know each other well, they are many friend's cousin's neighbours in the group, if you see what I mean. It is doubtful that any of them has met everyone else in the group."

"That's good. It weakens their arguments. Will they be brought to court for encouraging treason, for it was a treasonable action?"

"I'm not sure what is best. I have not yet heard enough to arrest anyone, but I know where the girls are based. They are based in villages far south of here, quite near the border with Pendroch. The villages are near one another."

"So, none of these girls have actually experienced the violation of the flag, nor met anyone who went through the experience?"

"Precisely. I also heard of peasant men grumbling about the monarchy and nobility in general and wishing that those who had violated the flag had overturned the whole system. However, it may just be people who are sick of war and poverty and want better faster than we can deliver it."

He did not look hopeful, so I reassured him.

"That occurs all over the civilised world. People always moan about their lot. Granted the peasantry have harder lives than us and are obliged to serve us, but in return we protect them and make the government work. Do not forget the revolt in Doggerdale in the eighties. Within a year, they were begging for their king to return. The country was in chaos. It is all very well holding a revolution and calling for change, but something must come after it, and it is not easy to make that something work."

My husband was slightly soothed and had come up with two good ideas by the time we went to sleep that night.

"If any of the maidens make real trouble and have to be called to court, I will not make martyrs of them. Instead, I will open their eyes and send them to Mendoc to help there. A week of charity and hard work there will soon open their eyes and stop their tongues. If not, the inhabitants of Mendoc will certainly educate them. If the peasant men stick to grumbling, I will not disturb them. Hopefully, the trial and punishment of the four, should they be found guilty, will give them faith in our justice and deter them from revolt. If not, let them face the same. We cannot let people think they are above the law.

"If the four are guilty, they must be executed and in public. The punishment must fit the crime, and the people must see justice being done. We cannot let rumours and legends spread. Everything must be open and honest. However, I will insist on execution by beheading."

"Why? That is not the usual penalty for violating the flag. It is too quick a death."

"I don't want to create martyrs, people who the discontented can hold up as examples, and I wish to be a merciful king. We need to get our rule off to a good start."

I agreed with him and respected his decisions as wise and right. We kissed and cuddled but did nothing else before falling asleep. I was glad. The day had exhausted me.

CHAPTER SIXTEEN

Although I would not play an active part in the trial, I needed to be seen there. I dressed soberly but richly to reflect my new rank. However, I was confident that all eyes would be on the four strangers and Ambrose. They were the most interesting people in the room.

I, too, could not stop looking at Isleen, Oliver, Rodnap and Ness as they were led into the Great Hall, which now doubled as a court of law.

They looked nervous but not overwhelmed with fear. They kept scanning the room, as if looking for help. My husband had described them well, and I could see that Isleen and Ness had indeed dyed their hair. Isleen's gown and the cloaks worn by all of them did not look as though they quite fitted. Her gown was too tight around the waist and baggy around the bust. Her cloak trailed along the ground, and the men's cloaks did not reach their mid-calves or ankles, the way a winter cloak should.

The hem of Ness's cloak looks like it has been let down, and he is the tallest of the group. Whoever made or altered Isleen's gown did a poor job of it, or there was not enough material around the waist to let it out properly. Everyone should be able to sew, especially the lowborn. I suspect they quickly changed their clothes to try to further disguise themselves. I wonder how they acquired these clothes and if they burned or exchanged their old ones.

A movement caught my eye, Madoc had slunk into the room, and he remained near the back. Ambrose rose to indicate that the proceedings had started. We all rose in response.

The day was a surprising and puzzling sequence of events, although I am not sure quite what I had expected, for I had never attended a trial before, let alone one in the Westlands or of such importance.

To avoid collaboration, they were questioned separately, and three remained under guard in far-off rooms at any time. At first, they all denied any wrongdoing. They had never been to Mendoc, they had never violated any flag, nor had they seen a dragon set fire to a church. When asked why they had been trying to cross the border without permission, their defence began to crumble, as their stories did not tally. Small but crucial details, such as what the weather was like at a certain point in time or who they intended to meet in the Woldsheart, did not match.

Although everyone present was legally obliged to keep silent and not communicate in any way with the accused, an atmosphere developed as the questions were answered. People exchanged looks and raised eyebrows. The four on trial desperately scanned the crowd. They all swore their innocence and begged for mercy.

Everybody thinks that they will be burned alive if they are found guilty. Only Ambrose, me and a select few know their fate will be beheading. We told Lady Isolde, Owen, Cerys and Marjory not to say anything, but it's not like they could have spoken with our prisoners, in any case.

Ambrose and his council of six retired towards the middle of the afternoon, after everyone had had the chance to speak. As his consort, I could not be one of the council. The accused were returned to a dungeon to await their fate. People began to move about.

Madoc made his way out of the room. I would not have noticed but for Rodnap's calling his name.

"My lord, may I beg mercy of you?"

Madoc looked briefly perplexed before telling the guard holding Rodnap that he would speak with the man.

What has this got to do with Madoc? Did Rodnap guess at his title or does he know him? His dress and demeanour indicate his high status. Is Madoc allowed to do this?

It appeared that he was not permitted to speak with the accused, but by the time a clerk had called this to the guard's attention, some seconds had passed, and the two men had had the chance to speak alone. Madoc slunk away, his head down.

Ambrose and his council of six returned to the Great Hall. Before they could give a verdict, Rodnap begged to be permitted to speak on behalf of the group.

Ambrose did not look ruffled at this unexpected interruption and consented.

Rodnap turned to address us all, although his remarks were aimed at Ambrose as his sovereign.

"Most gracious lord, we *all* humbly beg your pardon, for we are all guilty of violating the flag at Mendoc at Samhain. We did try to escape to the Woldsheart to avoid justice. We can only beg you for mercy and tell you that nobody else was involved in our misdeeds, nor have we committed any other foul acts of which this court is not aware. Between the time of Samhain and our capture, we simply wandered about the countryside, making our way to the border."

"How did you support yourselves?" Ambrose wanted to know. "How did you eat?"

"We begged at the roadside, and people were most generous towards us. They did not know what we had done."

"What would you *really* have done, had you made it over the border?"

"We would have begged a monastery, and Isleen would have begged a convent, to take us in. We had no plans beyond that."

"You expected to become monks and a nun?" Ambrose was incredulous.

Rodnap shrugged sadly.

"Like I say, most noble lord, we had no plans beyond being admitted to a religious house."

Ambrose looked disconcerted, then recovered himself.

"Your confession has been noted. You have voluntarily admitted your guilt, but you are still all guilty of an act that is punishable by death. Therefore, you will all be beheaded."

A murmur went around the court. Ambrose raised his hand for silence.

"Your executions will take place a week today, and they will take place on Mendoc Green. In the meantime, you will return to our dungeons. May the Gods have mercy upon your souls."

He sat down to indicate that the trial was over. Rodnap bowed his head and said nothing. I looked at his three companions but could not read their expressions. They were all looking at the floor. I looked for Madoc but could not see him.

The prisoners were led away, and the great room gradually emptied of people. I made my way to Ambrose, who was giving the clerk orders for the executioner. The man bowed to Ambrose, saw me, bowed to me, then left us.

We were now alone. Ambrose took my hand.

"Let us get some fresh air. I need it."

We walked around the rose garden, now bare of flowers, but people approached us. If we wanted privacy, we would have to go to our chamber. Even family could disturb us in the solar.

Lady Isolde was one of those who approached us. She was in a good mood.

"I am so pleased you were merciful, nephew," she smiled. "I told Clementia last night what you had planned, and she approved too. You have got your reign off to a good start! The violators of the flag have been caught, and they will meet death, yet you can still be seen to be merciful without looking weak."

"In future, let us tell my aunt nothing we wish to keep secret,"

Ambrose whispered after she had left us. "She sees the family as one large mass and not as different people."

"Very well, but I think your judgment did not look like a foregone conclusion, and that is the most important thing. You looked gracious without looking weak."

"True, but I need to keep my family, who should not have any influence over me and my actions, from having such influence."

This was put to the test that afternoon. Nessa, Madoc and Lewis requested an audience with Ambrose. I remained with him as support. He now knew that Rodnap had spoken with Madoc alone. He had since spoken with Rodnap, who had simply told him that he recognised Madoc as the king's brother and he believed he might have influence over him.

"Do you believe him? Did you talk with anyone else who might have overheard them?"

"I don't know what to believe. He may or may not have known my connection to Madoc and what he looks like. I can neither prove nor disprove that. I spoke with the guards, who could only tell me that the two men exchanged very few words and both were calmer afterwards. They both looked very anxious before."

"*Madoc* was anxious?"

"Apparently so, and I intend to find out why. They are coming now."

The three entered the room with smiles I could now never trust. They bowed and curtseyed with the respect due to their sovereign and his wife. I returned the courtesy, careful to hide what I felt.

"My dear brother," Madoc began. "We have a suggestion, a request."

"What is it?" Ambrose asked pleasantly.

"Pray behead the four who violated the flag as soon as possible. Do it as soon as the executioner gets here. It will surely not take him a week for him to arrive."

"Why do you wish to go against the ruling of a court of law?

Not only that, but against the law of the land. Those condemned to death must have a week between the sentence being announced and it being carried out. It gives them time to prepare their soul and time for any new evidence to come to light. Sometimes people come forward after a judgment has been announced."

Madoc's smile tightened. Nessa's face froze.

"I just feel that the sooner this sorry business is concluded, the better," Madoc eventually stated. "People need to see justice done as quickly as possible."

"I disagree," Ambrose returned. "Can you tell me what Rodnap had to say to you? Why did he approach you?"

"He caught me entirely by surprise. That's why I went with him. He thought I might be able to influence you. I assured him I would respect the judgment of my sovereign."

Ambrose raised an eyebrow. Madoc flushed, and the meeting was hastily concluded.

"What was that all about?" I wanted to know.

"Gods know. Personally, I think they just like stamping their authority where they can. Well, the sooner they learn they have no authority over me, the better. The executions go ahead as planned, unless I hear something extraordinary to convince me of the innocence of the four. The violators of the flag will be a magnet for troublemakers and a figurehead for rabble-rousers unless they suffer the death penalty."

The next week passed quickly. The condemned four made no further plea, and they insisted they had no kin or friends but each other. We doubted this was true, but Cerys told me that many sentenced to death said this, out of fear of their loved ones suffering revenge. A priestess heard their confessions and suspected they were holding something back, but they would not open up.

"It's most unusual, sire," she reported. "Normally, they are eager to tell you every misdeed they ever committed in order to clear their souls."

Ambrose thanked her for telling us and insisted that she keep her opinion to herself. The executioner arrived, and Ambrose briefed him on what was necessary; a quick death but also a public one.

"The people of Mendoc must see that justice is being done."

The man nodded thoughtfully. I tried to look at him discreetly. He looked so ordinary, yet his business was killing to order.

I shuddered. Executioners were necessary to a civilised society, but I did not want to be near one any longer than I had to.

The night before the beheadings, we lay in bed in each other's arms. We had made love again, for the fifth time since our wedding night. Ambrose grew more confident, and it pleased me to see him blossom. The thought of not ever being able to take a lover still worried me, but I was happier than I had hoped to be.

At any rate, there is a bond between us, and it's growing.

"Tomorrow will be a big day," I murmured.

"Aye, and it's one I am not looking forward to. Unlike you, I have attended executions before, but I do not wish to attend these. However, I must not shirk my duty."

"I will be with you."

He smiled the smile that always transformed his face and showed the man he really was.

"I know. I know I can trust you, Hawise."

We lay in each other's arms, easy with each other but not easy with what lay ahead of us.

"I've been thinking," I said. "You know the purse of coins that was found on the four? I think we should keep it and whatever clothes they do not wear when they are executed. There is a mystery there. It is clear we have not been told the full truth, and after they are gone, we will have nothing else to go on. One day more evidence may come to light or somebody may confess to something significant."

"I agree. We will do that, and we will have to see what happens tomorrow."

I woke up feeling very apprehensive the next morning. My

appetite was quite dead, a most unusual occurrence for me. Ambrose advised me not to eat anything and to only drink a little. What I was about to see, hear, and possibly smell would be truly stomach-churning.

I dressed in a similar manner to how I had for the trial, in a sober style but not one that could be mistaken for mourning.

This is something I can control. How I look. I can get that right.

Ambrose looked decidedly unhappy before we left the solar for the executions. I gave him as reassuring a smile as I could muster, and he squeezed my hand in return.

There was a knock on the door. Jane, the ten-year-old daughter of Nessa and Madoc, entered. She resembled her mother, for she was built like an Amazon, with a similar bone structure, excellent teeth, olive skin and a mass of black curls. However, I would not call her beautiful as I called Nessa beautiful. There were slight but significant differences in her appearance and many more in her behaviour. She was as shy and unhappy, as fearful of attracting notice, as her Aunt Clementia was.

Today the child stood awkwardly in front of us. She was dressed in a plain velvet gown, in a cut and a colour which did not suit her. Her hair was scraped back off her face in a manner that made her face look fat and her nose bulbous.

"Good morning, Jane," her uncle greeted her pleasantly. "We are about to leave for the executions."

She curtseyed clumsily, then spoke to the floor in a gruff voice.

"My father and mother send their apologies, Uncle. I am to go in their stead. My Aunt Clementia will also join us."

As if on cue, Clementia emerged. She was about the same size as Marjory, but far less noticeable, for she always shrank away into the shadows. For herself, she was plain, with a suet-coloured face, unremarkable features and mouse-coloured hair. I could not say what colour her eyes were because she never looked me in the eye. Today she was dressed as soberly as her niece.

We set off for the executions. I made an effort to talk but soon gave up. What could we talk about? It was no time for chat, and nothing important needed to be discussed. Ambrose saw the executioner's apprentice and made his way towards him with the intention of asking that any clothes which the condemned took off before being beheaded be brought to him as soon as possible.

"What is Uncle Ambrose doing?" Jane's face drained with panic. Her aunt suddenly looked decidedly worried. "Is he going to pardon them at the last moment?" Clementia looked ready to faint.

"No. He wishes to speak to the boy about something else." I saw no reason to give reasons to the pair. The fact that they would certainly report back to Madoc, Nessa or Lewis was an additional reason to stay silent."

"What does he want?" Clementia asked. Fear made her voice sharp. "The execution is going ahead as planned, isn't it?"

Now I was decidedly puzzled. I answered her second question but not the first.

"The sentence of beheading, which Ambrose ordered as King of the Westlands, will be carried out this morning. It is his express command and his right to issue it."

My choice of words silenced them, but neither looked satisfied. In turn, I asked them:

"Why are you so anxious?"

Clementia answered me quickly. Too quickly.

"Neither of us like bloodshed, but Jane's parents wish her to become accustomed to it, for she may have to attend these events as an adult. I have come here to support her."

Ambrose re-joined us, and the four of us were obliged to part. He and I made our way to the royal stand, where we would be as much on display as the condemned, while Clementia and Jane made their way to stand with the other nobles. I decided to tell my husband what had happened later. Now was definitely not the time. I steeled myself.

The event was over surprisingly quickly. The four were brought to the scaffold one by one by the apprentice. The men wore shirts, and Isleen wore a shift under a kirtle, in order to leave their necks bare. Whether they shivered from the cold December air or from fear of the hereafter, I cannot say. They looked dazed but were able to give short, comprehensible speeches, in which they followed the tradition of confessing their guilt, acknowledging Ambrose as having dispensed justice as a monarch should and begging those present to learn from the error of their ways. The crowds hooted and booed to such an extent that I only heard the words of the condemned because I stood relatively near them.

With a final plea to the gods, they knelt one by one in the straw, which became increasingly bloody. Ambrose lifted his hand every time the executioner glanced at him, to indicate that he had not changed his mind. The executions must go ahead.

I did not look where the axe fell, nor did I allow my eyes to linger on the still-warm bodies. Instead, I kept my gaze slightly to the side of the scaffold. Nobody could say I was turning away, but I wished to see as little as I could get away with.

Ambrose offered me his arm, for which I was grateful, and led me away. It was not customary for a king to give a speech after executions. I could hear the crowds making their way home. The spectacle was over, and justice had been seen to have been done. The bodies would be disposed of in the usual way. Soon nothing would remain of the four or their plot.

We just have to hope that we have caught everyone involved and that those who sheltered them will aid no other traitors.

On our way back to our chamber, we wished to be alone, we passed an open door, behind which stood Madoc, Nessa and Jane. The adults were too focused on their daughter to notice us, and the girl was too distressed.

"We need to be quite clear as to what you saw and heard," Madoc insisted. It sounded like panic was making him angry. "All four were beheaded?"

"Yes, Pa. It was just as Uncle Ambrose ordered. They are all dead."

"And their last speeches. What did they say? This is *important*. We *told* you it is."

Jane's voice shook, but she was able to reply:

"They did not say much, and we could not hear much. Truly, nobody could because of the roar of the crowd. There was such a crowd."

"Tell us what they said, you stupid little bitch!" Madoc thundered.

Ambrose looked at me, as appalled as I felt. We paused by the door, out of their sight but in earshot.

"They all said similar things," Jane wept. "They all confessed their guilt, acknowledged Uncle Ambrose as having behaved as a just king should, they said he had done the right thing, and they begged everyone present to learn from their errors. The only other thing they all did was beg mercy from the gods. I swear that is all I heard."

"Did they name anyone other than your uncle? *Did they?*" Nessa snarled.

"Only the gods, Mumma, only the gods. The crowd made such a noise, but I caught the gist of what they said. I am sure I would have heard any other names because my uncle's name stood out at me."

The wretched girl broke down. Ambrose strode into the room, and I followed.

"Is everything alright? I heard raised voices. Jane, why are you crying?"

Nessa replied to Ambrose before her daughter could respond.

"She is being a ninny. She was upset at seeing blood, but we warned her that is what executions are like, and there are far worse ways to die."

"Was she upset at the sight of blood or does she weep under your interrogation?" Ambrose demanded.

Madoc stiffened.

"It is up to us, as parents, how we raise our daughter."

"It is up to me, as your king, to ask questions that I wish you to answer."

Madoc reddened but said nothing straight away. I wondered if he and Lewis had the powers attributed to Fairy Folk, namely the ability to read minds, as well as the glittering blue skin. Ambrose thought not, they merely knew how to use their considerable abilities well, but I could not feel so confident.

Eventually Madoc spoke.

"We wish to raise our children to be fit to hold the noble stations they enjoy in life. That means being able to attend executions. We wanted her to pay attention to what was going on because she cannot turn her face from things which disgust her in life. That is why we asked her questions."

Neither Ambrose nor I believed him, but we could not prove anything nor force them to treat Jane with any kindness.

"At least she will be with us when we move to Castle Pendroch after Yule," I told him when we were alone that night. I sat down on our bed, gripping my gown.

"Yes," he agreed. "We can make sure she is treated properly then. Are you alright? Do you still feel sick? You look pale, as far as I can tell in this light."

I did indeed feel sick. The executions had made me sick, and seeing how Jane was treated made me feel even worse.

When I woke the next morning, I felt better. I remained in good health until mid-December when I felt so exhausted and nauseous that I thought I was falling ill. However, nobody else complained of any sickness.

"Are you sure you are unwell?" Ambrose asked me shortly before Yule. "Might you be carrying my child? I have read this is an early sign."

I raised my head from the pot. Could it be? My breasts had become heavier, but I thought it was due to overeating and had tried to curb myself. I tried to remember when I had last bled.

"My Goddess," I whispered. "I think you are right."

Ambrose was overjoyed. He hugged me as soon as I dared move away from the pot and promised to look after me. Whatever a husband could do to help his pregnant wife, he would do in a heartbeat.

I wrapped my arms around his narrow back, trying not to panic.

I need to give the Westlands at least one prince or princess, but what if I miscarry or die in childbirth? My only miscarriage nearly destroyed me, and I have lost aunts and cousins to childbed. Oh Bessy, would that you were with me now!

Chapter Seventeen

Narrative continued by Bessy the Novice

Hawise and I were able to correspond tolerably frequently in our code. Nobody challenged us, and if anyone checked our letters, I remained ignorant. I was confident that my friend still wrote honestly to me but no longer frankly. The way she described her husband made me believe that she had transferred her first loyalty to him. This hurt me, but it was only natural and understandable. She had to make her marriage work, and King Ambrose was not only her husband but also her monarch.

I could not quite imagine her as a queen, let alone as the queen of a land to which neither of us had had any connection less than a year ago. Hawise was always Hawise in my eyes; my lovely, lively friend.

I carefully put away the letter she sent me just before Yule, the one in which she wrote that she believed herself to be with child. Although I was delighted for her, I was also anxious. Childbed claimed too many female lives, even wealthy ones, and I knew how her miscarriage had scarred her. If it occurred again, I would not be there to console her.

Will King Ambrose be able to be what she needs him to be? Surely, he will care about her as a person by now and not just see her as a walking womb? Is there a bond between them?

I made my way to the herb garden. It was a frosty day, but there were still plants to be tended to. Sister Agnes and her three monks were still at the convent, still the same people they always were. She ruled with an eagle eye and an iron fist, Brother Harold trotted after her like an eager puppy, Brother Percy looked solemn and showed kindness in discreet ways, while Gethin looked as unhappy as I felt most of the time.

Is it better to be like me and to long for what you thought somebody was, somebody who is actually false and who never cared for you, or is it better to be like him? To love a good person and be loved in return, yet be parted from them until you both die and are reunited in the next world?

I saw Gethin's tall figure bent over a bush, his gloved fingers searching for medicinal berries. The haunted expression on his face told me that I was the lucky one.

He does not always look miserable. Indeed, I believe he is genuinely merry at times, maybe he even experiences moments of contentment, but that sadness is always there, somewhere beneath the surface. It must be like an old injury that's never fully healed. Every so often, he will knock the site and feel pain.

God knows my life is far more austere than I ever thought it could be, but I know I would not be happier in the civilian world. I would be in a marriage that must feel unnatural to me and still be parted from Hawise. Only seven months ago I could never have thought my life would be like this, but I know it could be worse. I must count my blessings and keep going.

Whilst looking around to see that we were alone in the garden, I called a greeting. Gethin looked up, smiled at me and returned the salutation.

"Sister Bessy, how are you?"

"I am well, thank you, brother. I hope you are too. I heard from Hawise again. She is likely to be with child."

His face lit up.

"Good. That's excellent news and just what the Westlands needs; the promise of an heir or heiress to its throne."

I agreed and told him the rest of Hawise's news which was not confidential. Gethin and I had long been in the habit of speaking openly to each other. We needed each other in order to cope with the hard life we were both obliged to live.

"Hawise tells me that she, King Ambrose, and their court will move to Castle Pendroch in the new year, where they will likely stay for some months. After that they will move around the Westlands."

"Does she look forward to it?"

"I think she has mixed feelings. She knows her duty, but she knows Castle Malwarden well and its people well, and she must now go somewhere new and strange. She will also constantly be on display and be carefully watched. Although she is a sociable person, it would be a considerable strain on anyone."

He agreed, and I continued, glancing round to check we were still alone.

"She will be glad to leave Malwarden lands for one reason, though."

"Oh?"

"You have told me more than once that Lords Lewis and Madoc and their wives are not to be trusted. Well, for the past fortnight, they have been offering handsome young men to Hawise."

"What do you mean? How can you offer someone to someone else?"

"You know how I told you how oddly they behaved after the executions? Well, their behaviour suddenly changed. Hawise describes them as being overly nice and always introducing her to people. Most of these people are men in their twenties and very good-looking, or at least charming. The men flirt with her as far as any man may flirt with a queen."

"How does your friend take it?"

"At first, she was astonished and polite, but she kept mentioning King Ambrose. Now she is polite but chilly, and she talks at them non-stop about King Ambrose. The men soon back off, but days later, another one appears."

"That is so strange. Those four have always been strange, but why try something so obvious to drive a wedge between their queen and her husband?"

"I don't know. Lady Nessa asked to be allowed to lead the investigation into the Deadly Favour, but King Ambrose refused. He made it very clear that it is in the capable hands of Lord Owen and Lady Cerys. They are working directly with the militia and other people, and they will report only to King Ambrose. Hawise is not sure if they enjoy stamping their authority where it is neither needed nor required, or if something more sinister is going on.

"You know them, brother. What do you think their motives might be?"

"I don't know. I can only guess, but from what I do know of them, their motives will be self-serving at best and malicious at worse. Whenever Marjory mentions them in her letters, she never has anything positive to say, which is most unlike her."

We stood in the cold, silent garden, both busy thinking. At last, I spoke.

"I wonder how Hawise will deal with Lady Jane as a demoiselle. She thinks the child has been groomed to spy upon her, but decorum dictates that she offer places to her husband's relations, and Jane is old enough. Can you tell me what the girl is like?"

"Physically, she resembles her mother, but she is less pleasing to the eye. Whether from nature or nurture, I cannot say, for her parents are cold at best to her. She always held herself as though she were something to be ashamed of. In personality, she is like her Aunt Clementia, to whom she was always close. Clementia has been the bedrock of her upbringing. She is more of a mother to her nieces and nephew than their own mother will ever be. I think the child will serve Queen Hawise well. She is a quick little creature, but your friend must remember that Jane's first loyalty will always be to her parents, not to her queen. Even if she marries the wealthiest man in the civilised world, her parents will expect her to obey them first and foremost."

"Maybe getting away from them by going to Castle Pendroch will do her good."

He shook his head.

"I doubt it, sister. Her parents' control is so great that were she to live amongst the stars, they would still find a way to influence her."

I thought how strange it was that a child who lived in a castle, niece to a king, could still have so little to look forward to in life. I was now almost halfway through my novitiate. I would only wear civilian clothes again when I made my final vows and when my corpse was prepared for cremation, yet I had more freedom than this girl ever would. Sister Agnes could only impose so far on me. She could not go against the law or the rules laid down by our founder.

Jane's parents and uncle are *the law as far as she is concerned and a most cruel and capricious law at that.*

As if partly reading my mind, Gethin asked me about my novitiate. How was I faring? Was I struggling with anything on my spiritual journey?

I was blunt in my reply.

"I chose the nun's life, even after Sister Agnes took over the convent, because it is preferable to what the civilian world offers me. I could never bring myself to lay with a man while any other option remains. For itself, this life is hard, yet it has its consolations. I like practising physic and working with herbs. It interests me, and I am glad to be useful, even if I do not always enjoy what I am obliged to do. I confess that I neglected my duty to the poor and needy in my past life. Devoting myself to meditation and prayer has helped me feel calmer and more at ease with the world.

"I can more easily give up luxuries, although occasionally I will be struck by a craving for something, be it a jewelled girdle or

Frankish wine, than I can freedom or the chance of love. However, nobody is completely free, are they, brother? We all have a duty to follow, laws to obey, nobody can ever do only what pleases them. As for love...well, I was fooled once, I don't know if I could ever trust again."

"Pray don't trust again," he interjected. "Sister, the penalties... Even I would no longer risk so much as a kiss or a flirtation."

"How do you fare, brother? Do you struggle?"

"I manage, and I do struggle. Celibacy is one thing, but to be parted from my family, my love and my true home is quite another."

He looked so melancholy that I thought he might cry.

"You have even given up your blue scarf."

"Not quite. I wear it tied around my waist under my robe. That way, it's still on me, and I do not want to risk hiding it in my cell. Ten to one, someone will search it, if they have not already."

"I know someone has gone through my belongings, and two other novices have said the same to me. One of them complained to Sister Agnes the other day, who only said that could not be true because we do not own anything. We merely borrow from the common store of the convent. Even our tooth cloths are considered to be loaned to us, although we do not share them, thank God."

"Brother Percy is the only human out of that three. Everything that she-devil does, Brother Harold backs her up with gusto."

We received proof of this later that day.

It was six days after Yule, which we had celebrated in a tame style, and three of the nuns decided this would not do. They wanted to celebrate it properly, albeit belatedly. Somehow they acquired a flask of mead and got very merry. It was extremely foolish. Sister Agnes saw what was going on almost immediately. She banished them to their cells for a week and had wanted to punish them even more harshly, but Brother Percy intervened. He begged her not to have them beaten in Landesmar's marketplace, as she threatened, because it would create martyrs.

"All three sisters are beloved for their gentleness towards the children they teach. More than one parent has also praised them for their knowledge and their ability to impart it. They will take their side if they see them treated so. Besides, would their children ever respect their teachers again and obey them?"

Sister Agnes backed down after much huffing and puffing, but the danger remained. The world we lived in less than a year ago was gone, never to return, and it had been replaced with something far nastier than we could have ever imagined. What was once unthinkable was now daily life.

Under this harsh regime, I prepared to make my final vows, and I corresponded with Hawise, grateful for this one freedom that still remained to me.

I told her of my struggles, not of eschewing creature comforts, but of working with the poor and monastics from humbler backgrounds. I was discovering sides of myself which I did not like, sides of myself that I had either ignored or been previously unaware of. In short, I was a snob, who both feared and looked down on those beneath me.

One benefit of my religious training and my friendship with Gethin was that I learned how to tackle my faults by facing them head-on. In the Spartan environment of the convent, there were few distractions from one's darker side. Demons had to be confronted because there was no hiding from them.

I realised I feared the unknown and what was alien to me, as well as feeling some guilt at my comparatively privileged status in life. Little by little, interaction by interaction, I started to see the people I came into contact with as separate human beings rather than one homogenous, puzzling mass. There were those I liked, those I did not, one man so determinedly stupid that I suspected he was descended from a turnip, and all was well.

"Providing you can be civil and treat people as you wish to be treated, nobody can ask for anything more," Gethin advised one afternoon in July as we walked back from a visit to Landesmar.

I nodded and turned my thoughts from my situation to his. I wondered how he coped without the crutch of fornication he had relied on for years. He sometimes looked tense and unhappy, but we did not tell each other absolutely everything.

Hawise must also do without what she once used to steady herself: lovers, rich food and wine. I do not think I will ever know her true feelings for he husband until we meet again, and Goddess knows when that will be. Oh, don't think of that and start crying! As for rich food and wine, her pregnancy and the need to present a good public image will limit her indulgences, and she wrote about the need to stay healthy. I wish I knew what she really felt. I wish I could reassure myself that she fares as well as she insists.

"You make your vows in exactly two months' time." Gethin changed the subject. "Are you ready? You still have the opportunity to leave this life."

"I'm as ready as any woman can be, and I don't want to return to the civilian world. It's not just having to marry, I feel a pull towards the monastic life, even though I don't agree with everything it involves. I believe I should become a nun. It is the best path for me."

The summer flew by. Hawise left Castle Pendroch for another castle held by a different Westlands house, aware that she would give birth there. I could feel her fear through her letters, able to read between the jolly lines after years of deep friendship. She always wrote well of King Ambrose, even gently laughing at him.

He has taken it upon himself to learn all he can about childbirth, she wrote during the last week of July. *People laugh at a man for taking such an interest in such a matter, but I am touched by his concern. He grew several herbs that help a birthing mother and had them made into tinctures. I keep them with me to humour him, for I appreciate his kindness, yet we both know I will have the best midwives when the time comes.*

I was due to make my final vows on 11ᵗʰ September 2016, one

of four novices to do so on that day. My clothes were ready. As was customary, I would make my vows dressed as though I were a bride at my wedding. I would wear a new outfit, the best my family could afford. I smoothed the cream-coloured shift, the heavy silk kirtle, which was a rosy pink, and the matching gown.

I admired the silver girdle and turned the silver circlet, studded with pink sapphires, around and around to catch the early autumn light. Aunt Illustra had sent it with the other jewellery I would wear for the ceremony; pink sapphire earrings and a matching bracelet.

I had a sense of needing to appreciate the fine clothes and ornaments because I would never see them again after the ceremony. Under monastic law, the clothes would go to the poor. (In my case, to a noblewoman in reduced circumstances rather than to a peasant in absolute poverty.) However, I did not want to say goodbye to my jewels. I had inherited many pieces of jewellery from my parents and sisters. I strongly did not want to have them given to charity.

Instead, I had visited my old guardians, and we agreed that my all old clothes and my possessions which were not of sentimental value to me might go to those in need. I was more than happy with that. My jewels and what I held dear would be split between them, my distant relations and Hawise.

"We can tell Sister Agnes that the bracelet, circlet and earrings are your family heirlooms and not mine to give away. Even she cannot dispute that. My other jewels and possessions are nothing to do with the convent. You have them safely stored away. She will not be able to interfere there."

Uncle Piers looked at me with tears in his eyes.

"Do you *really* want to become a nun, Bessy? It will be until the day you die, and it is *such* a hard life."

"Uncle, I am sure. I have a vocation."

I went to bed on the night of 10th September, still convinced this was the case. I thought of Jennet, thought of her deception and remembered my brief marriage.

No, this is your best choice, Bessy. The path that will suit you best.

I awoke on the morning of the 11th feeling calm but not joyful. A sense of inevitability hit me.

I was treated like a bride on her wedding day. The other nuns were in high spirits and pleased for me. They waited on me, helped me to dress in my fine clothes, fastened the circlet to my oiled, loose hair and handed me the cosmetics and perfume I had not worn for a year.

And will never wear again until I am dead and about to be burned.

I looked into the glass. What I saw pleased me. It was not vanity that made me think I looked beautiful. The other women cooed over me in a manner that confirmed what my eyes told me. Sister Agnes, as the abbess, was not present. None of the three monks were present because of their sex.

I pulled my eyes away from the glass. The other novices were also prepared, dressed in the best their families could afford. Only I was noble and wealthy, and our appearances reflected this.

"Let's go," one of them suggested.

During the ceremony, I had a spiritual experience. I felt as though the gods were speaking to me, welcoming me. Tears ran down my cheeks, and I did not check them. I made my vows with a sincere heart.

The final moments of my civilian life came. At Sister Agnes's command, we novices lay down in front of the altar. I felt the cold marble beneath me. The nuns and monks sang a lament as though we were dead whilst Sister Agnes walked up and down with a candle, to mimic cremation.

The song ended. Sister Agnes blew out the candle and set it down. Wordlessly, we rose and stripped naked. Nuns took away our clothes and handed us the garb of the convent. We dressed. More nuns came up to us with bowls and flannels. We washed away our cosmetics and all traces of perfume. The first group of nuns returned with scissors and cut our hair close to our scalps.

The second group presented us with kerchiefs, and we tied them around our heads.

I felt no shame whilst I was naked in front of men, nor did I feel loss when my mass of hair was taken from me. It was as though I had left my body.

We knelt in front of Sister Agnes. She placed necklaces over our heads; from each hung a pentacle.

"Rise, sisters. Rise and rejoice, for you are now nuns!"

The congregation broke into applause.

I rose, feeling giddy. I was indeed no longer Lady Millabess or Bessy the Novice but Bessy the Nun.

CHAPTER EIGHTEEN

The rest of the day was a bit of an anti-climax. I felt almost numb. The convent celebrated our taking our final vows with a feast, to which our families were invited. My old guardians attended, and they gasped to see me. Technically, they should have addressed me as 'Sister' or 'Sister Bessy', but they could not, and I remained plain Bessy to them. I handed Aunt Illustra a parcel containing the jewellery, the little bottle of perfume and the cosmetics which she had sent to me. They felt alien in my hands and not what they were only hours before. My cream and pink outfit was already lying in the convent's laundry, ready to be washed, ironed and sent to an unknown recipient.

The presence of my aunt and uncle was bittersweet. They, and the families of the other new nuns, did not fit in with the convent's plain interior and the religious habits that we wore. They looked alien. At the same time, I felt a sense that I was seeing them for the last time, even though I might still make and receive some visits. I thought of Hawise and my late family. It was all I could do to keep smiling and chat gaily.

Gethin understood. He approached me at the end of the day while we were helping to clear up.

"Nearly everyone feels strange after they take their final vows," he whispered to me. "It does not mean you have made the wrong decision, merely that you are aware of the enormous change in your life. Give yourself time, be it days or weeks, and come and talk with me when you can. The feeling will pass, and you will start to feel at peace."

He was correct. It took me nearly a fortnight of feeling a sense of rising panic and as though I were not part of anything, as though I were only watching life at the convent, before I became calm and clear-headed. The other new nuns confided they felt the same. It felt good to find common ground with them.

11th September was also a notable day for my oldest friend. At some point during our feast, Hawise gave birth to a healthy baby girl many miles away. She told me all about it in a letter later that month.

Darling Bessy,

I received your letter to say you are now a nun, but I cannot address you by your title any more than you can call me 'Your Grace.' Our friendship runs too deep for such formalities.

I am now a ma! I cannot quite believe my great good luck, but I neither died nor miscarried. Instead, here I am, happy, quite recovered and the mother of a beautiful baby girl. She is perfect, Bessy. Healthy and perfect. I think she looks more like Ambrose's side of the family than mine, and that is a good thing with my reputation. She has his very dark hair, and I think her eyes and skin will be the same as his. He says her face is heart-shaped like his mother's was, and her eyes are almond-shaped like hers were. She has dimples like my sisters had, and I rejoice in that small link. I do not care if she never resembles me, but her pa insists she looks like me when I'm happy.

Her name is Millabess, and we already call her Milly. Princess Milly, the heiress to the Westlands. I cannot believe I am writing these words. Millabess is your name and my mother's, and Ambrose's mother was called Milly, but it was short for Millicent. I wish I could ask you to be godmother, but protocol dictates that the role goes elsewhere.

All I can offer is update after update of everything she does, and I will send you a portrait, should your convent permit it.

Her birth was dramatic, but all's well that ends well. I bled more than usual and grew quite light-headed. It is fortunate that Ambrose had a large bottle of tincture of clotweed prepared. I dread to think how much blood I would have otherwise lost. The midwives only brought a small amount with them, which had hardly any effect on me, and they were impressed that a man should consider such a thing.

I love my husband more than I thought possible. I would feel the same if we were beggars, being queen has nothing to do with the deep love, respect, trust and admiration I feel for him. Oh, to see him dote on Milly would quite melt your heart! All this, and I feel such lust for him. I never dreamed I could have all of this in one man, let alone that he might return my feelings.

I broke off reading to wipe my eyes. My first feelings were relief and gratitude that my friend had had a safe delivery and a healthy baby, as well as a loving relationship with her husband. Beneath that, I felt empty. Hawise naming her child partly after me did not change this. I was sure I did not regret giving up the opportunity of motherhood, yet I knew I would never feel what Hawise felt. I could only pray I would never find a woman who made me feel what she felt towards her husband. The gulf between our lives was suddenly enormous.

It was some days before I could write a suitable reply and tell her about my becoming a nun.

We exchanged several letters over that autumn. She told me all about little Milly, as I expected, but she also mentioned other matters. She wrote of her demoiselle Jane, and how the child was far livelier and happier now she was away from her parents and uncle.

I would never call her a pretty child, but she is in better looks now she smiles more and does not walk about with her shoulders hunched. I am getting her to dress in a way which suits her, and she appreciates these little attentions. However, I do not trust her and would not write so if I were not writing in our code. I am convinced she has been told to spy on me. She is a quick child, and she always looks at me uneasily whenever she receives one of her many letters. I cannot check her correspondence without arousing suspicions, but neither Ambrose nor I can trust her, through no fault of her own. Instead, we watch her discreetly.

The rest of her letter was full of people I had never met yet had heard much about, thanks to her earlier letters. Lady Cerys and the investigation into the so-called Deadly Favour. So far nobody had been caught, but nor had there been any more reported disappearances. Her hosts at High Castle, Lady Bronwyn and Lord Gudarro, were so welcoming and a pleasure to spend time with. Young Lord Bran and his ambition to have an army of hawks and cats. Lady Cerys wrote he made some progress there, but they were hardly a force to be reckoned with.

I put down the letter, feeling sick. We now lived in completely different worlds. Did she miss me as much as I missed her, or was our correspondence merely a duty she felt obliged to carry out? Did she pity me in my bleak, monastic life?

A tear slid down the side of my nose. I pitied myself. The loss of brocade gowns, pearl-studded girdles, minstrels and imported wine I could easily bear. The loneliness and the loss of my freedom were a good deal harder to endure. Should Gethin leave or Hawise stop writing, I truly believed I would fall into madness and embrace it as the lesser suffering.

It's the monotony of the place. So little happens, and tomorrow I must deal with Son-of-a-turnip because he has stupidly put a spade through his foot again. Why could it not have been his neck?

I began to wonder if a second marriage would have been so bad before recalling my bracing myself to kiss Horace and his eyes when he realised what I was doing. No, I had chosen the lesser of the two evils, and there was no third option available to me.

At around the beginning of December, I was permitted to

visit my guardians for a week. Both the invitation and the permission came as a surprise to me.

An old friend of my Aunt Illustra had written to her to beg a visit. Her name was Maeve, she was originally from the Emerald Kingdom and had returned there after her marriage. Now widowed, she wished to take a holiday where she had spent several happy years. She also wished to bring her ward, Roisin, with her.

I write to you, Bessy, to beg your help. Rowena, Simon and their two will also be staying with us. Rowena is likely to give birth within the next month, and we will all have our hands full. I cannot put Maeve off, we were close as girls, and she was only recently widowed. Pray join us to help me with your cheerful face and calm ways. Put it to your superior as an act of mercy, which I can assure you is how I will see it!

Sister Agnes consented with surprisingly little persuasion and merely reminded me of the importance of behaving like a nun in my childhood home.

"Eschew all unnecessary indulgences. Do not overeat or drink to become merry. Pray as often as you pray here without turning it into a display of your virtue. Wear your habit as you wear it today, with no modifications, and shun perfume, cosmetics and ornaments."

"Yes, Reverend Mother."

I wrote a quick note of reply to my aunt, agreeing that I would come to the Castle of the Eastern Coast a week from that day, before spreading the news to my fellow sisters. Some of them envied my having the opportunity to briefly leave the convent, others did not.

"Will it not be too much of a contrast, Sister Bessy?" Sister Ida asked. "The castle must be so sumptuous, yet you will not be able to enjoy all the pleasures it offers, then you must return here. I think that must be harder than staying here."

I did not own that I longed for some variety, and this was the likeliest chance of obtaining it. Instead, I arrived at my old home on the dragon my aunt sent on the agreed day.

I slid off the dragon, grabbed my bags and patted her, telling her what a good dragon she was. A man greeted me with as much ceremony as he did when I was 'my lady', but he stared at my appearance before leading the dragon away. My uncle came out of the castle and embraced me warmly.

"Bessy!" He kissed me on the cheek. "It is so good to see you again." He partially released me to look at me more closely. "I cannot get over seeing you as a nun. I suppose I should call you sister."

"Nay, Uncle, please don't. I don't want to be anything other than Bessy or my dear to you and Aunt Illustra."

"Our guests might call you sister." The contented expression in his eyes fell slightly, and his voice became weary.

"By guests, I take it you do not mean Rowena, Simon, Henry or Clarice?"

"No, I mean Lady Maeve and her damnable ward, Lady Roisin." He sighed heavily, which was most unlike him.

I looked at him, puzzled, and he continued in the same flat tone.

"Lady Maeve is all very well, a pleasant, charming sort of woman, but one suspects her good nature does not run too deep, at least not when it would mean doing something that might inconvenience herself. She and your aunt get on, but between ourselves, I don't think this visit will be repeated. They are not as close as they once were.

"As for the girl, she turned fourteen in October, and she's a pain in the neck. She carries herself as though she were thirty-four and a great queen, yet she shows a nasty streak that I would have been ashamed of, if any of my children had shown at the age of four. Her behaviour is petulant, self-centred, at times downright spiteful, and she has an overweening sense of her own importance. She has brought her cat with her, and quite frankly, it has better manners than she does."

I was astonished. It was not like my uncle to run somebody down like this, let alone a young guest under his roof.

"Lady Roisin must behave badly indeed for you to say this to me. What does her guardian say? Does she not curb her?"

"I think it would inconvenience Lady Maeve to notice her ward's rudeness, let alone her occasional violence towards the servants, so she turns a blind eye or speaks to her mildly at best. 'Pray don't do that', you know, that sort of thing."

"*Violence* towards the servants?"

"Aye. She has pushed a few out of her way, and she slapped the maid who was waiting upon her for not doing something to her liking. I did not overhear all the conversation, but the girl had committed the mortal sin of fetching the wrong cloak, then the wrong boots or some such thing."

I stared at my uncle open-mouthed. It was sadly true that some lords and ladies treated their servants in such a manner, but I had never lived with anybody who would behave so badly. It would have never occurred to me to strike someone like that.

My guardian noted my shock and continued.

"I intervened then and told Roisin, in front of the maid, that such behaviour is not tolerated under our roof. She looked taken aback to be pulled up before sneering that she is used to better servants. I retorted that I was used to better manners. She replied that things are done differently where she comes from, and when she marries, for her guardian is already negotiating a betrothal, she will neither tolerate stupid servants nor stupid questions."

"She spoke so *to you*?"

"Aye. I left her at that point and went to find Lady Maeve. I related the tale in full, but her ladyship would only sigh and say that fourteen is a challenging age, and Roisin has suffered much. She lost her parents at five and the man she called Daddy before she turned fourteen. However, she agreed to talk with her. Whether she did or not, I don't know. We will have to see what good it does, if she has."

We entered the castle, and my head was full of these strange people whom I had yet to meet. Uncle Piers asked a servant where his mistress was, and the man replied that she was in the solar with

Lady Rowena. I went there directly whilst another servant dealt with my luggage.

It was not so long ago that I was waited on hand and foot. What a contrast it will be to return to the convent next week and to have to do everything for myself again.

My aunt and her daughter were indeed sitting in the solar. They jumped up in surprise when they saw me and embraced me, exclaiming how good it was to see me again. I wiped tears away from my eyes. I realised just how much I had missed them all.

"How are you both?" I asked before dropping my voice to a whisper. "Uncle Piers has told me about Lady Roisin."

Rowena rolled her black eyes, and my aunt spoke.

"All I can say is that I thank the gods none of you ever showed such unkindness and that they both go home soon. They leave for another friend's house the day after you leave us. I shall not invite them again. Maeve blushes for Roisin's bad behaviour but barely tackles it. It has made me lose all respect for her. It surprises me, for I remember her being a much stronger character when we were younger."

"Maybe their loss has affected them?" I tried to be charitable, but Rowena only laughed.

"Oh Bessy, that convent has made quite a saint out of you already! No, they speak often of the late Lord Sean, but they do not seem so overcome as to lose their wits. Lady Roisin talks more about the boy she hopes to marry, the great Cormac of Ballywoods, just seventeen and already a fearsome warrior. Lady Maeve is in contact with his family, and it is likely that they will agree upon a betrothal before Imbolc, then marry as soon as she turns fifteen. However, they may not talk about him back home, so she makes up for lost time here."

"Eh? What do you mean, they may not talk of him back home?"

Rowena rolled her eyes again.

"Apparently, many girls of high birth would like to marry this elusive warrior. Roisin tells me how handsome, how clever he is and so forth. However, due to the nature of his work, he has to be careful as to what he tells people about his whereabouts. Roisin should not tell anyone in the Emerald Kingdom about him until just before they marry. Nobody would harm her once she is his wife, but she would be in danger as his betrothed."

"I've never heard of anything like that. Is she lying, or do they do things differently over there? Every warrior I have ever met has been quite open about what they do. Those who are on secret missions do not create mysteries to draw attention to themselves. If he is such a risk, why is he considering marriage?"

Rowena shrugged her narrow shoulders.

"Goddess knows. She is not making him up. She has shown me his portrait. Lady Maeve has mentioned him on more than one occasion, and I have seen Lady Maeve send letters to post. She says they are to his father. Still, Roisin will settle with him somewhere in the Emerald Kingdom or the Land of the Leprechaun. Either way, she will not return to anywhere where we're likely to be, thank God."

"Amen to that," Aunt Illustra added. "I have heard quite enough from her, about her betrothed, her rank and her mark of royal blood."

"Mark of royal blood?"

"She says she has a birthmark shaped like a star on her collarbone. Every female descendant of some queen who died over a hundred years has the same. She insisted on showing it to Rowena."

I was full of curiosity by the time I met these guests at dinner. By great good luck, or to give my guardians a break, I was sat between them for the meal. I had learned their mother tongue, Banshee, as a child, but my uncle assured me they spoke fluent Suvvern.

Lady Maeve was a pretty woman of about forty. She had rich red hair, a milky complexion and green-grey eyes. When she spoke, she had a definite Banshee accent, but words never failed her. I found her an agreeable companion at dinner. We talked about her homeland for some time, she was impressed with my knowledge of her language, and about my life at the convent.

Lady Roisin was completely different, apart from her accent, which was as strong as Lady Maeve's. For a start, she was one of the most beautiful girls I had ever seen. She was willowy without being lanky, fair without looking washed out, her hair was like a wheat field, and her eyes were an intense purple-blue I had never seen before. Her conversation revealed a sharp mind, a conceited personality and an education that had been thorough in everything but developing self-knowledge or real consideration for others.

I could not put her cold judgments and arrogant presumptions down to a recent bereavement without lying to myself. I tried to make conversation with her but only received monosyllabic answers in response. Admiring her manicured nails was more interesting to her than anything which passed at the table. Lady Maeve's pale cheeks reddened, but she made no effort to reprimand her ward. Instead, she turned my focus on herself and asked me questions. The subject turned to Hawise, and I realised that neither Lady Maeve nor Lady Roisin knew that the Queen of the Westlands was also my dearest and oldest friend.

The effect it produced on them was interesting. Lady Maeve was surprised and made polite enquiries. She showed the curiosity one would expect on suddenly finding that the person one is talking with knows royalty. Lady Roisin's reaction made me bite the inside of my cheeks and avoid catching anybody's eye. At first, she froze in amazement before asking me if this really was so. When I assured her that yes, Queen Hawise and I were once both wards at the Castle of the Eastern Coast and became as close as sisters, she sat up straighter and gave me her full attention for the rest of the meal. Her manner was not exactly deferential, but she certainly treated me with a good deal more respect.

I was not the only person to notice this new appreciation or that it was also directed to my old guardians, their daughter and her husband.

"Gods, Bessy," Rowena whispered to me as soon as she might be confident we would not be overheard. "I never saw such a transformation effected so speedily. What a silly girl! That will teach her to treat people with respect."

"I cannot imagine why she bothers," I replied. "Hawise and I correspond, but I can hardly influence her. Besides, what favours could she need from the Queen of the Westlands when she will soon be settled in either the Emerald Kingdom or the Land of the Leprechaun?"

Rowena had no answer, then Lady Roisin entered the solar with a book in her hand. Her cat, a friendly ginger creature called Pan, followed at her heels. She curtseyed silently, we returned the greeting, I petted the cat, and she began to read. The light was not strong enough for her, so she called for candles. I made no objection, but I did speak up when she began to abuse the man who brought them for not bringing them quickly enough.

"That is rude. Nobody speaks to anyone like that here."

She looked at me with a red face, and her new respect for me vanished.

"Back home, things are different."

I raised an eyebrow at her.

"You are not at home now."

She looked around the solar and sneered: "I see that."

I refused to dignify her with a response. Rowena was about to say something when Aunt Illustra entered the room with Lady Maeve. They were talking in concerned tones about the violation of the flag in Mendoc.

"It was a terrible event," I chimed in. "Hawise told me all about it. The village church and several homes were completely destroyed. Many other buildings were badly damaged. There were many injuries, but fortunately, nobody was seriously injured or killed. Luckily, they caught the culprits and beheaded them about a year ago. It's a better fate than they deserved."

Lady Roisin looked appalled but not for the reasons I assumed.

"That is not the true story!"

"Pardon?" I was too surprised to take offence at her scorn.

"You were told lies. Freedom fighters demonstrated peacefully and lit a bonfire as part of the traditional Samhain celebrations. They *were* freedom fighters, not terrorists. They just wanted to protest against the brutal treatment of the people by the local militia and against the incompetence of the Council of the Interregnum. Nobles lived in luxury, ignoring the plight of the people. When the four realised they were going to be unjustly condemned, they fled, for few had the courage to shelter them. They did not receive a fair trial. Instead, they were killed to strike fear into anyone else who might dare to stand up for themselves."

She sat back satisfied. Her guardian fiddled with her bracelet and tried to change the subject. Aunt Illustra looked aghast. Rowena raised her eyebrows.

At last, I replied.

"Do you honestly imagine I was lied to? I passed on eyewitness accounts to my aunt and uncle. Official reports back these claims. The four who were executed received a fair trial and a lighter sentence than they might have expected. King Ambrose and Queen Hawise saw the damage to Mendoc and spoke to its people. Indeed, King Ambrose was there when it burned."

"All lies! The fire was contained to a bonfire."

"How do you know you were not lied to? Where have you got your information from?" I wanted to know.

She paused before stating: "From my betrothed. The man who will soon be my betrothed. Cormac of Ballywoods. He is well-connected and a man of honour. He wrote to me the day after Samhain, and he sent me news before and after the trial."

"Why should you believe him over everyone else? Was he there?"

"No, but as I say, he has many connections, and he would never lie to me."

"Who are these connections? How do you know they did not lie to your betrothed?"

She smiled serenely with a look of pity in her eyes and said nothing.

"I will trust what I heard from my oldest friend," I told her.

She continued to gaze at me with the same expression. I turned to Aunt Illustra and Lady Maeve and joined in their conversation about their plans for Yule celebrations.

"Goddess, Bessy, what a smug brat," Rowena hissed later that evening when I was about to go to bed. "She thinks she's something special, doesn't she? Like she knows more than anyone else and as though the usual rules of society, like basic manners, do not apply to her. Does she believe her birthmark is a passport to do as she pleases?"

I could only agree and add that she and her guardian would soon be far from us and the Woldsheart.

In bed that night, I thought about what had passed that day, what I had said and done and if I had sinned in any way. The convent was making its mark on me.

I stayed calm, and I did not descend to her level. Besides, it is not my place to try to teach her anything. That is Lady Maeve's responsibility. Nor is it my place to tell Lady Maeve that she is failing her ward by allowing her to behave so badly.

I once also thought that the rules did not apply to me. I must admit to that. When I first came to the convent, I did what I liked, but so did everyone else. No, I did no harm there, whereas Lady Roisin does cause harm through her words and her deeds. I do not delude myself there.

The rest of my visit passed in the same manner. Although I was glad to see the back of Lady Roisin, incorrectly assuming I would never see her or her guardian again, I was truly sorry to bid farewell to my guardians, Rowena and her family. Rowena promised to let me know when her baby was born.

I set off for the convent, exactly one week after I had left it,with a heavy heart. Sister Ida was right. It was such a contrast to get used to.

Chapter Nineteen

The routine of convent life was briefly broken by the Yule celebrations. Nobody dared to smuggle contraband into the convent or break any rules this time. I cannot say I was happy, but I did feel content. Hawise wrote to me from another castle in another part of the Westlands. Reading between the lines, I could tell that she struggled with what was expected of her; to always be on display, to support the most important man in the kingdom and to always appear happy. If I had not already known that money cannot buy happiness, I did now.

It just protects one against certain evils, not all of them.

Hawise also wrote of more disappearances, carried out in the manner of the so-called Deadly Favour. I wondered whether or not to pass this news on to Gethin. I knew how anxious he was for his children. In the end, I did not, but he learned anyway from a letter from his sweetheart.

Rowena gave birth to a second son, named Paul, in the second week of the new year.

An everlasting peace was declared between our house and our allies and our enemies, namely the House of Ishelmer, the House of Merendysh and the House of Malwarden. The celebrations were muted, for nobody was sure it would last. Tucked away on the Eastern Coast as we were, the fighting had scarcely touched us. I am ashamed to say that I did not feel the weight of such an announcement, bar that it strengthened Hawise's position. I could only hope the peace would last so she felt safe.

"This is the first time that the House of Lothwold has not been at war in my lifetime," Sister Ida, who was almost forty, told me. The announcement affected her more than it had me. "Peace was declared between us and the Kingdom of the Isles almost four years ago, and it held. The peace between the Woldsheart and Doggerdale has lasted for almost thirty years without so much as a skirmish."

Her hazel eyes glowed with pleasure.

"Do you think we will be able to live in peace and harmony with *all* our neighbours *for ever*?" The thought stunned me. Conflict and strife seemed to be the natural way of life throughout the ten kingdoms on these islands. "Peace, everlasting peace has been discussed for a good ten years, but it seems too wonderful to come true."

"It is coming true, sister," she beamed. "Look at what has happened so far. So many wars have ended, with both sides agreeing not to reignite the conflict. Many hostages have been returned to their homes. We will live in a better world."

Her optimism was heartening to see, but I felt slightly knocked off balance.

The world and what we can expect from it are changing rapidly. When I entered this convent, less than two years ago, I could never have guessed that I would end up living under such a strict regime. I could not have guessed that it would still be preferable to a second marriage. Whatever hardships I face, I know I made the right choice.

What will happen next? Will my life change once more? How will Hawise fare in the Westlands?

Within two months something else happened which changed

both my life and Hawise's. It also brought me back into contact with Lady Maeve and Lady Roisin, and it changed my opinion of both the woman and the girl.

CHAPTER TWENTY

Narrative continued by Brother Percy of Lothwold

I stared at Sister Agnes in horror across the table. I could not quite believe what she had just gleefully reported.

"I beg your pardon, Reverend Mother? Do you mean to say that monastics may be punished retrospectively for misdeeds which they committed before the High Priest announced that the rules must be properly enforced? And, in instances when the sin has been great, their nearest kin or friends should also be punished?"

The window showed a lovely March day. Green leaves were beginning to cover branches. Fluffy white clouds moved rapidly across a clear blue sky. Inside, it was deepest winter. I sat with Sister Agnes and Brother Harold around a round table to discuss convent business as we did every week. We still formed a sort of interim council for the Convent of the New Moon. Brother Gethin would also have been present, had a peasant's wound not turned poisonous and called him away.

It has been over eighteen months since she seized power, for want of a better phrase. Why has the bishop not insisted that a permanent abbess be installed? Does she intend to stay here for ever? I want to go back to my old monastery and stop being a part of her foul schemes.

Sister Agnes shook her head sadly.

"No, not quite, brother. That is the proposal which I sent to His Holiness, the High Priest, yesterday. Naturally, I cannot expect a reply so soon, but the idea came to me in a dream the night before last. It is as though the gods had spoken to me."

She cast her eyes down modestly. Brother Harold stared at her adoringly. I tried to master myself. I knew I had to tread carefully, just as I had been treading carefully since the summer of 2015.

"Sister, how would that work?" I eventually asked. "The new rules, for that is how we must see them, have been in place for less than two years. Can we morally condemn people for what they did before then, if they have broken no rules since that time? Can we morally punish people for the crimes of another?"

She exchanged a pitying look with Brother Harold, a sight I had grown all too used to seeing. Neither of them credited me with much intelligence because my mind worked very differently to theirs.

"Brother, these rules are hardly...*new*," she stated in a slow voice. "They have been in existence for over a thousand years, in the case of this convent. Monastics have merely escaped a just punishment when they sin."

"But to punish their closest connections?" My voice faltered. "How is that just?"

"Some sins are so heinous that they spread from the culprit to those whom they love. Besides, this will encourage people to check the behaviour of others, thus reducing the likelihood of someone sinning in the first place."

I said nothing. I had so little power. I had made what small changes I could inside the convent to try to mitigate the petty cruelties which they sanctimoniously dealt out, but if the High Priest approved of her insane notion, my hands were tied. For the millionth time, I cursed myself for volunteering to help with something that I had not understood. I had truly believed I would be doing good by helping corrupt convents and monasteries to mend their ways. Sister Agnes's reign of terror, backed up by those above her, had soon disabused me of that notion.

I must get hold of Brother Gethin as soon as I can and warn him. He may face castration.

Brother Harold appeared to read my thoughts.

"The so-called new rules are certainly being appropriately enforced. I daresay you have heard of a brother in Doggerdale who paid the price for giving in to his lust."

We had not, so he continued in the same tone, the tone of a child telling tales on another child.

"My cousin, who is the prior at this monastery, not forty miles from us, told me in a letter which reached me this morning. Apparently, it will soon be common knowledge. This monk, Brother Henry, was caught *in the act* with a local peasant woman. The woman fled, and I do not know what will happen to her, but he could not deny his sin. The abbot insisted that he be castrated, and so he was, that very day."

Vomit rose in my throat. I swallowed. Sister Agnes looked calm but curious. He spoke as though some great wrong had been righted.

"This all took place four or five days before my cousin wrote to me. He believes Brother Henry will soon be well enough to return to his duties. Although the operation was carried out in private, it had quite an impact on the other men and boys there. My cousin believes the deterrent worked, for the atmosphere at the monastery has been most solemn since then."

"As it should be," Sister Agnes stated. "I believe that the more public these cases are made, the less likely such punishments will need to be carried out."

What a disappointment that will be for you both. Don't pretend that you volunteered for this mission to save anyone's soul or to improve the standing of the church. It was to be able to bully people according to your whims, pure and simple.

Later that day, I pleaded a toothache and went to find Brother Gethin.

I checked that we were alone in the infirmary.

"There is nothing wrong with me, brother," I whispered. "However, I need to speak with you urgently and in confidence."

He looked surprised and bade me sit down in a loud tone. He fetched some instruments to support the lie that he was examining me, should we be interrupted, before pulling a stool close to mine.

I told him what had happened at the meeting that morning. The colour drained from his face.

"I know you used to wear a blue scarf. I have not seen it for a long time, but I am sure I was not the only person to notice it and believe it is of sentimental value. For the love of the saints and all that is holy, get rid of it as soon as you can. I cannot believe you have lost it or that you threw it away."

He stood up, glanced at the closed door, and then briefly lifted his robe. I saw the bright cloth tied around his waist. He sat down and explained its importance to him.

My eyes filled with pity for him.

"It would quite kill me to be parted from it." His voice cracked. "It...it kills me as it is to be parted from Marjory and our children, only able to communicate by writing letters."

"I am confident those letters are being read. As I left the meeting, Brother Percy urged Sister Agnes to be more vigilant, and she replied something along the lines of checking everything regularly. I know she searches through people's cells and possessions. She knows people correspond, which is permitted, but as I left, I heard her mention Bessy, the queen and a code. I know our sister was brought up with the Queen of the Westlands, and they are as close as sisters. I assume they write to each other."

"They do, and they write in a code. Sister Bessy told me. Marjory, the children and I write in Suvvern. We are bilingual in Book Language, our boy is fluent, and the girls have a little knowledge of it, but we know no other languages or any codes. Every educated person has some Book Language. Its use as an international means of communication renders it useless for my needs." His face fell. "Must I burn my letters, my scarf, and ask Sister Bessy to tell my family, through my queen, to stop writing?"

"To save yourself and the boy you call your son, yes, yes you must."

"They would not dare touch Bran. I would die first! I cannot believe they would dare to think such a thing." His face flushed.

"Brother," I said gently. "Would you have believed two years ago that we would be having this conversation? I could not have believed it only a year ago."

He slumped forward, almost ready to faint.

I pulled a piece of singed cloth out of my purse. He looked at it in surprise. The cloth was bright blue, thin and mottled with soot and scorch marks.

"This is part of a child's petticoat which was donated as alms for the poor. I noticed that the colour and texture greatly resembled your scarf. Most of the garment is now down a privy. I tore off part of the skirt and attacked it with a candle.

Brother Gethin looked at me with an open mouth.

"When I say 'get rid of your scarf,' I mean you should send it to your sweetheart via Sister Bessy. Sending a parcel from the convent would arouse suspicion but not if she sent it from Landesmar, which she could easily do. You are both called to the village frequently to help people. I will present this cloth to our so-called superior tonight and say you gave it to me. Such submissiveness might save you and stop them from suspecting my real thoughts."

"Brother Percy, that is a stroke of genius!" He embraced me with tears in his eyes. "Sister Bessy and I plan to go to the village tomorrow, I will speak with her directly." He took a moment to compose himself before continuing.

"You think they suspect you of not agreeing with them?"

I answered honestly.

"I fear they do. Don't get me wrong, I believe that the church needed to reform. Convents and monasteries were hotbeds of idleness and indulgence. Monastics neglected their duties. That's why I volunteered. However, the current situation is a thousand times worse. This is as far removed from what is right, from what the founders intended, as hell is from heaven.

"If I had my way, I would have stopped you from your swiving. However, I would have issued some more humane punishment and warned you. If that failed, I would have thrown you out of the order."

"But nobody may leave the monastic life except through death?"

I shrugged.

"I would say that if someone sins greatly enough, and persistently enough, then they should be thrown back into the civilian world. They have broken their vows, and they refuse to change their ways. Had I the choice, I would leave the church and return to farming. I did no harm in the fields, and the church has become even more corrupt but in a different way."

"You were a farmer before you joined?"

"I was a farmhand. My family has worked on land some thirty miles south-west from here for generations. I married a blacksmith's daughter when we were both nineteen. My Blissmina died within the year, leaving me heartbroken. I had no children and no appetite for a second marriage, so I joined the church. I believed it was the right thing for me to do. That was a decade ago last Yule. How I wish our lives had been different! At first I thought I was on the right path, but now...now I feel I cause suffering, instead of relieving it."

We sat in silence for a minute, lost in our own regrets before he spoke in a firm voice.

"Brother, I am grateful to you. If I can ever repay you in the future, I will."

We shook hands, and I left him. It was a relief to know that someone I liked and admired did not look down on me. I could only guess what the nuns thought of me.

RUTH DANES

I presented the scorched cloth to Sister Agnes after supper that night. We were alone, and I told her how Brother Gethin had handed it to me in the infirmary.

"It was a token from his past life that he feels he should have given up long before now. He tried to burn it, but the material would not burn completely, so he gave it to me with his humble apologies."

She smiled her terrible smile, the one she always made when she knew someone was unhappy because of her, and took the cloth. It was a cold enough evening to justify a fire. With one neat movement, she threw the piece of petticoat into the flames.

"Thank you, brother. You may go now."

CHAPTER TWENTY-ONE

Narrative continued by Bessy the Nun

Gethin spoke to me in confidence before we set out for
Landesmar. His eyes were wild, and his voice was rapid.
I agreed to write a note to Hawise, enclose it with his
parcel and letter to his sweetheart and address the parcel to
Hawise in my own writing. I knew that she and King Ambrose
had recently returned to Castle Malwarden, where Lady Marjory
lived.

"Of course, I will do this. We will send it to post at the inn," I
promised. "Good gods, brother. I cannot believe we have come to
this. Every last thing is being taken from us. Every last comfort.
Should I stop writing to Hawise?"

"No, I believe you are safe because you write in code and
because of her position. They do not dare admit to spying on us,
they won't ask you to crack the code. Besides, you have not
committed any sin. I have."

He kissed the parcel with such a desperate look in his eyes as
to make me feel quite worried.

"Farewell, Marjory. One day I will come for you. As soon as I
can, I will," he whispered as though he were praying.

He composed himself and became calmer once he saw me hand over the parcel at the inn. We visited the people who required our help, and I noticed how much easier I felt around them. I was able to examine them, comfort and advise them and give physic without feeling awkward.

Progress indeed. I really am a nun. I feel connected to these peasants, connected to all my sisters and connected to a man from a foreign land. I truly have become part of general humanity and am no longer a lady of Lothwold of the Woldsheart. By giving up that role, I became part of something much greater.

I did not share my thoughts with Gethin. His face showed how distracted he was.

Within a week I received a letter from Hawise. The letter was almost a package, it was so thick. I did not think Gethin had received anything, I did not know if he had any correspondents other than Lady Marjory and their children, so I wondered if Hawise was trying to contact him via me.

Please don't, Hawise. It puts me and him in such danger.

I opened the letter as soon as I was alone in the infirmary with Gethin. I gasped before I could stop myself.

He was by me in an instant.

"What is it, sister? Is it my family?"

I was able to reassure him there.

"No, they are safe. Hawise merely writes that Lady Marjory has your note and scarf, just like I requested. The problem relates to the Emerald Kingdom. I must beg leave from Sister Agnes."

I handed him the letter. It was easier than trying to explain.

Dearest Bessy,

I received your parcel. I am sorry to learn that life at the convent has taken such a turn for the worse. Rest assured, I passed Brother Gethin's letter and scarf to Marjory. I used Cerys as a messenger, for she is closer to Marjory than I am. I saw Marjory later. She is as unhappy with the news as you might imagine, but she understands and promises to send no further messages to Brother Gethin. She has also explained to their children why this must be so in terms appropriate to their ages.

I hope you will be able to speak with them soon, for I must beg your presence and aid as soon as possible. Be assured that we are all well. This matter refers to Lady Roisin.

Lady Maeve is a distant cousin of Owen. Yesterday evening we received a message from her by gold sprite. She and Lady Roisin are both living at her castle, Castle Kinselk, on the Eastern Coast of the Emerald Kingdom. She requests that Owen fetch Lady Roisin discreetly and as soon as possible. She asks that he take her off her hands permanently, or she will be obliged to take more stringent measures. Lady Maeve is willing to pay sufficient money to apprentice her ward and for her keep until she begins to earn enough to support herself. Lady Roisin need not be treated as a noble maiden, but instead as any other apprentice at his castle.

You may imagine Owen's astonishment at receiving such a letter. Indeed, we were all amazed, for it is such a bizarre request, and it is far from how you described the relationship between guardian and ward last December.

We all fear that more stringent methods may mean execution or a prison somewhere far from anyone that the girl knows. These words are dramatic, but what else could her ladyship mean?

I have enclosed a diplomatic passport, signed by Ambrose and Owen, and a letter from them to your Reverend Mother. Bessy, I beg you to go to Castle Kinselk and bring Lady Roisin to Castle Malwarden as soon as you can. I ask you because I know your abilities: your fluency in Banshee, your level-headedness and your courage. You are also a nun, which makes you less likely to be detained or questioned. The inhabitants of the Emerald Kingdom and the Westlands have as much respect for monastics as we do in the Woldsheart. You will also been seen as non-partisan, which I feel will be vital.

Whatever has happened at Castle Kinselk is very worrying indeed. I fear the girl has meddled in what does not concern her, and now her very life is in danger.

"Good Gods," Gethin whispered. He handed the letter back to me. "Well, sister, will you go?"

"Yes, I will. I will find Sister Agnes right now. I have no idea what Lady Roisin has done, nor why she cannot go to her betrothed's family, but it is my duty to save her if I can."

I had no trouble persuading Sister Agnes to release me to go to the Emerald Kingdom, even though I could not tell her when I might return. Despite her egalitarian principles, she could not ignore a royal command. Likewise, she adored having her own way, but she had the sense not to upset what might involve international politics.

I packed and prepared to leave in a very different state of mind compared to before I returned to my old guardians a few months ago. I felt more confident in myself and sure that I really was a nun. It was the right path for me. I knew I would fit back into convent life again.

Early the next morning I set out on a dragon, one fuchsia pink Gryngolet. As she took off, I realised I had not been alone for so long. So few nuns were alone for any length of time. Apart from private contemplation or sleeping at night, I was nearly always with someone and doing something.

Naturally my thoughts turned to what lay ahead of me. It was such a mystery. I could not think of any reason why the indulgent Lady Maeve had suddenly turned her back on her brat of a ward, and so cold-heartedly.

Sure, Lady Roisin's behaviour is disgraceful, but why punish her by banishment, and why do it now? I don't understand why Lady Maeve does not simply send her to Cormac of Ballywoods. She may not marry until she is fifteen, which is half a year away, yet she might live with his family until then. Has she done something so bad that he has broken off their betrothal?

Betrothals were sometimes broken off, but it was rare among the upper classes, where marriages were even more likely to be guided by practicalities and politics than love. From my knowledge of the Emerald Kingdom, I could see no reason why a match between two nobles would be dissolved, unless something very bad was discovered about one of the party or an allegiance had fallen through.

My heart beat fast for most of my journey west. It was both exhilarating and nerve-racking to travel so far alone and through lands that were only recently the enemies of Lothwold. However, my good manners, my nun's habit and my passport served me admirably. I was treated well and encountered no dangers. Gryngolet was as curious as I was as we saw unfamiliar countryside and towns, but she was discreet for a dragon and made no rude remarks. I could only be thankful for the peace and wonder what part King Ambrose had played in bringing it about by accepting the crown of the Westlands and what part Hawise had played by marrying him. Together they had ended an interregnum and provided an heiress to the throne. Maybe the longed-for peace would last, and people might enjoy stability and the opportunity to travel easily.

Towards noon on the second morning of my journey, I was escorted to Castle Malwarden by a pair of young guards. They looked at me with the same ill-concealed inquisitiveness which Gryngolet showed, but they had the manners to say nothing. I was curious to see where my friend now lived.

Castle Malwarden quite took my breath away. The mountains were impressive enough to me, a girl used to the Wolds and flat country, but I was amazed at how the builders of the massive castle had incorporated them into the defence of the castle. The guards smiled at my praise, and the younger took Gryngolet and my baggage while the elder begged me to wait in the Great Hall whilst he fetched his king and queen.

I looked about discreetly. Hawise had described the place well. It was richly furnished and spoke of centuries of power.

Suddenly she appeared, calling my name. Her behaviour was what it had always been, merry but mindful of etiquette, yet her appearance had changed. The gold necklace around her neck contained diamonds, and her gown was cut in the fashion of the

Westlands. Her brocade gown and her white shift, visible at her neck and wrists, were of a far higher quality than I had seen her wear before. She carried an infant in her arms, well wrapped against the chill of the spring day.

We embraced, then I remembered myself. She was now royal, and I curtseyed as deeply as any woman should to a person of such a high rank.

"Oh, Bessy, don't. Not you, you are my oldest friend. You should not curtsey so to me."

"You are a queen, I must."

"Aye, and you are a nun." She took in the change in my appearance, then she smiled. "This is my daughter, Milly."

"She is adorable, so sweet." This was true. The child was an unusually pretty little girl, but I could not see much of a resemblance to Hawise in her.

"I still think she favours her father's side of the family." Hawise dropped her voice. "Which is no bad thing. I will return my little dumpling to her nurse, then we must talk in my closet. Do you want any refreshment?"

I reassured her I would wait for lunch and followed her. The women in the princess's nursery curtseyed with even more reverence than I had, and the one who took Milly from her mother curtseyed first to the baby. All three women looked at me curiously, but we did not speak.

How odd that my oldest friend's child will one day rule the women who now care for her. They must raise and guide her, like any other infant, but she will be their monarch.

All the rooms I encountered were both grand and comfortable, even Hawise's comparatively small closet.

"I cannot believe you really live here," I told her, once we were safely alone. "You really are a queen and have given birth to the next ruler of the Westlands."

Hawise laughed. It immediately felt like old times again.

"Aye, I can't believe it myself at times. Oh, it is so good to see you again!"

She hugged me, then sat back down.

"Are you happy?" I asked.

"Mostly. I know I live in splendour that I could not have dreamed of, even two years ago, splendour that most people will never even see, and I do love Ambrose. He is an excellent man, and the best husband I could have. Milly is the best thing to have ever happened to me. I know I am unusually lucky...yet all this comes at a price. I have to be careful and crafty to carve out any privacy, I still feel very foreign at times, the world watches us, and so much is at stake. The peace is as fragile as it is new. People are grateful to Ambrose for accepting the throne, but will their good-will last when we encounter bad times, as we inevitably will. At times, it honestly feels that if I sneeze too loudly, another war will break out. I live in fear of putting a foot wrong."

I smiled. My life at the convent had its downsides but nothing like this. Hawise continued.

"When I look at Milly, I feel love like nothing else, and through her, we secure the throne, but what an inheritance for such a tiny girl! So much responsibility will lie on her shoulders. The world will watch her as she grows up, she will be mother to a nation, and she, of all girls, will have to marry for politics over love."

"All this comes at a price," I sympathised.

"Yes, but I agreed to this. Nobody tricked or forced me into marrying Ambrose or bearing his child. I suppose nobody knows what it is like to be queen until they are crowned, but I did go into this situation with my eyes open. But enough about me. Tell me about you. Tell me everything that you could not tell me in your letters."

I was only too glad to do just that. I told her everything. I finished by telling her about Gethin and the scarf.

"Ah, that is a sad tale. Will you see Marjory yourself this after-noon? I know she, and possibly her son, would like to speak with you about him. They want to talk to someone who spends time with him."

"Of course. How did they take my message?"

"We are not close, so I asked Cerys to break the news. They were shut away for some time. When I next saw Marjory, her eyes and nose were red and swollen. She now always wears a purse I had not seen before on her girdle, and she keeps touching it. She must keep his scarf in there. We have not spoken about it, but I can see how it has devastated her and her son. The two girls are too young to be told the full truth yet, although they naturally miss their father. Owen looks full of remorse and avoids the little family. Marjory and Bran appear to be avoiding him."

"What an unholy mess."

"I know." She sighed and looked lost in thought before continuing. "We have another unholy mess to resolve. Lady Roisin."

"Yes, I told you everything I could in my letters. This is as much a mystery to me as it is to you. I will head off straight after breakfast tomorrow. With luck, I will return late the following day."

"Thank you. I wish I could tell you more, but we only know what we have been told. Owen wrote to Lady Maeve to offer to take her ward off her hands and said that you would come to her within the next few days. We have not received a reply."

A gong sounded.

"We should go to eat." Hawise rose and threw her arms around me. "Oh Bessy, having you here is like old times again."

I hugged her back, swallowed my tears and laughed.

"Like old times? Queen Hawise, look at yourself in the glass before we leave your chamber. When did you ever wear a gown with gems stitched around the neckline and wrists or wear diamonds around your neck when we were at the Castle of the Eastern Coast? How Uncle Piers and Aunt Illustra would stare to see you now. As it is, they can barely believe I wear a nun's robe and kerchief."

She laughed and led the way to the Great Hall.

"Will I see Lord Bran and his private army?" I asked. "How does he get on with such a venture?"

"You will meet him, but I do not think he has been as successful as he had hoped regarding his hawks and cats. Still, nobody has the heart to discourage him. Besides, stranger things have happened."

CHAPTER TWENTY-TWO

Once in the Great Hall, Hawise introduced me to several people whom she had described, some in more flattering terms than others, in her letters. It was gratifying to be able to make their acquaintance at last. I was especially eager to meet her husband and monarch.

King Ambrose caught my eye and kept it. Naturally I could not admire a man like most women, and I could not even say he was conventionally handsome, but there was something there that made me want to keep looking at him.

It is not just his position. A child might see how everyone defers to him, but independent of that, he is interesting. Hawise is lucky. I never saw her like this with any other man, not even Adam. If only I could meet a woman who made my eyes sparkle like that, and be able to be with her without risking terrible burns.

King Ambrose was gracious to me. Indeed, everyone was pleasant and polite. After the meal, he, Lord Owen and Hawise stayed with me to discuss my business in the Emerald Kingdom.

"I do not think she will resist you," Lord Owen said. "However, no matter if she does. She must be made to understand this is one situation where she cannot throw her weight around. If she is stubborn, Lady Maeve or her guards might force her to go with you."

"Of course. I cannot imagine what I will find. This is all so very different from what I experienced from them back in December. I understand Lady Maeve is a kinswoman of yours, sir. Do you know her well?"

"Not really. I have only ever met her twice. Once shortly after she married Lord Sean and once a few years after they took Roisin in. They had four or five, maybe even six, children of their own, all of whom were older than their ward. I can remember Roisin as being an exceptionally pretty and precocious little girl. She was quite sweet, nothing like her behaviour under your guardians' roof."

"How did Lord Sean and Lady Maeve behave towards Lady Roisin?"

He paused to think before eventually saying:

"I honestly can't remember anything about their behaviour that sticks out. I think they were kind and attentive to her in the way that most parents are towards their small children. I cannot remember anything that might explain what is behind Lady Maeve's sudden desire to get rid of the girl she has raised for almost ten years."

Later that afternoon I was approached by a thin woman with dark red hair and an anxious look in her eyes.

"Sister Bessy?" she asked. "I am Lady Marjory of Malwarden. You were kind enough to send my...a scarf to me about a fortnight ago."

"Yes, my lady, that's me."

I curtseyed, and she returned the greeting.

"Pray come with me," she begged. "I have so many questions that I would like to ask you. Do you have the time?"

"Of course."

I followed her. Hawise did not get on well with her, and this reflected in her letters, but she had tried to be fair to her. She had not mentioned her appearance beyond describing the blue scarf, which I could see tucked into her gown, and I had not spoken with her sufficiently to judge her behaviour. All I could safely say was that she was a lady suffering under a great strain.

She bade me to be seated, and I looked at her sympathetically. Hawise had not described her as a bad person, and I had heard much about her from Gethin. She did not deserve what was tightening her mouth and making her eyes look haunted.

"What would you like to know, madam? I can assure you that anything we say will not leave these four walls. You know that Queen Hawise and I are as close as sisters, but I am not obliged to tell her everything, nor would she expect it."

Lady Marjory looked slightly more at ease, smiled gratefully and began to speak

"You must know what has passed between me and Gethin."

"I do. He has told me. I do not judge you, madam. I just wish to help two people who are in a wretched situation which they do not deserve to be in."

"Five people, actually. Our children suffer too. Our son knows he must never have contact with his father again and why. You may imagine his suffering. Our daughters know they may not write to their father nor receive letters from him, but they do not know this will be for ever. I cannot bring myself to crush them as Bran, Gethin and I have been crushed. Not while I can avoid it and distract them."

She looked into the distance, heaved a great sigh, and then bombarded me with questions about the man she loved.

How was he? Was he in good health? How did he find life at the convent? Was he in any danger? Was he treated well? Did he lie with anyone? Did he confide in me? Did he have any messages for her, Eluned, Isabeau or Bran?

I answered her as best I could. I could reassure her that he was in excellent bodily health, although his estrangement from those he loved made him unhappy. I could confirm that he did confide in me, he did not so much as flirt with anyone, and he spoke of her often and with the greatest of love. He was treated no worse than anyone else at the convent. I believed he took pride in his work as a physician. The villagers, nuns and Brother Percy respected him. Sister Agnes and Brother Harold liked nobody and only cared about their self-righteous mission.

"Providing he obeys his so-called superior, he is in no danger. None of us are until we break the rules. He had one message for you. The last time I saw him, he said that he would come for you as soon as he could. One day he will come for you."

She broke down and sobbed piteously.

"He always says that. Oh, that will be in the next world now! After his corpse has been stripped of his monk's robe, dressed in a civilian jacket and breeches and been burned to ashes. Gods, how am I to get through my remaining years without him? If I did not have the children, I swear I would have..."

Her voice dissolved into tears. I broke etiquette by laying a hand on her arm. She wept on my shoulder for some time. Tears of sympathy trickled down my cheeks.

"His scarf and the one he gave me are all I have of him now." She wiped her eyes and indicated the blue cloth around her neck and the leather purse at her waist. "I've swapped them."

"Pardon?"

"This," she touched the scarf around her neck, "is what I gave to Gethin. I want it to touch me because it once touched him. The one he gave me is in this purse." She tapped the little bag.

"I'm sorry." I had no other words.

We sat in silence for a while before she pulled herself together and turned to me.

"I thank you for what you have done for me, Sister Bessy. When you return to your convent, pray tell Gethin that he has all my love and always will. The children and I desire nothing more in the world than to be with him. As it is, I will raise them as best I can and consider his wishes in all things. I will send no more messages via you, for fear of endangering you both. I beg him to show the same restraint. I will only contact him through you, should I or our children...should we be dying. Would you grant me the same favour? Providing I hear nothing from you, I may rest easy that he is alive, albeit alive and unhappy?"

I swallowed and nodded. I could not speak.

She went to bathe her face and asked if I might see her children. I gladly obeyed.

I found Lord Bran, instantly recognisable by his dragon, chatting to two little girls, who looked very like each other but nothing like him. I correctly guessed they were Isabeau and Eluned. I introduced myself and explained I came from the convent where their father was staying.

How the little girls pounced on that information! Lord Bran looked excited but remained silent whilst they bombarded me with as many questions as their mother had. I was careful how I answered them, neither willing to break their hearts nor give them false hope. However, I was able to satisfy their curiosity and make them grin. They were in high spirits when their Aunt Cerys called them away.

Lord Bran fixed me with an intelligent stare. I knew I could not and should not attempt to lie to him. Instead, I told him a watered-down version of what I had told Lady Marjory.

"I thank you, sister," he said with an unusual dignity for his age. "But pray tell me, is there no hope that we may meet him again in this life?"

"My lord, I will not lie to you. I wish it were otherwise, but no, there is not. I fear that even if you were to write to him, he might be punished in such a manner as to maim or even kill him. The rules are so harsh, and they are enforced without any consideration to an individual's circumstances. Those in charge would not consider the need for a father to have a relationship with his son. They would just see it as a breach of his vows to the gods."

His face crumpled, and he begged leave of me. His dragon

wordlessly moved away, carrying him from my eyes. As they moved away, Lord Owen passed. The creature shot him such a look that I would never wish to receive, and the look in the eyes of the Lord of Malwarden reflected guilt I could only be glad never to have felt.

CHAPTER TWENTY-THREE

G ryngolet and I left Castle Malwarden early the next morning, both feeling apprehensive at what we might find in Castle Kinselk. We flew over the sea and arrived without incident. I was very quickly aware I was now in a foreign country, more so than when I was in the Westlands. Here, people spoke another language, and they dressed differently. Wealthy women trimmed their outfits with something called lace and even wore it as a veil. I saw several dressed in such a manner while a guard checked my passport, and I had to hiss at Gryngolet not to stare.

My Banshee served me well. I could both understand people and be understood. Another guard escorted me to Castle Kinselk. He complimented me on my accent. In return, I asked him about the family who lived there. It turned out his brother was a guard at the castle.

He told me what his brother frequently told him. Lady Maeve was a cold, proud sort of woman but reasonable enough towards those who served her. Lord Sean had been of a similar nature, but he had had a hotter temper. Their children, now all grown up and living elsewhere, apart from their eldest daughter who would one day inherit the castle, were very like their parents.

"A man can get on with them providing he remembers his place and shows he is respectful," he told me as we headed towards the castle.

"What of Lady Roisin? What is she like? I have heard her described as a most beautiful girl."

"Very like those who brought her up. She clearly thinks a great deal of herself and of her rank. She's not the sort of girl to go out of the way to be unpleasant, but you wouldn't want to cross her. Yes, she is lovely, to look at, that is."

"I hear she is now fifteen." I told a small lie. "I suppose she will marry and leave the castle at some point in the next few years."

The guard shook his head.

"No, I think she is a little younger than that. In any case, my brother has not mentioned any betrothal, and that sort of news spreads quickly in these parts."

We had now reached Castle Kinselk. A priest passed by, and the guard called to him.

"Father Declan, this is Sister Bessy, who has come all the way from the Woldsheart to speak with Lady Maeve. She has a passport. Do you know if her ladyship is about?"

The priest nodded eagerly.

"Aye, she is. Will you take the dragon to the stables, and I will take Sister Bessy to her ladyship."

I thanked him and the guard, patted Gryngolet and told her to behave, then followed Father Declan. As soon as we were out of sight of the guard, he whispered in my ear.

"Do you come from King Ambrose or Lord Owen of Malwarden?"

"Both. I have been told to take Lady Roisin to Castle Malwarden."

He visibly relaxed.

"Thank the gods for that. I fear she will go mad otherwise or her guardian will kill her."

I stared at him aghast.

"Father, what has happened?" I explained what little I knew about the situation and added that nobody in the Westlands knew any more.

He told me far more than the guard had. Both the guard and Lord Owen had described Lord Sean, Lady Maeve, their ward and their relationships accurately. However, the tender bond between the woman and the girl had changed as recently as it had dramatically.

One day near the beginning of March, a man and a woman came to the castle, requesting to see Lady Maeve. Both were lowborn and shabbily dressed, the man looked to be his mid-forties and gave his name as Finbar the Executioner. He was indeed once an executioner, but he had since been banned from that profession for taking bribes to unlawfully prolong deaths. He admitted to wandering about the countryside for the past ten years, committing petty crimes to get by, falling in and out of various groups of ne'er-do-wells. The woman was at least two decades his junior and so attractive that people stared at her, despite her grubby appearance and worn clothes. She gave her name as Mairead and said she was not only Finbar's daughter but Lady Roisin's half-sister. Finbar had sired them both.

"You may imagine people's amazement when she announced this in the Great Hall, sister. Lady Roisin was also present, and she could not speak. However, Mairead was good-looking in the way that her ladyship is. Tall, slender, creamy skin, lots of silky blonde hair and very unusual eyes set in an angelic-looking face. Once you saw the resemblance, you could not stop seeing it. Certainly, neither looked like Finbar.

"Lady Roisin was most displeased at this announcement, as you may imagine, and insisted Mairead was lying for some foul purpose. In response, Mairead took off her shawl and pulled down her bodice enough to reveal a birthmark shaped like a star on her collarbone. She insisted Lady Roisin do the same."

"The mark of royal blood," I whispered.

Father Declan laughed sadly. "Oh yes, how Lady Roisin used

to brag about that. She would even insist on showing people her birthmark when she was younger. I have worked at this castle from a time before she was born."

He continued in the same sad tone. Lady Roisin recovered herself sufficiently to insist that Mairead was trying to fool her for some reason. She told her to wash the birthmark because she believed it had been painted on. Before Mairead could reply, Lady Maeve stepped forward and told Finbar, Mairead and Lady Roisin to come to her solar to talk. She asked Father Declan to accompany them as a witness.

They left the aghast group of servants in the Great Hall and followed Lady Maeve. Once in the solar Lady Maeve made a full and frank confession without blushing. It disturbed Father Declan and Lady Roisin but came as no surprise to the other two present.

Lady Roisin had been adopted by Lord Sean and Lady Maeve shortly after her fifth birthday. She could remember little of her life before then, only that she had not lived in such comfortable circumstances, and her family was not respected. She could not remember the particulars, only a sense of being feared and loathed by their neighbours and living with both parents and older siblings in a poor neighbourhood. Her most precise memory was of her father having to travel for work.

When Lady Maeve and her late husband took her in, they told her it was because her parents and all her siblings had died, and they were friends of her family. She was led to believe that she was highborn, and her family had been reduced to poverty. Over the years she was dissuaded from asking about her birth family to the point where she barely thought of them and believed what she had been told.

"She was told lies, sister. Lady Maeve explained to us that while her mother and brothers had died during an epidemic, her father and sister, Finbar and Mairead, survived. Lady Maeve and her late lord took Roisin in, I should say Roisin, for she has no title, and Mairead stayed with Finbar."

"Why? Why was Roisin given up but not her sister, why did Lady Maeve lie to her ward, and why have Finbar and Mairead returned now?"

"Finbar had been expelled from his profession, and Roisin was too young to work or be married off. Fourteen-year-old Mairead could join him in a life of crime, but the five-year-old was a liability. So, he made the best use he could of her. He knew the lord and lady through executing their prisoners and asked them to take his youngest child but lie about her parentage."

"Why did they accept?"

"Because they will get a good price for her when she marries. They agreed to give him a small portion of it."

"Are things done differently over here? How can her guardians get money when she marries?"

"Things are not *legally* done differently here. Lady Maeve calmly admitted that Roisin would be sold as a bride when she turned fifteen. Such good-looking, bright, healthy young girls fetch good money in the forbidden trade of humans."

"That has been illegal all over the civilised world for over one hundred years."

"Murder has always been illegal, but people still kill."

I struggled to take all of this in. We paused outside the castle itself in order to be able to keep talking confidentially.

"I cannot believe Lady Maeve admitted this so casually," I said. "Did Cormac of Ballywoods know he was getting a bought bride or was he involved as well? Is that why she could not tell people about him?"

"Cormac of Ballywoods does not exist. He was an invention by Lady Maeve. She concocted the story to stop anyone seeking Roisin's hand and to stop her asking for a match to be arranged in the near future. Besides, she needed a reason to persuade Roisin to travel with her when the time came. Lady Maeve intended to take Roisin to her owner soon after she turned fifteen. That was when Finbar was supposed to come to Castle Kinselk for his money. He came here several months in advance because the buyer for Roisin has pulled out. The buyer lives in the Westlands, and the new peace there has made trafficking people near impossible. Finbar wanted to take her back to use her to make money for her family. I would not be surprised if he intended to prostitute her out."

"Goddess, what a story! What happens now? Where is Roisin?"

"She is locked in a dungeon and will remain there until you can take her out of the country and off Lady Maeve's hands permanently. Lady Maeve does not want her to go with Finbar because that way she would remain in the Emerald Kingdom, and she might try to return. She is less of a risk over the water. This is why I was told to be a witness, so neither Finbar nor Mairead might come back to claim Roisin on false pretences."

"I cannot quite believe it, father. Lady Maeve and her ward visited my old guardians just before last Yule. She was so kind and indulgent towards her. This is incredible. It was just an act?"

He nodded.

"Are you quite composed, sister? Can you face Lady Maeve? Time is of the essence, for Roisin grows increasingly hysterical. They even took her beloved cat away and gave him to a farmer. She is completely alone and broken. I fear she will go mad, if she has not already."

"Yes, father, I am ready. Do you think Roisin will agree to come with me? When I last saw her, she was extremely fond of her own way."

"She will, she definitely will, for Lady Maeve has told her on more than one occasion that if she does not go to the Westlands, she will keep her locked away and keep everyone away from her until her corpse has rotted."

I was even more appalled. The priest noticed my face and nodded.

"Yes, her ladyship has revealed her true colours. I knew she had more than a sliver of ice in her soul, but nobody could have dreamed she would threaten the girl she brought up as her own with death from thirst and hunger. Indeed, nobody could have guessed she would be sold or banished from the country."

"Does Lady Maeve not fear retribution? What she has done is surely against the law here. Besides, I cannot believe that this sort of behaviour is any more acceptable here than it is in the Woldsheart."

"Her family rule this area with an iron fist and keep pirates away. I doubt even our queen herself would dare to upset the apple cart."

We entered the building and fell silent, unable to talk any further without risking being overheard. Father Declan approached a servant and bade him to take us to Lady Maeve.

"Tell her that Sister Bessy from the Woldsheart has arrived. She is expecting her."

The man soon returned and begged us to follow him. He led us to the solar where her ladyship awaited us. I curtseyed and tried to see any outward change in my aunt's old friend, convinced Aunt Illustra had been deceived as to her character and equally convinced that I must tell her the truth at the first opportunity. However, I could see no change in the woman before me, beyond minor changes in her dress to allow for the warmer weather. She greeted me with a smile and courtesy that chilled my blood more than screamed threats would have.

"Sister, I am glad you made it here. Will you come to my ward now? Then, pray take some refreshment and take her to Castle Malwarden. I think Lord Owen explained what is required."

"Yes, madam. If that truly is still your will, then yes."

I could not quite match Father Declan's words with her cheerful politeness.

Her smile did not falter.

"It is. I will take you both to the dungeons now."

We followed her and went to the part of a castle that every castle must have but which I had never entered. We left the main building, entered a heavily-guarded smaller building and passed through three locked doors before we saw Roisin.

My heart quite broke for her, and I forgave her for her behaviour under my guardians' roof in an instant. She was still finely dressed in lace and damask, and her cloak looked new, but both she and her clothes were filthy. Her hair was greasy and tangled, it looked as though she had been tugging at it in despair, while her face and hands were grubby. It was also clear that she had been crying and biting her hands in extreme distress. The clothes were stained with dirt and even what looked like days of menstrual blood. Clearly, she had been left to bleed with no cloths.

Upon seeing us, she rushed at Lady Maeve and begged for mercy. Without blinking, her guardian struck her around the face, knocking her off her feet. I believe she would have kicked her, had I not intervened.

"No, I beg you, do not do that, madam."

A nun's word carried as well in Banshee as it did in Suvvern. She stepped back and addressed Roisin coldly.

"Get up. Sister Bessy is come to take you to the Westlands, from where I expect to see and hear nothing of your existence ever again. Contact me, and you will return here to your tomb. Servants will bring you soap, water and a change of clothes. Be ready to leave within the hour."

Father Declan begged that Roisin be allowed to eat and drink before her journey and be permitted to take cloths for her bleeding with her. In a dull tone, the girl told him she now did not expect to bleed for another month. Lady Maeve nodded and bade me to take some refreshment in her solar before my journey.

We left Roisin in her prison, and she was brought to me an hour later. She was now clean and tidy but dressed like a peasant in a sheepskin coat over a gown of rough cloth. She carried a bag in her hands, which she pulled at incessantly.

Lady Maeve briskly explained that the bag contained a change of linen and a few other necessities, but once at Castle Malwarden, it would be up to its Lord and Lady to provide for her.

"They have already received the money I sent for her keep,

and they may do what they wish. I have now washed my hands of her and desire nothing more than for you to both leave this land for ever."

Roisin opened her mouth, but I cut her off before more violence could take place, by curtseying to Lady Maeve and taking the girl's arm.

"Thank you, sister."

With that, her ladyship turned on her heel, and we were dismissed from Castle Kinselk.

"Come on. We will make good time on my dragon and should be at Castle Malwarden by nightfall."

She obeyed, looking dazed, and we found Gryngolet. Once we had permission to leave the Emerald Kingdom and were flying high above the sea, I decided to talk with her. So far, she had sat silently whilst I spoke to officials and Gryngolet.

"Are you well after your imprisonment? Would you like to see a physician once you are at Castle Malwarden?"

The proud girl I met in December would have scorned such questions. The subdued person beside me merely shook her head and whispered, 'No, thank you'.

"Did you have something to eat and drink before we set out? If not, I have supplies with me. What have you brought with you? I need to know what else you will need."

I found it came naturally to me to have these concerns and to take care of her. It was neither a sign of weakness nor of being a nun. It was simply being human.

Roisin broke down.

"Oh Gods, sister, those are the first kind words anyone has said to me since I was dragged away into the dungeon. After all I have suffered, sufferings I could never have predicted would ever occur, and after I was so rude to you and your family."

She cried for a while, and I told her, truthfully, that I forgave her.

"I was angry at you," I admitted, "but I never wished such a fate on you. Nobody with any humanity in them could. Were you badly treated in the dungeon?"

"Not really. The guards barely spoke to me, never mind touched me, and they brought me food and small beer and emptied the pot fairly regularly. It was cold, but I had blankets. I was just left to bleed..." Shame stopped her voice, then she continued in a more determined tone. "What you saw Lady Maeve do was the worst that I suffered. She struck me in a similar manner when I would not go into the dungeon, then I did not see her until you did. To think she was my guardian and I called her Mammy, for she was a mother to me."

"And until your real father and sister turned up, she was always as gentle towards you as she was when I saw you at the Castle of the Eastern Coast?"

"Oh yes, no girl could have wanted a more tender, caring mother. Lord Sean was equally gentle towards me. The whole family made me feel so welcome and so wanted. The saints know what their children, whom I called my siblings, knew or what they've been told. I know Lord Sean was in on the plot, but I don't know about them. Their eldest daughter and her family live at the castle, but they have been away visiting other relations. They set off the day before Finbar and Mairead turned up."

"Had you truly forgotten your birth family? Did you honestly not recognise Finbar and Mairead? Did you suspect nothing about Cormac of Ballywoods?"

She paused, thinking deeply.

"I believe I made myself forget where I came from soon after I arrived at Castle Kinselk. I honestly did not suspect anything when I saw Finbar and Mairead. When she pulled down her bodice to reveal her mark, I felt sick inside, but I still did not fully know the truth, if you know what I mean. I sensed something bad, but I did not quite know what.

"As for my so-called fiancé...I can only say that I then had no reason to doubt my guardians. They produced a portrait of him, showed me letters and took letters from me to post to him. They spoke in such detail about this boy and his family. I swear, sister, the wisest of us would have been taken in."

I was about to ask her who had told her about the burning of Mendoc, as it was obviously not Cormac and what her guardians knew, but judged it prudent to say nothing. She looked overwhelmed, and the ordeal of arriving at Castle Malwarden, to start a new life as a lowborn maid amongst strangers, awaited her. Instead, I focused on what she had in her bag and what she might need to settle at the castle.

We made good time and arrived at the castle before nightfall as I had promised. Gryngolet was pleased to be back and to be able to chat with the other dragons. Roisin looked as though she had landed on the moon and clutched her bag to her chest.

"Come," I said in Suvvern. "I have known Queen Hawise since we were girls, and I have met King Ambrose, Lord Owen and Lady Cerys before. Everyone will be kind to you if you behave well to them and try to fit in."

She answered me in the same language, the foreign tongue she would have to speak for the rest of her life, and followed me into the castle.

CHAPTER TWENTY-FOUR

Narrative continued by Queen Hawise of the Westlands

Bessy's return was announced shortly before dinner. Ambrose and I were spending a rare hour by ourselves, lying in our chamber, when a servant knocked on the door. We hastily dressed and went to the solar to receive them. We had already agreed that this was a reception which should not take place in the public of the Great Hall. Once we had spoken with Roisin, Cerys and Owen would be called to meet her.

The four of us had made other decisions before my friend had even set off from her convent. Fully aware of Roisin's unpleasant nature, we agreed to present a united and firm front. She could be apprenticed to someone near or at the castle, anyone who was not a soft touch, and apply herself like any other apprentice or live in a dungeon. She was to be plain Roisin and forego all items now forbidden to her under the sumptuary laws, such as jewellery of precious metal, cloth of silver and certain perfumes.

"We should not be cruel," Cerys stated, "but she must be made to fit in with life here and understand she is no longer a lady with a lady's expectations. With a bit of luck, the fiction of Cormac the Warrior will have put her off men, and she will not be sniffing after lads and marriage. If she is as pleasing to the eye as Bessy the Nun writes, she will almost certainly attract notice, regardless of plain clothes and a lack of ornaments. However, she will hopefully do nothing to prolong any such attention."

We agreed, then I turned the subject as to what story she should tell other people at the castle about herself and her history.

"Her story will draw attention to her, attention that she does not need. However, would she be able to maintain a lie for the rest of her life?"

In the end, we decided that she should tell the truth but a misleading version of it. All she need say was that she had been taken in by a couple in the Emerald Kingdom, one half of whom knew Lord Owen. Due to a recent bereavement, she needed to find somewhere else to live and quickly, for she had nobody else.

This settled, we were prepared for the girl's arrival. I had told Ambrose more than once that I did not want her lording it over anyone, and he quite agreed with me.

"She can live as the other apprentices do, obey as they do, and be glad she is far from Lady Maeve. I'm not having her strike people or expect them to run round after her."

I was not quite sure what to expect when I finally met Roisin, but once I had met her, I was surprised.

Bessy had not exaggerated. She truly was one of the most beautiful girls I had ever seen. Standing opposite her, even whilst wearing a gown trimmed with sapphires that everyone said suited me, I felt like an old dumpling. What I could see of her hair, damn her to Hades, was a plait as thick as a ship's rope, simply pinned around her head, partly covered by plain brown cloth, which emphasised its blondeness.

I had to stop myself from touching my own finger-width plaits that were held in place with gold pins under a silk veil. I ignored the difference between my hair and hers, just as I ignored the fact she was half a head taller than me yet probably weighed less than I did, and instead, focused on the business in hand.

Roisin either did not notice the contrast in our looks or was too sensible to show that she did. On the whole, I believe the former was true because I was even more struck by the terrified expression on her face and her trembling hands than I was by her looks. Had I not had every faith in Bessy's veracity, I would have believed she had not told me the truth about the fourteen-year-old's behaviour last December.

She almost fell into a curtsey at our feet.

Ambrose addressed her in a neutral tone.

"I welcome you to my kingdom, Roisin."

"I thank you, sire. Believe me, I am most grateful. I honestly believe that if you had not taken me in, I would be dying of thirst by now."

She shivered.

Is this an attempt to manipulate us, or does she genuinely think that her old guardian would let her die, and let her die a terrible death?

"Lady Maeve has told more than one person that if Roisin did not come here, she would be locked away and left to die," Bessy said. "Roisin, this must now be your home forevermore, or at least, you must never return to the Emerald Kingdom. I don't think I need to say anything more on this subject."

The girl nodded and was about to speak when Ambrose cut in.

"You did nothing to deserve such a fate," he told her, "but we are all well aware of how you behaved at the Castle of the Eastern Coast when you were a guest there in December. Lord Owen and Lady Cerys also know and are equally appalled."

She blushed and looked at the floor. He paused for effect before continuing in the same cool voice.

"I do not think I need explain how inappropriate such behaviour is, nor that you will be severely punished if you indulge in it here. You know how to conduct yourself. Do it."

She opened her mouth, then closed it without speaking. She looked lost for words.

Ambrose continued.

"You must have realised you will no longer live as a lady of rank. You have returned to the station in life into which you were born. You will live here and be apprenticed to someone at the castle. We are willing to let you choose between falconry, physic and a cloth business, and you have until tomorrow morning to decide. We will shortly go into dinner, where I will introduce you to the lord and lady of the castle, before you dine below the salt."

She nodded and seemed relieved not to be facing a harsher fate. She thanked him again, and he told her what to tell everyone about her background.

Owen and Cerys received her with calm politeness and as though they were welcoming a new servant to their castle, not a guest of high rank. Rosin accepted their greeting meekly and followed an apprentice tanner to the correct table.

"I think that went well," I whispered to Bessy as we sat down. "Let's talk more after dinner. I want to know everything."

My friend beamed.

"Me too. I want to hear everything that has happened here too. I want to hear about everyone whom you have mentioned in your letters. I can recognise a few people from your descriptions."

"Not everybody is here who usually is. We are quiet tonight, but I understand that some people will return later this evening."

Ambrose passed her the bread basket, and she chose a roll with wide eyes.

"This is such a contrast to the convent. The food, the wine, the hangings on the wall, everything. I have so much to tell you and so many questions to ask."

Ambrose left us to talk in my closet, undisturbed, until supper. We had so much to catch up on. Until Bessy was sitting in front of me, telling her tale of convent life, I had not realised what a poor substitute letters were. I was concerned about the constant surveillance she suffered.

"I am not afraid," she said. "I do nothing wrong and am careful to say nothing that could be misinterpreted. Besides, I spend much of my time in the infirmary or tending to the sick of

Landesmar. It is rare that I am under the eyes of Sister Agnes or
Brother Harold for long, and they know I love women, so Gethin
and I may work together without suspicion."

"I've noticed you never give Brother Gethin his title. You
always write of plain Gethin."

"I think it's because we are close friends, and he should not be
a monk. He has no vocation, though he is an excellent physician.
However, I am careful to call him brother to his face and when
talking to others."

"Ah, poor man and poor Marjory. Poor Bran, Eluned and
Isabeau too. I may even add poor Owen because the guilt eats
away at him."

"I know. It is an unholy mess and not one that can ever be
resolved in this life."

We turned the subject to my marriage, and I was able to truthfully tell her how happy I was.

That night, as Ambrose and I prepared for bed, he saw me
frowning at my hair in the glass. It was soft to touch, I had no
bald patches, and it glinted gold in the candlelight, but I was not
happy with it.

"There's nothing wrong with your hair," he told me. "So you
don't have thick plaits when you dress it, so what? You can buy
false hair that looks real, if you wish. It's better than trying to
acquire a false personality."

"How did you guess what I was thinking?"

He smiled at me.

"I know you rather well after over a year of marriage, my wife.
I also saw how you looked at our new arrival's head earlier."

"Gods!" I blushed. "Do you think anyone else noticed?"

"Doubt it. Your friend was watching Roisin to see how she
was behaving, and Roisin could barely look anyone in the eye. It
will be interesting to see what she says and does once she has
gotten used to living here. I fear her true colours will show before
long, and then what are we to do? We will have to lock her away as
we threatened, or she will walk all over us. I doubt she will be able

to maintain this meek façade for more than a month. Once she stops feeling alien and nervous, she will slip up."

"Yes." I got into bed and settled myself. "However, that may be after we have left to go to the Lord and Lady of Merendysh. Roisin will be Owen and Cerys's problem by then."

He blew out the candle and climbed in beside me.

"Yes, that will be one less problem to deal with. The Deadly Favour may have returned, a young man was reported as having vanished from his village, a place twenty miles from here, a week ago. The council will meet tomorrow to discuss it. The day after we will receive the Doggerdale ambassador, who will stay for a fortnight. It is a promising sign of faith in the peace, but it is all so tiring."

"It never stops, does it?"

"So long as I have you by my side and little Milly nearby, I believe I can do anything. You've made the man and the king that I am, Hawise."

He kissed me, and I felt loved. I knew that I was able to be a better woman, a woman capable of high office and royal dignity, because of his support and influence.

Roisin approached us both just before breakfast. In a shy voice, she begged to be allowed to apprentice herself to the falconer.

"I love animals and would very much like to work with them."

"After breakfast I will introduce you to Master Evan," I told her, inwardly relieved that she appeared to have accepted her new situation and had not suggested something stupid. "Come to me when the meal is over."

She obeyed, and I sought out the falconer. Cerys came too, keen to keep an eye on what the newest inhabitant of her castle was up to.

"There," I said. "That is him there, the little man wearing yellow, stood at the end of the bench, talking to Lord Madoc, the blue gentleman in a grey outfit."

The girl blanched and grabbed at my arm, a major breach of etiquette, but she looked ready to faint. Her gaze was fixed, and her mouth hung open. Cerys caught her and sat her down.

"What's wrong?" she asked. "Your hand is like ice."

I could see no reason for this sudden change in her.

"Does...do both of those men live here?" Roisin eventually whispered.

"Master Evan is our falconer. He and his family have lived at the castle from a time before I came here," Cerys explained, looking perplexed. "Lord Madoc lives here with his family, but both he and his brother, Lord Lewis, are often called away on business."

"Lord Lewis is here too?"

She turned grey and started to fall forwards. Cerys quickly pushed her head towards her knees. We exchanged puzzled looks whilst Roisin tried to recover herself. Cerys kept a gentle hand on her quivering shoulders. Eventually the girl sat up. She was still shaking.

"Why are you so scared?" I asked. "How do you know Master Evan, Lord Lewis and Lord Madoc?"

"I...I don't know them as such. Indeed, I have never met any of them. Lord Madoc knew my late guardian. Yes, Lord Sean sometimes spoke of him and his brother. I fear they will give me away. May I go and be apprenticed somewhere else? You are of the House of Lothwold, madam, may I not go to some old acquaintance of yours? I would happily do anything." Her voice grew stronger as she finished her short speech.

Cerys and I exchanged another look.

"No," I said bluntly. "You are to stay here at Castle Malwarden and take up an apprenticeship like we agreed. It's that, or you go to the castle's dungeon."

"I will go there if you promise that only you or King Ambrose have the key and visit me with what I need."

Now I was completely baffled. I had never expected her to give such an answer.

"No, you will take up an apprenticeship with Master Evan, just as you agreed to." Cerys spoke as she spoke to her children when they were particularly stubborn. "Lord Owen asked him the other day if he had room for another apprentice, and he said yes. Are you even telling us the truth? Why would Lord Madoc or Lord Lewis recognise you? You say you have barely met them, you have no title, are dressed as a peasant, and the history you will give of yourself will not involve Lord Sean or either of them."

"I would just feel safer, madam. That is all."

"You are perfectly safe as it is." Cerys turned towards Master Evan. Madoc was walking away from him, their conversation over. "Master Evan, I have a new apprentice for you."

Roisin cringed but stood up and followed Cerys to the falconer. Master Evan looked surprised then pleased and talked to Roisin, who looked at the floor, but she answered his questions. Her manner was shy rather than arrogant, and he did not act as if he were offended.

I looked away. The Great Hall was now nearly empty apart from us and Madoc. Madoc heard Cerys pronounce Roisin's name and started. He turned to us and quite stared at her for some moments before hastily leaving the room.

Roisin claimed not to know Madoc, but he certainly knew her.

CHAPTER TWENTY-FIVE

I got hold of Ambrose as soon as I could and told him what had passed. He frowned.

"It would be so like either of my brothers to be at the bottom of any trouble that is going on. Neither of them have ever mentioned a Sean, a Maeve or a Roisin before, or Castle Kinselk, but they never tell me anything, and I know they have links to the Emerald Kingdom. I will get hold of Roisin and question her myself. There is no point in either of us approaching them or their families. We will only be lied to."

"Will it do any good? She would not admit anything to Cerys or me, and we have no way of proving anything. Maybe it is best to let matters lie and ask Master Evan to keep a discreet eye on her. If he reports anything suspicious to us, we will be in a better position to act."

"That is a better idea. We just need to make it clear that he must hold his tongue. The Gods know that man has a good heart, but he is such a gossip."

Ambrose did just that. Cerys and I also agreed to keep a watch, and she warned Owen and Marjory.

Later that day, I happened upon Jane talking with Roisin. There was nothing obviously wrong with that, I had given my young demoiselle a couple of hours leave, nor were apprentices forbidden to chat with ladies-in-waiting, but neither girl looked at ease. Roisin kept trying to leave the conversation, but Jane was determined to stay with her. From a distance, it looked like Jane was asking her questions.

It is far too much of a coincidence that Madoc's timid daughter should be making Roisin unhappy. He has put her up to this.

I approached the pair. Roisin looked relieved, whereas Jane looked guilty.

"Jane, I crave a word with you. Roisin, please return to your duties."

The elder girl quickly curtseyed before hurrying away. The younger looked apprehensive. She turned away.

"No, Jane. We will speak in my closet."

Her face fell, but she obeyed me.

"Tell me," I said, once we were safely alone. "Tell me what happened just now in the garden."

"Lady Roisin and I were just chatting, my lady. I saw she was new and tried to make her feel welcome."

"Why do you call an apprentice falconer 'lady'?"

Her eyes widened, and for the second time that day, I thought a child was about to faint.

"Pray sit down. Put your head between your knees. Now, why do you give Roisin a title?"

"I made a mistake, ma'am." Jane lifted her dark head slightly, then quickly hid her face again.

"Sit up now. I can see you are no longer in danger of swooning. That is a strange mistake to make. How does your father know her? Is it the same way that your uncle does? I suppose one of them or your mother sent you to her. What were you asking her? What is it that they want to know about her?"

My demoiselle froze like a hare before the hounds. She did not speak. I waited, then played my next card.

"I shall find your parents and ask them myself if you have nothing to say."

"No, madam, I pray you do not do that. They will kill me!"

She grabbed my sleeve with both hands, looking on the verge of hysteria.

"Why should they kill you, you, their own child? Have you heard of other parents, or guardians, having their children killed, or have they threatened you?"

She screwed up her eyes and shook her head vigorously, as though she might shake me and my questions away.

"Tell me the truth, Jane. Are you or Roisin in danger? What has been said to you, and what have you said to her? I cannot help either of you if you will not speak frankly."

The girl suddenly dragged herself up and surprised me.

"I am going, madam. You are my mistress and my queen, but I fear you less than I do my parents!"

With that she gathered up her skirts and fled, sobbing loudly.

I let her go, certain I would get nothing else out of her and worried that I never would, now I had put her on her guard.

I observed her, Roisin, Madoc, Clementia and Nessa at dinner. Had Lewis not been away, I would have watched him as well.

Jane sat with my other ladies, red-eyed and quiet. Nobody paid her much attention, apart from her mother, who looked at her sternly several times, and Clementia, who looked sympathetic. Roisin held herself well amongst the other apprentices. She talked little but appeared interested in what was being said. She occasionally glanced nervously around her.

Madoc and Nessa spent most of the meal blatantly staring at where the apprentices sat. Whenever they caught Roisin's eye, they smiled and smirked, causing her to redden and look away. They did not care who saw them. Clementia watched them timidly but barely opened her mouth.

Bessy was as confused as I was and could offer no more explanation than anyone else could. We parted the following morning and shed tears in each other's arms. I was missing her already and promised to write.

"Thank God we have our code," she whispered. "I do not want to make you paranoid, Hawise, but it would not surprise me if Lord Madoc, Lord Lewis or Lady Nessa were spying on you and trying to read your letters."

"It would not surprise me either. I will take care, my friend, and I will find out what is going on between them and Roisin. I will also try to protect Jane. She clearly suffers, poor thing."

"And I will tell you everything that passes at the convent. I will also pass on anything concerning Gethin for Lady Marjory's eyes, if necessary."

"Yes, please do. It is so cruel that a pair who have loved each other for so long should be kept apart."

"I agree. When I consider my situation, I am glad to have done with love. When one cannot act on it, it is a torment that even Sister Agnes would hesitate to inflict."

Chapter Twenty-Six

Narrative continued by Roisin the Apprentice from the Emerald Kingdom

I stood before King Ambrose, Queen Hawise, Lord Owen and Lady Cerys in the solar on my second morning under their roof. I had seen many people in my life and had experienced many changes, but I had never felt as unnerved as I did on that April morning. They watched me like Master Evan's hawks watched their prey.

I thought I would be safe here, with the sea between me and my old life. I knew Lord Madoc and his family were of the House of Malwarden, but I did not know they lived here. I always imagined they lived nearer to the coast. For the second time in my life, I believed I was moving to a better life, and for the second time, I can see I have fallen from the frying pan into the fire.

I bit my lip to keep from crying. Up until now, everything had gone so well for me at Castle Malwarden. I had been treated far better than I had dared hope. My prayers to escape from my guardian's dungeon seemed to have been answered. It was nothing to wear a peasant maid's clothes. Indeed, they were at least as comfortable as what a noble girl wore. Nor was it much of a challenge to be polite and deferential. I had behaved in that manner before the couple whom I struggled not to still think of as Mammy and Daddy took me in.

I honestly thought I was safe, and I stood a chance of happiness. Now I would only be worse off if I were in Castle Kinselk's dungeon, going mad with fear and thirst.

"I understand you wish to speak with me?" I curtseyed deeply, then stared at the floor.

"Look at me, Roisin," the king commanded.

Reluctantly, I obeyed. This otherwise ordinary-looking man now looked every bit the powerful monarch. I swallowed. He continued to speak like the voice of the gods.

"Lord Owen and Lady Cerys agreed to let you live and work in their castle. I signed the passport which permitted Sister Bessy to kindly fetch you and bring you here. Master Evan agreed to take you on and train you. Money has changed hands, that is true, but more is required in return. We demand honesty from you."

I began to shake. I clasped my clammy hands together, but it made no difference.

"Answer our questions and answer them fully and honestly. Omit nothing and add nothing. Do not attempt to be disingenuous," he warned.

"Sister Bessy has told us your opinion of the events in Mendoc during the Samhain of 2015. You boldly stated those who committed arson, causing devastation and injuries to people and livelihoods, were freedom fighters peacefully protesting against the government. When asked how you knew this, you said from Cormac of Ballywoods, who although not present during the mayhem, was well connected and no liar. What is the truth behind your statement?"

"My former guardians deceived me, sire. I never met anyone claiming to be Cormac of Ballywoods. Instead, I received letters, sent letters, sat for a portrait and received a picture in return. I know I was rude and ignorant, and I beg pardon for it. My guardians must have written about Mendoc, and Lady Maeve encouraged me to give my opinion whenever I wished. Either she or Lord Sean must have written the letter, for I well remember reading it."

If they did not, Lord Madoc, Lord Lewis or Lady Nessa did. One of those three must have informed Mammy and Daddy of what was happening in the Westlands.

King Ambrose nodded, then spoke again.

"Did you receive any other information about Mendoc and those who partially destroyed it? Did you ever have any correspondents in my realm?"

"No, sire."

It is technically true. I never wrote to them nor received any letters.

"What did Lady Jane say to you yesterday?"

"She just welcomed me to the castle, sire. She chattered a great deal about nothing in particular."

Oh Gods.

"You were both observed to be acting in a very agitated manner, considering you were only chatting about trivia."

"I cannot account for Lady Jane, but I know I was feeling overwhelmed yesterday. It was all a lot to take in, and I was tired from the journey. The past few weeks have been very hard on me, you all know why."

Please believe such flimsy lies, or at least, stop asking me questions.

"I spoke with my demoiselle, Lady Jane, after she spoke with you," Queen Hawise stated. Her cold, calm manner was nothing like the merry liveliness I had become accustomed to seeing in her.

Sweat stung my armpits.

"She called you Lady Roisin."

"Madam, I swear by every saint that I cannot account for that. I never saw her ladyship in my life, until yesterday, and I have not used my title since I left Castle Kinselk. I would swear to that on anything you hold dear."

The second and third statements are true, at least. Oh Goddess, what have her parents said to her?

The queen ignored me and continued her questions.

"We know that you know Lord Madoc and Lord Lewis, brothers to the king, and Lady Nessa, the wife of Lord Madoc. There is no point in denying it. We have seen them notice you and discuss you. It is very clear to Lady Cerys and me why you asked to leave the castle yesterday morning or go to its dungeon. It is even clearer why you begged that only the king and I might visit you in the dungeon or hold the key."

I could not speak. It was hard enough to keep upright.

"Have any of those three, or Lady Clementia, the wife of Lord Lewis, spoken to you or passed on any message to you?"

"No, madam."

Lady Jane begged me to come to her family's apartments, and I declined, being a humble apprentice. She called me 'your ladyship', and I nearly jumped out of my skin, but denied having any such title. I have no idea what awaited me there. I have no real idea of what any of those four are truly like. I met both lords and Lady Nessa at Castle Kinselk. Daddy was especially close to the men. They made a fuss of me, which I, fool that I was, just accepted. I know they did business together but not what sort of business. I know I was going to be sold after I turned fifteen. Was it to them? What could they want with me? Lord Madoc, at least, loves his wife.

The four stood in front of me, motionless and silent, for what felt like an eternity. Lady Cerys broke the silence by changing tactics. Her voice was gentle, and her expression was concerned.

"Roisin, we wish to keep you, as well as everyone else, safe in our castle. We cannot do this if you lie to us about something so important."

"My lady, I can only promise that I am not lying about anything."

Lord Owen sighed heavily and dismissed me.

"You may leave us, Roisin, but don't think this is the last of the matter. We, and others, will continue to watch you very carefully."

I curtseyed and left the room, still shaking but also feeling relieved.

If they keep that so-called threat, I will be safe. I can tell they do not think highly of Lord Madoc, his brother or his wife. The more other people watch me, the less likely they are to get hold of me. I have managed to avoid them so far, but I have not been here for two full days. Already, they have sent someone to fetch me. Oh God, how will I survive here? I am meant to stay here for ever.

I left the castle and made my way to where Master Evan had told his apprentices to wait for him. Only Lord Bran was already there. He saw me, smiled and waved. I returned the greeting with genuine joy. I already liked him. He had been kind and welcoming and would have put me at my ease had it not been for three certain people.

It was a jolt to start an activity from scratch. My abilities place me with children of ten or eleven, but I can live with this. I have suffered no worse than a few questions about my accent and one of the lads looking at me for longer than was necessary. His sweetheart is none too happy about that, she gave me a very cold look at break-fast, but she is not an apprentice falconer, and we barely see each other. He is respectful and does not harass me. The pair will have to sort themselves out. They cannot harm me.

I've had this before, boys staring and lasses glaring, when I was the beloved ward of Lady Maeve and Lord Sean. I rather liked the effect I produced. However, I wish to make no enemies here, and I cannot help what I look like. At least Lord Bran treats me like a friend in the making. After the fiction of Cormac and what happened to me, what might still happen to me, I want nothing to do with love or lust ever again. Gods, how do I keep myself safe?

"Are you alright, Roisin?" Lord Bran asked, squinting against the sun. "You look nervous."

"I just feel very new, and I miss my old guardians."

He was sympathetic, even Desdemona looked concerned for

me, and I changed the subject. We chatted about his cats and hawks until Master Evan arrived.

I liked the ugly little man exceedingly. He was the perfect teacher, patient, encouraging and fair to his pupils. I wanted to earn his praise.

That would be worth something. My looks have been praised so many times, but really, what are they worth? I have been complimented for other things too, such as my fluency in foreign languages, but I do not know if the beloved ward of the lord and lady of Castle Kinselk received those flattering words or if Roisin did. Here, if someone tells me I have done well, I will know it to be true.

More apprentices appeared in the distance, along with Lady Jane, trotting away on some errand with an anxious look on her sallow-brown face.

My greatest achievement will be to stay safe and alive. How I wish I could fly away like one of these birds, yet never return.

CHAPTER TWENTY-SEVEN

Narrative continued by Lady Jane of Malwarden

Queen Hawise sent me to bring Aunt Clementia to her. I did not know why and felt even more nauseous and lightheaded from nervousness than I usually did. A churning stomach, a dry mouth, clammy hands and a feeling of having left my body from fear were so normal for me that I only noticed such sensations when I was far from my parents and Uncle Lewis, and they magically vanished. Both my siblings and all my cousins felt the same way.

I could feel myself relaxing as I met Aunt Clementia's eye. Were it not for her presence in my life, I knew I would have gone mad and been locked away, like my parents occasionally threatened when I irritated them. I called Clementia Aunt out loud but Mumma in my heart, for she was more of a parent to me than either of mine were. Her constant, discreet and steady presence saved not only her children but also me, my sister and my brother.

"The queen wants you," I told her.

She nodded and said in a low voice.

"Wait a moment before we go to her, Jane. You looked terrified just then. What is the matter?"

I looked into her pale blue eyes and saw the sympathy she so often displayed. Years of marriage to my uncle had not damaged her humanity.

"Aunt, I am terrified, more so than usual. Ever since that Banshee girl arrived, things have gotten worse. My parents and Uncle Lewis are even worse. They want something from her, but I do not know what. They tried to use me to get her to our rooms, but I failed, and now the queen is suspicious. She must have told the king and my lord and lady. What will become of me? I love being a demoiselle because it keeps me away from them, especially when we are not living at this castle."

"The king, queen, our lord and our lady are good, just people. They will not punish you unfairly. Indeed, they might protect you from your uncle and your parents."

"I don't think they can. I truly don't. They obey the law, whereas I know my uncle and my parents do just as they please, so they are more powerful."

"Times are changing, child. Peace, a real, everlasting peace might just hold. That means governments can concentrate on maintaining law and order. Those three will find themselves facing awkward questions very soon, should they be committing crimes. King Ambrose is anxious to set a good example to his realm. Being his close connections will not spare them."

I shook my head.

"No, they are above the law. I have heard them say so themselves, heard them boast of it. They speak rudely of everyone at the castle, but themselves. They might as well be gods, such is their power."

"Hush, now! Do not say such blasphemies." She quickly made the sign of the circle, and I automatically copied her. "Nobody is immortal, and nobody is almighty. Times are changing, the attention given to war and defence will soon turn to upholding justice and making society run smoothly. What is a blessing for us and the kingdom is a thorn in their sides, and by the saints, I hope it stings them."

"I don't. I don't know what I want. I only know that when they are driven to anger, they do all sorts of foul deeds. They are plotting something now. I know it. Them trying to get me to take Lady Roisin to their private rooms was the start of it."

My blunder over the new girl's name made me blush again, but I had no secrets from Aunt Clementia.

"*Lady* Roisin? Jane, that girl is lowborn. Why would a noble maiden, unless impoverished, apprentice herself like that? Even if she were a lady and suddenly made comparatively poor, we would have been told about it. Bran is a lord and an apprentice, after all."

I told my aunt everything I knew. It was a confusing jumble of facts, yet they were adding up to something dangerous, and I feared, as I so often did, that worse was to come.

"My father recognised Roisin as a lady and spoke with my mother and Uncle Lewis about it. They were shut up together for a great long time. I did not overhear much, only that Pa believed he could get a good price for her after all, providing he delivered her young, pretty and pure. He said something about surprising a customer who had been told he could not have something after all.

"Mumma complained about Uncle Ambrose not being loyal to them, his true kin, and how he insists that the guards, militia and warriors maintain order. She said something about life going too smoothly for business. Pa then said, 'We can do something about that. I can ensure our brother is out of his mind', and then they moved towards the door, so I had to run away."

"When was that, Jane?"

"Early yesterday morning. Later that morning Mumma told me to fetch Roisin and bring her to our rooms. I asked what I should tell her, and she said to tell her that she wanted to talk about her late guardians and console her. I did not dare ask anything else, you know what they are like, and I went to find Roisin. I eventually found her, but she refused to go with me, she was clearly suspicious, then Queen Hawise came and asked me so many questions..."

I broke off in tears, and my aunt comforted me.

"Queen Hawise is now acting like nothing has happened," I concluded. "However, I don't know what she wants with you."

"Let us find out."

I wiped my eyes, blew my nose and followed her to the rose garden, where I had left the queen.

I never learned what my mistress wanted with my aunt. Nothing much happened for the next three weeks, although I was continually on tenterhooks. Roisin avoided me and my family, and my parents were content to let this happen. I did not see much of my parents or Uncle Lewis, for which I was grateful. My father left the castle towards the end of the three weeks, such a common occurrence that I was only glad he was not near me, and returned in a good mood. Once again, he shut himself away with my mother and uncle. This time it was impossible for me to eavesdrop. Lady Cerys wanted me in the nursery.

I observed how happy she was with her children. All five happened to be with her, and she had recently announced she was expecting a sixth. They looked so relaxed in each other's company. Lady Cerys not only listened to what they had to say but appeared interested. She smiled and did not sneer, spoke gently instead of snapping, and delighted in her children's company, instead of shunning it.

Why can't my life be like this? What is so different about me that I am marked out for disdain and cruelty, whereas they are cherished? Why did the gods inflict such a fate on me, Drogo, Blissmina and our cousins?

Lady Cerys greeted me, and I dreaded questions from her about Roisin. However, she only wanted to talk about my leaving with the other demoiselles when the king and queen quit Castle Malwarden for another place in May. I brightened. This was something to look forward to.

Goddess willing, we will leave within a month and not return for a year. Much can happen in a year, and in the meantime, I will be free.

My face fell.

I will be free but the others won't. They will have to stay here and suffer.

My mother got hold of me as I left the nursery. She insisted that I accompany her to our apartments immediately.

I did not dare say that the queen was expecting me to return to her. Instead, I followed her to the hated rooms.

My father and Uncle Lewis were inside, waiting for us. They were suspiciously pleasant to me.

"Jane, we have little job for you," my father announced.

"What is it, Pa?" His breezy tone put me on my guard rather than at my ease.

"You go to the nursery often, don't you?"

"Fairly often, yes. Only when I am sent."

"Good. When you are next sent, put a couple of drops of this down Princess Milly's throat or in her food or drink. It does not matter which, and you will only need a few drops. Just make sure nobody sees you."

He handed me a tiny bottle made out of silver or pewter. It was no bigger than his thumb.

"Put it in your purse, and take the next available opportunity," my mother commanded.

"What is it?" I examined the bottle carefully before putting it away. There was no engraving or label.

"Never mind what it contains. That isn't important. What is important is that you do as you're told," Uncle Lewis snapped. He then recollected himself and spoke in a more casual voice. "The child will hardly complain. She's just a baby and babbles away to herself like all infants do."

"What will it do to her? Why must I do it secretly?"

My father smashed his fist onto the table.

"God's blood, girl, stop asking questions, and do as you're bid." He strode over to me, grabbed my shoulders and shook me. "You are our property, just as these boots on my feet are my property. I will throw these boots away when they no longer serve their purpose. Think on that!"

He shoved me out the door, causing me to fall over. My mother laughed. I picked myself up and scurried away.

Near to tears, I fled to behind the privy, a place where I knew from experience I was unlikely to be disturbed. I took the bottle out of my purse and opened it. I sniffed cautiously and pulled my face away in disgust. Whatever it was, it stung my nostrils. The top was a pipette. Carefully, I squirted two drops onto the leaf of a nearby bush. Immediately two black-rimmed holes appeared, spreading rapidly across the once healthy leaf.

With a hammering heart, I replaced the top and put the bottle back in my purse.

God's wounds, what do I do now? Whatever this is, it is obviously poison. Do they mean to kill the little princess? Why? Why do they want to hurt her, the king and the queen so badly?

I stayed half-hidden behind the wooden structure for some time. My mind was all racing with confusion. What could I do? They would know if I had not poisoned the princess, and what might they do to me then? They had always hinted that whatever I suffered, they could make it far worse. Simply throwing the little bottle away was not an option.

Yet my only other choice is murder. The murder of an innocent child.

I felt the bottle through the leather of my purse. There was another choice, to swallow the contents of the bottle, but I could not bring myself to do that. Running away was also out of the question. I had tried that twice before and had not got very far before being found, unceremoniously escorted back to the castle and punished. Whatever punishment might await me this time would be even worse.

Maybe they will make me drink the bottle. Nothing would surprise me now.

I began to cry and could not stop. I saw a man walking towards the privy and fled, determined not to be seen. I staggered about, weeping myself into a state of oblivion to my surroundings. Eventually I nearly collided with Master Evan.

The falconer was most concerned to see me in such distress. He carefully asked what was wrong in the most soothing voice, which made me cry all the more. Why could this good-hearted man not have been my father? I had seen how kindly he and his wife treated their sons. Life was so unfair and about to get even worse.

Unable to get anything out of me, he fetched Aunt Clementia. He left us alone in the rose garden whilst I cried and told her what had happened. She looked aghast, but before she could say anything of consequence, my mother and Lady Marjory appeared. They saw us, but only my mother realised the cause of my tears.

Lady Marjory tried to ask me what the matter was. She was genuinely concerned. However, my mother managed to sweetly send her away. I tried to follow her ladyship, tried to get away, but my mother grabbed my gown.

"Listen to me, you little shit, you will do as you are told, or else I'll pour it into your eyes. Oh, I know you're not completely stupid. You will have smelled it, maybe dripped some onto the ground, you will have tried to find out what it is, but I know you have had the sense not to taste it. You would not be here, were that not the case. Now, wash your face, then go to the nursery. Send the nurses away to Lady Cerys, tell them you were told that she needs them, and you will watch the babies. Then do it. Do it, or go blind. You have no other choice."

I became too hysterical to speak. Mumma continued in a sickly-sweet voice.

"The poison is on your person, Jane. What if I called the guards? What if they found it on you? You have no way out of this but to obey me. Your noise will rouse half the castle as it is. You have sealed your fate."

"No." Aunt Clementia put her hand on my purse and looked at my mother in a way I had not seen her do before. It showed her real strength of character and quick thinking.

"What do you mean, *no*? I can already hear people coming to see what the commotion is. Jane either comes with me to wash her face, or I tell whoever first reaches us that I have found something suspicious on her, and she became hysterical when confronted. Throwing it away will do no good. Any half-witted physician will be able to deduce what the bottle contained."

"Aunt, let me take the poison," I shrieked. "I would rather die than go blind. I cannot carry on as it is!"

"No, Jane. I will do that. I will set you free and thwart your foul scheme, Nessa. I will show you what a true mother is."

With that, she opened the purse at my waist and took out the bottle. The voices and footsteps of many people came closer. She opened the bottle.

"You would never dare," my mother sneered. She sounded confident.

Aunt Clementia answered her by squeezing the pipette until it was full and squirting it down her throat. The movement stunned me into stillness. My mother lost control of herself and began to scream and scream. My aunt froze, her eyes wide with shock or pain, before collapsing without saying a word more.

Lady Marjory returned with Lord Owen and Master Evan. I turned to them, fear for my aunt overcoming fear for myself.

"My mother tried to force me to poison Princess Milly by giving her what is in that bottle. She threatened to blind me if I did not. My aunt would not have it, so she swallowed the poison herself. She is dead because of me."

I, too, collapsed. Blackness enveloped me.

CHAPTER TWENTY-EIGHT

I came to in a strange bed in a room I did not recognise. It was richly decorated, even by the standards of the castle. I sat up, feeling dizzy and scared. I remembered all too well what had happened. Lady Cerys and Queen Hawise were present and noticed my movement.

"Where am I?" I asked. "Where are my mother and my aunt?"

"You are in my chamber," the queen replied. "Your aunt is in the infirmary, where the physician and the apothecaries are trying their best. There is still hope for her. Your mother, your father and your uncle Lewis are being questioned. We know that if one of them is involved in something, the other two will be tangled up in it."

"Madam, they tried to kill your daughter, the princess. They tried to make me do it, although I swear I would never do such a thing. That's why Aunt Clementia took the poison; to save me and Princess Milly."

"An apothecary has tested what remained in the bottle and what your aunt vomited up. It is indeed poison, a very fast-acting one which is not easily obtainable in these lands."

"I think my father went away to buy it. How...what time is it?"

"It is just after three o'clock. You were not unconscious for long. We took you here directly from the garden."

I sat silently, all too aware of my aunt's enormous sacrifice and what would happen next.

Lady Cerys appeared to read my thoughts.

"Jane, if you wish for anything to change, speak now and tell the *whole* truth. We will protect you. We can send you away, if necessary. Tell us everything about the poison, Roisin, your parents' business and what they commanded you to do."

With no other path to take, I told them everything.

"I don't know why harming Princess Milly would help them with their business, but they thought it would," I concluded.

"They want to distract the king and me with the most horrible grief and distract us from the business of government. It would also jeopardise the succession. They hope that would lead to chaos, under which cloud they might carry out whatever crimes they are committing. Yes, they are crimes. If they were not committing criminal acts, they would not need to stoop to such lengths."

Queen Hawise looked grim and determined.

"What happens now?" I whimpered.

"We will send you to my friend, Sister Bessy, who lives in a convent far from here. It is near to where I come from. You will be quite safe there, and you will only stay until we have sorted this matter out."

"What about Blissmina and Drogo? What about my cousins? And my aunt?"

"We will take care of them," the queen promised. "Your aunt will receive the best care and be kept safe. We will write to you often. Whatever happens, your parents' reign of terror is over."

"But you don't know what they are like," I dared to contradict. "They have always done whatever they please, and nobody can stop them."

The queen smiled a grim smile.

"On the contrary, they are about to discover they are quite mortal and as obliged to obey the law as the rest of us are."

She was as good as her word. Within an hour, I was sitting on a dragon with a bag and a guard, who held a passport and a letter. It was then that I started to believe there were people in this world who were more powerful than my parents or Uncle Lewis.

CHAPTER TWENTY-NINE

Narrative continued by Bessy the Nun

Sister Adeliza, the convent's portress, received a nervous child, an excited dragon and a straight-backed guard early one morning. They were unexpected visitors and caused quite a stir. I was even more surprised to be summoned to them and to be handed a letter by the guard.

"My mistress, Queen Hawise of the Westlands, has written to you, sister."

I took the letter and was amazed to read its contents. I had never expected events in the Westlands to take such a nasty turn. Recovering myself, I turned to the girl.

"My name is Sister Bessy, and I am one of your queen's oldest friends. I welcome you to the Convent of the New Moon. I will take you to Sister Agnes, who is the mother superior here."

The guard went off with Sister Adeliza to deal with the dragon, and I took Lady Jane to where I thought Sister Agnes might be. I tried to look at her without her being aware of it, while we walked through the convent. I was sure I had not seen her during my visit to Castle Malwarden. The girl looked dazed from her recent experiences, and I pitied her.

"Will I have to become a nun?" she asked.

"No. Convents and monasteries open their doors to people in need or those who are fleeing unjust persecution. Your parents may not touch you here. You may stay here for a while as a civilian and help out with the running of the convent, nothing unpleasant or too demanding, just helping with the daily chores as we all do. Children also come here to receive lessons. Perhaps you will attend some."

"I see. How long will I stay here for?"

"I don't know, but I do know you will not be sent back to the Westlands until it is definitely safe."

She laughed bitterly. It was an odd sound from someone so young and polite.

"Then I might as well stay here until I am an old woman. So long as my parents or my uncle live, I am in danger. I dread to think what they are doing to my sister, my brother or my cousins."

"They can do nothing," I assured her. "Queen Hawise promises that, and she does not lie."

Lady Jane made no reply, but I could see she was not convinced.

We found Sister Agnes, who was a little taken aback to see our visitor and to hear what I had to say, but she agreed that Lady Jane could stay for as long as necessary. She welcomed her to the convent and told her what to expect. The child looked quite over-whelmed, but she remained polite and held herself well.

Lady Jane of Malwarden was not our only new arrival that week. At breakfast the following morning, Sister Agnes told us that three nuns from another convent would be joining us permanently.

"Their names are Phyllis, Idelinde and Maude. Their convent, the Convent of the Equinoxes, is closing due to low numbers. It is no longer sustainable to run, so the nuns are joining other convents. We expect them tomorrow afternoon."

This was not surprising news. The enforcing of the rules had led to fewer novices taking their final vows, causing many convents and monasteries to become unviable. However, people still chose to leave the civilian world and join the monastic life. Our way of life was not going to die out just yet, and numbers might even grow in the future.

The time when people could permanently live in a convent without beginning a novitiate has passed. Unless you are like Lady Jane, you are either in or you're out. However, I think numbers will rise again. There will always be people like me who will shun marriage, no matter what the sacrifice. We might even become something to be proud of, now we truly do dedicate ourselves to the gods and good works.

The three women were introduced to us at dinner. I was too distracted by Hawise's letter and my thoughts of what was happening in Castle Malwarden to pay them much attention.

However, when Sister Idelinde knocked on the door of the infirmary the following morning, I could not stop looking at her. She was about my height and age but much thinner with freckled, almost translucent skin, a snub nose and arched, dark eyebrows. Her eyes were a colour I had never seen before, nor could I define it. They were definitely dark, but whether they were a shade of dark brown, grey or green, or some colour in between I could not tell. I did not think they were blue or black, but I could be no more precise than that, no more than I could stop looking at her.

Her voice was low but clear and sweet, and her accent was one I had not found attractive until she spoke. For herself, she came across as polite, intelligent and interested in what was going on. Her sudden smile lit up her face, and it was impossible not to return it and hope I had nothing stuck between my teeth.

Sister Idelinde had worked as a herbalist at her old convent, and she had been told she would work with Sisters Judith and Leah to tend our herb garden.

"This will mean I will also be working with you," she told Gethin and me.

"I look forward to it," I told her.

She smiled, quite transforming her face and mine.

We exchanged a few more words and showed her around the infirmary before answering her several questions. Brother Percy then arrived at the infirmary to ask Gethin something, and Sister Idelinde took her leave.

I was lost in my thoughts. Gethin pulled me back into the real world as soon as Brother Percy had left.

"Don't, sister. It is far too risky; for you and for her. Keep away and stay pure. The threat of hot irons has not gone away, nor will it."

"What do you mean, brother?"

He laughed gently, but his eyes were grave.

"It's obvious. I can see it like words on a page. You've taken quite a shine to Sister Idelinde, and it is not in the least bit sisterly."

I laughed. He knew me too well for me to deny anything.

"There's no harm in liking an agreeable person, is there?"

"No, but keep it to polite friendliness. You are grinning like an idiot, and I have never seen your eyes so bright. For the love of the saints, be careful."

Chapter Thirty

Narrative continued by Queen Hawise of the Westlands

E vents moved quickly at Castle Malwarden. Jane was dispatched to the Convent of the New Moon before she had the chance to protest. I received a note from Bessy to tell me she had arrived safely and was permitted to stay for as long as need be, without having to make a novitiate.

Nessa, Madoc and Lewis were held separately and questioned by Ambrose and members of his council. I was not involved. Instead, I dealt with a tearful but determined Roisin, who sought me out. It was no secret that Jane had been sent away, that Clementia had swallowed poison or that her near relations were being interrogated.

"Madam, I can no longer be a coward and remain silent. I must be inspired by Lady Clementia's courage and tell you everything I know."

She did just that, and I could only conclude that the secret business of the wretched three was the trading of humans. I passed this on to Ambrose as soon as I could.

After a week of careful nursing, Clementia had recovered

sufficiently to tell us everything she knew about her husband and her in-laws. The poison had turned her teeth black, made her voice sound raspy and had sapped her energy. The physicians told us these symptoms were unlikely to ever improve, and indeed, it was a miracle that she had not suffered further. Her very survival was seen as marvellous.

It was the longest time I had spent in her company since we were first introduced to one another. I paid her more attention during those hours when she poured out her heart and told us vital information than I had ever done before. I also admired her more than I would have ever believed I could.

Clementia's tale tallied with Roisin's. She could also add information about the man called Eoin whom Ambrose had mentioned to me when he told me about his family.

"Eoin was a Banshee man, from the Emerald Kingdom. He was a notorious trader of human flesh. His reputation as a clever, wicked fiend was well-deserved, for he caused more suffering than every imp in Hades put together. He saw himself in Lewis and Madoc, and so made them his heirs. Roisin was destined to be the toy of a wealthy man in the Pendroch lands, somewhere far south of here. I know nothing more about what was planned for her, nor how it came about. If you search their belongings, you will find papers relating to her sale."

Clementia made the sign of the circle and was too weary to continue her tale. It did not matter. We had plenty of evidence against the three. I thanked her sincerely for saving my daughter's life, promising to give her whatever care she needed in the future, and left her to rest.

The private apartments of Lewis, Madoc and Nessa were searched, but nothing incriminating was found. Ambrose told me how coolly they had answered every question put to them.

"We certainly have enough evidence to bring them to trial, but I cannot guarantee that we will find them guilty. I believe it, yet I am not sure if we will be able to prove it." He groaned deeply with despair. "If I were another sort of king, another sort of man, I could just execute them and be done with it. I could even arrange for them to meet an unexpected accident. However, I cannot. I have set myself up as a just monarch, which is why we have order in our lands, and nobody has rebelled against me, to my knowledge."

"Truth will prevail," I said with far more confidence than I felt. The thought of them being found innocent was terrifying. It was frustrating. Ambrose could easily order their deaths, with no regard to the trial they were entitled to, but to do so would damn his government as corrupt and destroy his reputation.

Bessy wrote to me from her convent. It was a chatty letter. She told me how well Jane had settled in, so well in fact that she spoke of becoming a nun.

Gethin and I have dissuaded her from making any decision. In any case, she is too young to become a novice, but he knows what it is like to become a monastic and live to regret it. We neither of us would have her make the same mistake.

Bessy went on to describe a new inmate of the convent, one Idelinde. She wrote as she would have spoken had I been with her, about the woman with whom she was falling in love.

Take care, my friend, I thought as I folded her letter. *This Idelinde may be another Jennet, someone who will use you, or she may not even love women like you do. Even if she returns your feelings, you risk torture if you are caught. Is it really worth it?*

I broke the news to Roisin of how she had nearly been sold and to whom. We felt she had the right to know the full truth about what concerned her, now we knew the truth about Lewis, Nessa and Madoc. She was shocked but not surprised. Later she told me that she had suspected such a fate, but she had not known the details.

The information disturbed her, and she kept returning to the subject. Her guardians' deceit troubled her greatly. She wondered aloud why they had fed her falsehoods about the burning of Mendoc. I suspected it was because they were involved in some way, mayhem suited them as much as it suited Nessa, Lewis and Madoc as a distraction from their crimes, but I said nothing because I could not prove it.

The lack of proof of any crime committed by them was a constant worry. Time was ticking, and the date of the trial loomed. By law, we could not defer it without good reason, and we had no good reasons. Ambrose needed to not only be a just ruler but be seen to be a just ruler.

"If we do not think we can find them guilty, we must let them go," he wept in my arms one night in early May. "For if we try them and they are found innocent, people may sympathise with them, and they will get away with attempted murder. People will also judge me and you harshly for questioning them."

"We have saved Milly and Jane," I soothed him. "We can insist that Jane stays at the Convent of the New Moon because she feels she might have a calling. She is too young to be obliged to act upon it, but no parent could drag their child back if they say that, especially now the church is reforming and being taken more seriously. The High Priest's diabolical dictate has caused much suffering, but it also offers Jane a sanctuary.

"They now know we are suspicious, and they have narrowly escaped execution. That won't stop them, but it does hinder their schemes and give us an excuse to spy on them. You have behaved wisely, not weakly. You followed the law instead of killing people for a dreadful crime of which they were not convicted."

Ambrose was slightly mollified, but it was him who had to comfort me when it became clear we had no strong grounds for a trial. Reluctantly, albeit with a delighted look on his face, Ambrose formally released his brothers and his sister-in-law. There were great displays of reconciliation that fooled nobody. I plastered a smile on my face whilst fantasising about torturing those who had attempted to kill my daughter and threatened to blind their own.

"I would give anything to see them suffer a painful death," I sobbed into Ambrose's chest the night after their release. "Justice has not been done, nor will we ever have the opportunity of carrying it out. If you were to order their deaths, you could no longer be called honourable by the people."

I did not realise that part of this wish would be granted before the year was out.

CHAPTER THIRTY-ONE

Narrative continued by Bessy the Nun

Hawise sent me the sad news that the three whom we were convinced were guilty would not be brought to trial. I took a deep breath and went to find Lady Jane. She needed to know this and know she was still safe.

I found her having a private lesson in Book Language with Brother Harold. When they had finished I broke the news.

The child was saddened but not surprised.

"They get away with everything," she whispered. "They might as well be gods, they are so powerful."

"Come now, do not blaspheme, and certainly not in here. No, they have not gotten away with this. Princess Milly is safe, thanks to you and your aunt. They know they are being watched and will have the sense not to harm her or any other child, including their own. Your aunt is making a good recovery. She is up and about and being kept away from them. You are also safe. You may remain here, where they cannot get at you."

"I will become a nun first."

She repeated this statement whilst she was helping Gethin,

Idelinde and me with making ointments later that afternoon. Gethin tried to dissuade her.

"Child, do not make vows without a vocation. As I have said before, if I can offer you any advice in life, it is this: A monastic life is hard but fulfilling *if* the gods have chosen it for you. If they have not, it is a dreary hell indeed. Besides, you are what? Twelve at most. No girl can begin her novitiate until she is sixteen at the youngest. Unless a love of the gods calls you, as opposed to a terror of anyone mortal, you would be best off staying here for a few more years, then looking to marry. The queen and Sister Bessy have many local connections and could get you a good husband."

Jane did not argue, although I did not think she looked convinced. When we had finished the ointments, Gethin turned his attention to preparing tinctures. She had many questions. I observed the consideration he took when he answered her questions. His behaviour to her was almost always paternal.

His daughters are roughly the same age as her. Does being with her make him think of them?

Idelinde interrupted my thoughts by asking that I help her to gather blossom in the orchards. I agreed, and we left Gethin and Jane together.

My heart began to beat faster as we reached the trees, the furthest part of the convent's lands from any building. We were quite alone on the sunny spring afternoon, far from anyone's eyes or ears. My attraction to Idelinde had grown and grown. I constantly wanted to be with her, yet this felt different from any other passion or relationship I had experienced before. I also felt more comfortable in her company than I did in anyone else's, including Hawise's.

We were not the same. Her nature was shrewder than mine, she was more inclined to silence and hiding her thoughts than me, yet we fitted together like pieces of a puzzle. I did not flatter myself when I noticed that she talked more to me, and more openly with me, than she did with any other inhabitant of the convent. She also laughed more loudly and merrily with me.

Careful. Hot irons aside, she might not even like women in the way you do.

We spoke of casual matters before she found the tree she wanted to harvest. Armed with scissors and baskets, we snipped away in silence, gradually moving so we ended up facing each other.

Our eyes met through a gap in the frothy white mass. She smiled, and I spoke.

"You know, I've finally worked out what colour your eyes are. They are a colour I have never seen before, but I would call it slate mixed with coffee."

I blushed. What a foolish thing to say.

She laughed.

"That sounds like such a funny colour, but it makes sense. I have never been able to say what colour my eyes are. Other people always have different opinions on the matter. I know we are not meant to consider our personal appearance beyond neatness and hygiene, but I like to hear you speak so. It makes me remember I am a woman as well as a nun."

She looked at me significantly. My heartbeat increased. Did I delude myself?

"Ah, yes. We are supposed to be a community of women, living as sisters."

"*Supposed* to be?"

"Yes...I think it is impossible for a nun to regard every woman in the convent as her sister. It is certainly impossible to regard Sister Agnes as a mother. Unless one had a very unpleasant mother, of course."

She laughed, such a joyful sound that I found myself smiling. She then grew serious.

"Do you regard *every* woman here as a sister?"

"No. I do not. I cannot." My fingers trembled. I had to look away.

"Who do you not see as a sister, Bessy?" Her sweet voice was so thoughtful.

"Well...our Reverend Mother, of course. I can only see her as a curse on the convent, and the sooner someone else takes over, the better. Her appointment was only ever meant to be temporary." I drew up my courage. She had called me by my first name alone. "There is one other woman, Idelinde, who lives here and wears a nun's habit, but I will never see her as a sister."

I made myself hold her gaze. She moved around the tree, towards me.

"Who is she, Bessy?"

I reached out, almost touching her, but not quite daring to believe my senses.

"I think you can guess, Idelinde."

She took hold of my hand with her warm one.

"Say my name again. Nobody else says it quite like you."

"Do I mispronounce it? Is it my accent?"

"Oh no. I love your voice, and I love to hear it pronounce my name."

I took her other hand in mine. We were so close.

"We run a great risk, Idelinde," I whispered. "But I think some risks are worth taking. Do you?"

She removed her hands from mine, put them behind my head, pulled me towards her and kissed me. I kissed her back. Electricity shot through me.

"There is your answer, Bessy. We will be together. We will run this risk. We will call each other 'sister' in public and our true names in private."

"And every endearment we can think of."

She laughed, and we kissed again for as long as we dared.

We made our way back to the convent with our baskets of blossom and a promise to each other. I tried so hard to keep myself from grinning wildly.

Gethin's behaviour towards me was a strong indication that we had both succeeded. I knew he would have pulled me aside the moment he suspected something, but he did not.

CHAPTER THIRTY-TWO

Narrative continued by Lord Owen of Malwarden

The council and the general running of my castle and my lands kept me very busy during the summer of 2017, busier than usual. Nessa, Madoc and Lewis remained quiet and polite, their very lack of suspicious behaviour raised everyone's suspicions. The council and Hawise agreed that they were likely to have been masterminding the Deadly Favour disappearances, especially as nobody had been reported missing since March.

"They are either biding their time, or they have learned to be more discreet," my wife said, and I agreed with her.

Cerys gave birth to our sixth child towards the end of September, a sweet little lad with her eyes, whom we named Simon. Whilst she was still lying in, I went riding in the Forrest of a Thousand Pines. I deliberately went alone because I happened to be in a bad mood that morning and wished to clear my head.

The exercise, the peace and the beautiful countryside soothed my soul. I was happy in my thoughts when Flame, my horse, suddenly stopped.

"What is it, boy?" I asked, automatically talking to my horse as though he were a dragon who might answer. I saw what, or rather who, had startled him.

A young man of about twenty staggered towards us, then froze. He looked thin and filthy, his appearance spoke of living rough and suffering for it. His clothes were that of a peasant, and his eyes were terrified.

"Good day," I called. "Do not be alarmed. I mean you no harm."

He nodded dumbly, his eyes fixed on me and Flame.

"Do you need anything? Can I help you?" As far as I knew, nobody lived in the forest, and he gave the impression of being in want, as well as being distressed.

"I don't know...I come from Grey Mountain, a small place not a day's walk from here, but I'm not sure if I can go back."

"Why? Have you committed a crime?"

"No, sir, but I was taken from there, and I fear I will be taken again if I go back or my family will be harmed."

"You mean you were kidnapped?"

"Aye, sir, but I escaped, and I have been lying low ever since. There's plenty to eat in the countryside in the summer, and the nights are warm."

Not for much longer they won't be, and the harvest is nearly gathered.

"Come with me. I will get you something to eat, and we can decide what to do next. Here, you can ride on my horse with me."

The youth obeyed, and I was almost overpowered by his smell. It reminded me of Ambrose in the old days.

"What is your name?" I asked as we approached the castle.

"Morgan, the third son of Peter the Miller and Isolde of Grey Mountain. Who are you, sir?"

"Lord Owen of Malwarden. I am taking you to my castle."

He nearly threw himself off Flame, making the horse start.

"Steady! What is wrong? You have no need to fear me."

"I have every need to fear your castle, or rather certain inhabitants of it. I'd rather be hungry and cold in the forest."

"Who are these inhabitants?" I had a shrewd idea.

He shook silently. I urged Flame on.

"We will go to the castle anyway. You need to eat."

"No! I beg you, my lord, *no*."

"I can sneak you into the castle, to my private apartments, where we can talk."

"Please do, sir. Can Lord Madoc, Lady Nessa or Lord Lewis come into your apartments?"

"Certainly not."

I felt him relax.

I gave him my hooded cloak, and thus disguised, led him to my rooms, loudly calling him Anselm and talking about the harvest. Once settled, I called for food and ale for him and insisted he sat nearest the fire. He looked about in wonder.

Morgan ate and drank enthusiastically. I did not interrupt him until he set down his mug.

"Thank you, sir," he said sincerely.

"That's quite alright. In return, pray tell me all you know about Lord Lewis, Lord Madoc and Lady Nessa."

"Will you keep me and my family safe?"

"I promise."

Morgan sat back and told me an extraordinary tale.

He worked as farrier in his village, where he had happily lived all his life. He was married to a local girl, but as yet, they had no children. At the beginning of March, a well-dressed gentleman approached him with a horse that needed his attention.

"The gentleman said he had heard I was the best farrier for miles around, which I confess flattered me, my lord. He paid me more than I charged. He returned the next week with his friend's horse and was so agreeable. My Martha and I hoped he might become a regular customer, for he insisted on seeing me and not either of the other farriers in the village."

The gentleman, who gave his name as Rhodri, asked if Morgan might be interested in working for him at his manor. He named a place neither Morgan nor Martha had heard of, but he said it was a newly built house some thirty miles away yet still in Malwarden lands. Rhodri named wages twice what Morgan then earned. He explained that he was a merchant who had made his fortune, and he wanted to settle down as a landed gentleman. He was in the process of acquiring staff.

To move so far from their village was a great decision for Morgan and Martha, but Rhodri's offer was most tempting and unlikely to be made twice. Rhodri offered to take Morgan to see his property the following week, on the condition that neither he nor Martha spoke about it or his offer to anyone.

"Rhodri told us that many resented a man of humble origins rising so high, so he wanted everything to be settled before making it public. That was why we had not heard of his home, Plas Green, before. What he said made sense. Indeed, I knew there were those in Grey Mountain who would begrudge our good luck, so we agreed to keep quiet."

Morgan met Rhodri on foot at an agreed time and place, at a crossroads five miles from his village. Rhodri had a dragon and greeted Morgan in high spirits. Morgan climbed on board, and they set off.

Rhodri remained in a convivial mood until after they had landed. They landed in a forest clearing, seemingly far from anybody. Rhodri gave the excuse that he needed to relieve himself. Morgan suspected nothing and waited for Rhodri to return from behind the trees.

When Rhodri returned, he returned with a dozen other men and their dragons. He was no longer smiling. Morgan realised he had been fooled but could neither fight nor escape. He asked what was happening and was told to shut up and get back on the dragon. With no other choice available, he obeyed. They all flew off and remained silent until they landed at an isolated manor.

"They then told me I had been sold to the lord of that manor, a man called Bryn, and I was his to do what his pleased with. Lord Bryn wanted me to be his farrier but for no wages. All of his staff were slaves, not free peasants."

Morgan learned from the other slaves that Rhodri was Lord Madoc of Castle Malwarden, and one of the men who had been in the forest was Lord Lewis. They, and Lord Madoc's wife, ran a business, abducting and selling humans to order. People would tell one of the three what they were looking for, and they would source such a person, lure them away and sell them for a hefty price. Their names were whispered with dread, for they were renowned in the criminal underworld.

Morgan soon learned Lord Bryn was a cruel man and that he was living in a place a week's journey from Grey Mountain, within the Westlands but not in Malwarden lands. He despaired of ever seeing his family or his village again. There appeared to be no way out.

Lord Bryn was a cruel man, but fortunately also a careless one. Towards the end of July, he sent Morgan to the nearest farm to see a horse. Morgan left the manor and fled. He lived off the land, cautiously hiding from people and heading towards his home as best he could, for he had no exact idea where he was.

"As I got in sight of Grey Mountain, my heart sank, sir. If I returned there, Lord Madoc would know how to find me. He had likely already been there to look. I feared he would harm my family or friends if he thought they were hiding me. I did not dare believe he would see me as Lord Bryn's problem now I had escaped, for if I told the truth, he would be doomed. That's why I have been living in the forest for I do not know how many days or weeks now."

He sat back, exhausted from speaking for so long. I was thinking hard.

"Morgan, that is an incredible tale, and I believe you. Lord Madoc, Lord Lewis and Lady Nessa must be brought to justice, yet neither you nor anyone else must be harmed. You may stay in my rooms for now. Pray take a bath and borrow some of my clothes whilst yours are washed and mended. We are roughly the same height."

He thanked me profusely. I smiled, called for a servant and began to plot.

I found Ambrose and discreetly brought him to Morgan, who was now washed and clean-shaven. He was quite overcome to be in the presence of his monarch, but Ambrose put him at his ease and gently asked questions. We soon established where Lord Bryn's manor was.

A plan was formed, but we had to be so careful how we carried it out. I did not dismiss the women in Cerys's chamber but instead waited until we were in bed together that night before whispering in her ear. Ambrose informed Hawise in the same manner. The council was not due to meet for four days, and we did not bring the meeting forward. The wicked three living my castle must suspect nothing. The minimum number of servants waited on Morgan, and I ensured they were my most trusted servants.

I need not detail the reaction of the council when I told them everything Morgan had told me. I could only caution them to be as quiet as possible on the subject and stress the need to act quickly.

"By tomorrow morning, we can gather three dozen militiamen, who will attend the midday meal as guests of the castle. They will be needed in case Lord Madoc, Lord Lewis or Lady Nessa resist, or if their servants try to fight for the masters. The presence of as many guards would raise suspicion, and we need them to be calm until the last possible moment. The militia will have weapons hidden on them, and they will dress to blend in.

"I will get up once people have started eating and fetch Morgan. I will lead him to where Madoc is sitting and call him Rhodri. I shall introduce Morgan of Grey Mountain to him, and his reaction, and Lewis's and Nessa's, will prove their guilt. The three will be led away to the dungeons, and we will hold a trial as soon as possible. Once the three are safely locked away, a party will head to Lord Bryn's manner to arrest him and set his slaves free. Morgan has given me a good idea of where it is. We will try to find out who else has been sold and to whom and do what we can to liberate them."

The room buzzed with agreement. Ambrose went off that afternoon to discuss a minor matter of business with one Captain Llewelyn, a military man with whom he often worked closely. That night I told my wife what was to happen.

"How I wish I were recovered enough to eat in the Great Hall tomorrow," Cerys whispered. I could see her eyes glint with enthusiasm, even in the dark. "Still, the midwife says I should be up and about the day after tomorrow."

"Do not risk your health, my love. I will tell you everything, you know I always do. You will be able to attend the trial and see justice done, which is the most important thing. Their executions will make our land safer, and our neighbours'. It will send a clear message that this sort of trade will never be tolerated anywhere. People will remember tomorrow, 12th October, for the rest of their lives."

As it happened, the following day was memorable but in ways nobody could have foreseen.

CHAPTER THIRTY-THREE

Narrative continued by Lord Bran of Malwarden

We apprentices had the morning of the 12th off. Master Evan needed us to gather after the midday meal to practise hunting, but until then we were free to do as we pleased. Roisin and the other older girls went to read, the younger children played Hare and Hounds, and the older boys asked me if I wanted to join them over some happy herbs that one of them had recently got his hands on.

I declined. I needed a clear head for the afternoon, and I had plans for the morning. My training of the cats and hawks was not going as well as I had hoped, not nearly as well as I had hoped. The hawks would generally obey me, but I could not make them attack the targets I set up. Instead, they flew away or fought with each other, causing me to panic. The cats were even worse. I had succeeded in getting them to follow me, not chase the hawks, not flee from the hawks or squabble with each other, but nine times out of ten I would turn round and see them lolling in the sunshine or grooming each other instead of standing to attention.

Maybe everyone else was right. Maybe this is a pipe dream. Why should I succeed where others have had the sense not to try?

They probably did not try for a good reason. I can manage the birds as well as any other apprentice, and Master Evan often praises me. Must I be content with that?

As I made my way to where I would find my birds, I saw Jerome hurrying past, looking most anxious. I did not know him well. All I could say about him was that he sat on the council, where he acted as a clerk, and he was a widower without children. I could only wonder what had disturbed him.

Sometime later, I could not say exactly how long, I was busy trying to stop Gremlin from wandering off, when I saw Lord Madoc, Lord Lewis and Lady Nessa together. This was not an unusual sight, but their expressions and actions were. They all carried a bag, and they were walking very quickly, but they were not quite running. They looked terrified.

"Puss, come here. Gods know what they are doing, but it is not that interesting. Not as interesting as working with me, I promise."

Gremlin fluttered her wings, turned to me, and I led her, Magdalena and two less experienced hawks to a meadow far from the castle. Desdemona ignored the two younger birds flapping at each other, but it was hard work keeping Gremlin from batting them with her paws or Magdalena from intervening by pecking at them.

I had hoped to also train some other cats and a falcon, but they had been so uncooperative that I had had to leave them behind. The falcons behaved perfectly by themselves but not with the other birds, and the two other cats had a tendency to join in any mischief going.

I decided to see what the animals were like near water, it had proved to be a distraction in the past, and led them to a river that bordered the meadow. By the time I reached the water's edge, I noticed that all of my animals, apart from my faithful Desdemona, had vanished.

I cursed. It was going to be a challenge to round them up,

especially as this was not familiar territory for them. The temptation to explore was too much.

Desdemona and I flew for a little way down the river, Magdalena had always been particularly fascinated by water, but we saw Jerome before we saw any other creature. We froze. There was nothing obviously wrong, he was standing by a small boat, but his expression was almost as worried as it had been when I saw him earlier. He was clearly looking for someone, and it was not to give them a pleasant ride in his boat.

I began to direct Desdemona away from the water's edge, back up the meadow, when we heard voices. The voices belonged to Lady Nessa, Lord Lewis and Lord Madoc. The men called to Jerome.

"I said I would not let you down," he answered.

"Aye, you have been a good friend to us over the years," Lady Nessa said. "Without you informing us of council discussions, we would be looking death in the face by now."

Desdemona moved slowly away from them with my full support. Whatever they were talking about made no sense to me, but I knew I was in danger if they knew I had observed them. It was better to let them get away and then raise the alarm.

Something, I was never sure what, maybe a noise, maybe a movement, caught Lord Lewis's attention. He bellowed and pointed at us. Desdemona tried to accelerate away, but before I knew it, Jerome had pulled out a bow and arrow from the boat and shot her underneath me. She screamed as only dragons can scream and collapsed. Lord Lewis grabbed me and dragged me off her, pulling me to the river, cursing all the time.

"Let go of me," I demanded, trying to sound older than I was. "I don't care about your boat trip, why should you disturb me? Leave me alone, and I will leave you in peace."

They laughed. Desdemona tried to fly or run to me, but she was bleeding heavily from her side. The despair in her eyes mirrored mine.

"By the blood of the gods, you have killed her! You will hang for this. Let me go!" I was so appalled that I forgot I was in no position to make threats. My legs were as useless as ever, although I doubt many boys of sixteen could have fought off four adults, at least one of whom was armed.

They laughed again.

"Let you go?" Lord Madoc mocked me. "No, it's only your legs that are defective. You have heard and seen quite enough to go telling tales. Once we have drowned you, we will finish off your pet."

I screamed for help and tried to struggle, but it was no good. The two lords dragged me into the water. Within seconds, I was up to my waist.

"You won't get away with this. You will be stopped. You will not kill me. I won't let you!"

"Oh yes?" Jerome left the boat and waded towards us. "Who's going to stop us, then? You and whose army?"

"My army! The army who will go wherever I command. The army of your worst nightmares, for you always underestimated it."

"No, Bran," Nessa said. "We are your worst nightmare come true. You never thought we would dare kill you, but—"

Her voice cut off. There was a distinct sound which was growing louder. It sounded like the beating of wings. The four turned back to me, and the two lords dragged me to the middle of the river, where the water was the deepest and the current was the strongest.

I screamed in terror. I was so overcome that I did not realise that the others were also screaming. The two men suddenly let go of me. I opened my eyes and saw why.

My army had arrived.

Gremlin, the idlest cat in the civilised world, led a dozen other cats. Their furry wings beat furiously as they flew in a V formation. Coming from the other direction was Magdalena and all of my birds of prey. They also formed a V, heading determinedly towards us.

Now free of the lords' grip, I was able to swim using my arms and get back to the safety of dry land. I heard screams behind me but did not turn around until I was safe on the muddy shore. The animals were attacking the humans, scratching, pecking and biting, keeping them from leaving the water. Weighed down by layers of wet clothing and assaulted constantly, they saw their own watery graves.

I did not move. I could not quite believe what was happening.

"Bran!"

I turned and saw my Uncle Ambrose running towards me. He saw the scene ahead of us. Blood mixed with the river water, and the cries for help were becoming less frequent and weaker. Wounded, terrified faces and shivering hands appeared less and less often above the water.

I was torn as to what to do. They had just tried to murder me, but it was a horrific sight to see people drowning and with such injuries.

"What do we do?" I whimpered.

"We do nothing. As your uncle and as your king, I forbid you from going into the water. When they are definitely drowned, I will explain everything. In the meantime, do not call your army away. They do good work."

"Desdemona. She is dead? Let me go to her."

He permitted me to drag myself to her. Using my upper body alone, it was painful and exhausting, and my cold, wet clothes added to the strain. However, my uncle could not stop watching the river to help me. He had to be sure they were dead.

I reached her, my most faithful companion and bravest friend. She was not dead, but she was badly injured. She lay her head in my lap. Our tears mingled.

At last, my uncle joined us. He declared they were indeed dead.

"Uncle, Jerome was waiting for the other three in a boat. He said something about not letting them down. Lady Nessa told him that if he had not kept them informed about council discussions, they would be dead or looking death in the face, something like that. They saw me, shot Desdemona and tried to drown me. They told me it was because I had heard and seen enough to go telling tales. What was happening? We must take Desdemona to the animal doctor."

"I will fetch help immediately and explain later. Thank you, Bran. You and your unbelievable army have saved many lives."

CHAPTER THIRTY-FOUR

Narrative continued by Lord Owen of Malwarden

The flight of Nessa, Lewis and Madoc was a shock. How their flight ended and the discovery of Jerome's treachery were even greater shocks. Bran was quite the hero of the hour. At first we could not believe that his band of cats and birds had done what even he thought they could not do. Fortunately, Desdemona's injuries proved to be superficial, and she was set to make a good recovery.

I introduced Morgan of Grey Mountain to the rest of the castle. His being hidden away so successfully was only another surprise to them after a series of surprises. We also told those who did not know the tale of Lewis, Nessa, Madoc and Jerome, careful to exonerate Clementia and the children. Morgan and a party of militiamen, headed by Ambrose, went to Lord Bryn's manor to free those still enslaved. I made the shorter journey to Grey Mountain to tell Morgan's family that he was alive and would soon return to them.

I quickly found Peter the Miller and his wife Isolde. She went to fetch her daughter-in-law Martha, and their joy brought tears to my eyes.

The expedition to the manor was successful. Dozens were freed, and Lord Bryn was brought to trial. As Ambrose began the investigation into who else might have been sold and to whom, I returned to Grey Mountain to see how Morgan fared and to see if he or any other villager could help with the investigation.

The first person I met whom I recognised was Martha, who was talking to a man who looked vaguely familiar. His clothes indicated that he was lowborn but not poor, yet I was sure I had seen him in very different clothes and in grander surroundings.

Martha appeared unsure as to how to introduce the man. He stepped in and introduced himself as Henry of Merendysh, a distant kinsman of hers. This was a surprise, his accent was nothing like I would have expected from a man from any part of the Merendysh lands, but I said nothing. I met with Morgan and was pleased to see he was doing well. He and Martha were able to answer my questions, which gave me a better idea of the extent of the trafficking of humans that had gone on.

Henry of Merendysh followed me as I made to leave the village.

"I know you know me, sir," he said.

Now I was puzzled.

"You look very familiar." I played for time.

He laughed.

"Come now. You are a poor liar, Lord Owen. You know the High Priest when you see him, and you can deduce when he is visiting his bastard daughter."

"Your Holiness, I don't know what to say."

That was certainly true. He quickly took charge of the situation.

"Look, you have saved my son-in-law and ended my daughter's torment. You have been instrumental in ending a reign of cruelty. I should like to give you a reward. Call it a reward, call it a bribe for swearing on your life not to breathe a word to anyone about my connection to Martha, call it what you like. You may name anything you like that is in my power to grant, and I will give it to you."

An idea hit me like lightning.

"Your Holiness, I swear to forget ever meeting you, if you can do one thing. I don't want money, gold, land or a new title. All I want is this..."

CHAPTER THIRTY-FIVE

Narrative continued by Bessy the Nun

It was customary in most convents and monasteries to sew outfits for the needy three times a year. The Convent of the New Moon was no exception, and as the end of October approached, it was time to start considering winter clothes for those who did not have the means with which to acquire them.

This was also the only time we would try on civilian clothes whilst still alive, for we each put together an outfit and tacked the seams together. We did not finish the stitching or add darts so the clothes could be more easily altered for their eventual owners.

At around this time, we learned that the centuries-old sumptuary laws had been abolished. A few of our items were made out of silk and velvet, forbidden to those not of noble or royal blood. The lower-born nuns and novices had refused to try on any outfits containing these fabrics, such was the power of the sumptuary laws. Now all fabrics were permitted to all who could afford them, some of them gleefully posed in silk petticoats and velvet gowns, stroking the fabrics with their fingers and posing in front of the looking glass. The other lowborn nuns still did not dare touch these materials any more than was strictly necessary. (Sister Agnes was absent from the convent, of course.)

Idelinde had made a kirtle out of heavy purple-coloured silk. As a merchant's daughter, she had been used to having many material possessions but certain luxuries were forbidden to her. It gladdened my heart to see her stroke the rich fabric and twirl about in it.

"It suits you," I dared say.

Sister Maude said she did not like wearing civilian clothes, however briefly, because they reminded her of what she would be burned in. She then described an outfit they had sewn the previous autumn for a nun who died.

"She was the widow of a master craftsman, so we dressed her finely but not too finely. She had light brown skin and dark brown hair, so we chose a primrose-coloured gown and a red cloak. I made the cloak, and I was mighty proud of it. It was the colour of rosehips and fitted to a nicety."

Later that day Idelinde was called over to our neighbouring monastery, where Gethin, Brother Percy and Brother Harold had gone to make men's clothing. She came back looking terrified.

"What is it?" I asked as soon as I could get her alone.

She burst into tears, and I held her for some time, one ear listening for Sister Agnes, who was not due to return to the convent until the following day, but we could never be too careful.

"Bessy, you must be brave. I went to the monastery as planned. I did not see anyone we know apart from Brother Harold. He did not see me, and he carried on talking with another monk, whom he called Brother Rickynd.

"Brother Rickynd appeared to be in charge of sewing outfits for the needy at the monastery. Brother Harold told him to make sure the outfits modelled on Brother Gethin and Brother Percy were ready by tomorrow."

I could not see why this upset her, but she continued in the same fast whisper.

"Brother Rickynd described putting darts into the breeches and jackets. He asked something that I did not catch, and I distinctly heard Brother Harold say, 'They just need to be outfits suitable to their ranks before they took their vows and suited to the time of year. Never mind if it suits their persons or their tastes.' Brother Rickynd asked if it would go ahead. Brother Harold replied something along the lines of no questions having being asked yet, but anyone could guess their answers. He then talked about a second shirt, pair of under-breeches and stockings, and the men moved away.

"Bessy, we both know what this means. Our friend and good Brother Percy will be executed! These outfits are what they will be burned in."

I was stunned but not quite despairing.

"No. No, that cannot be. They have not been tried, let alone been found guilty of anything which carries the death penalty. The High Priest rebuffed Sister Agnes's suggestion that monastics be punished retrospectively or that their families be punished for their crimes. Other men clearly need these outfits urgently, that's all."

"Then why refer to the clothes as needing to be suitable to their ranks before they took their vows? Why sew them so they fit them properly and not another pair of men, who will not have identical measurements? Most of all, why talk about knowing the answers to questions that have yet to be asked? He referred to a show trial without naming it."

"Why talk of a second shirt and so forth if they are to be executed?" I knew I was grasping at straws.

"Brother Harold might not have been referring to them when he mentioned those clothes. Didn't we all make up more than one pair of drawers and shift each but only one kirtle or gown? They are quicker to make, and they need changing more often."

I sat in stunned silence. Whatever was going on was going to be awful, yet neither of us could quite work out what it might be.

Someone must be planning their executions not their murders, for no murder victim has an outfit ready for cremation. They will certainly be set up and a show trial will take place. Oh Goddess, what can I do? Must I say nothing whilst two innocent men die?

Neither Idelinde nor I could keep our feelings hidden that evening. Fortunately, all three monks and Sister Agnes were not expected back until the following morning. It was hard enough to not tell the other curious nuns and novices everything.

I barely slept that night. I could not eat any breakfast. Once in the infirmary, I could not work. I sat down and stared at the wall with gritty eyes.

A knock on the door startled me. Sister Ida poked her head around it.

"Sister Bessy, Sister Agnes has told us we must gather in the refectory immediately. She has something very important to say."

How I walked there I do not know. The walls were spinning, and I could not speak.

The three monks were also present. I could not look at them. I stared at the floor whilst Sister Agnes announced her first piece of news. She and the monks would leave us in either November or December. Their work was done, and a permanent abbess would be appointed.

"My second piece of news may affect some of you more than others."

I closed my eyes.

"The High Priest has made an unexpected announcement. All monastics who have taken their final vows are to be given a year and a day, from today, during which they may leave their orders, without penalty. Without penalty in this life, at least. He feels that the recent changes in monasteries and convents are so great that those who took their vows some time ago, might have believed they were committing to a different sort of life. Therefore, he wishes to release those who did not realise what they were agreeing to." She did not bother to hide her disapproval. "Those who choose to leave will be given a set of clothes appropriate to their station in life before forsaking the civilian world, a change of linen and enough money to live on for a month. Those who leave may also apply for a character, should they wish to seek employment."

I could scarcely believe what I was hearing.

"Those who wish to think about...leaving may come and find me later this morning." She made to dismiss us, but Gethin and Brother Percy both immediately stood up.

"Reverend Mother, we will leave!"

Chapter Thirty-Six

Narrative continued by Gethin the Monk

Once Brother Percy and I had announced our intention to return to the civilian world, events moved very quickly. Brother Harold handed us the clothes we had sewn with a look in his eye that suggested he had expected no better from us. Sister Agnes gave each of us a purse of money and requested that we leave straight after breakfast the following morning. She also handed me an official-looking document and a second purse.

Feeling very curious, I opened the document. It was a diplomatic passport, written by Lord Owen of Malwarden and authorised by King Ambrose III of the Westlands. Owen had enclosed a note requesting that I come to his castle as soon as I could. The money in the purse was enough with which to buy a dragon.

I turned to Sister Agnes, feeling very puzzled indeed.

"May I ask when you received this?"

"Exactly seven days ago, but the gold sprite who brought it also had a message for me. Lord Owen did not wish me to pass it to you until this morning."

"But...how could he or Ambrose know that I would be able to

come home? When did the High Priest announce that monastics may return to the world?"

"He made the announcement four days ago, and every abbot and abbess was informed three days ago. A massive flock of gold sprites was sent out so every religious house received the news on the same day. We were ordered to tell our brothers and sisters this morning."

"When were civilians told?"

"Monarchs were informed this morning. How they spread the information is up to them."

"Then how did Ambrose or Owen know more than a week ago that I would be able to come home?"

Nobody could answer that.

Brother Percy and I went to Landesmar that afternoon to buy a few things which we would need for our new lives. I also bought a bright orange dragon called Clarence. Brother Percy intended to go to his cousin who owned a farm some thirty miles away.

"We've stayed in touch over the years, and I know that if he cannot find work for me on his farm, he will not mind me staying with him until I can find something. Goddess, brother, I cannot believe it. We are finally free. It is as though an angel has whispered into the High Priest's ear."

"I know. I cannot think what has brought this about."

Did Owen or Ambrose meet with the High Priest? How could they? The High Priest's visits to any castle are rare, planned far in advance and always made much of. It looks like Owen knows more than Ambrose about the matter or has had more influence in it, but even if he knew the High Priest well, how could he bring about such a change in church matters?

"You are in a daze, brother."

"I just can't quite believe our luck."

We said goodbye to those we knew in the village. On returning to the convent, we had further farewells to make.

I knew I would particularly miss Sister Bessy, and we shed some tears.

"Will you also leave?" I asked her.

"No, I still believe this is the right place for me."

"You give up all hope of freedom by staying here, all hope of love."

"I still feel this convent is where I belong. I will miss you, brother. I cannot drop that title just yet, the habit is too strong. I suppose you leave for the Westlands straight after breakfast tomorrow?"

"Yes. Tell me, did your friend Queen Hawise tell you about this? About my getting a passport or about the High Priest's decision?"

She shook her head.

"No. I was as amazed as you were. I received a letter from Hawise yesterday morning, and she mentioned nothing about this. Because we write in code, I know she would have written about this, had she known. She knows only I can read whatever she writes."

That evening we had a ceremony of sorts. Brother Percy and I entered the chapel dressed in civilian clothes. We knelt at the altar, placed our necklaces with the pentacles on it, and bowed reverently. We signed a document to state we dissolved our vows, and we dissolved them of our own free will. Sister Agnes led prayers for our welfare with a face more suited to smelling rotten meat.

Nothing she or Brother Harold might do could affect me now.

We bade our final farewells early the following morning. Brother Percy and I agreed to keep in touch. I felt confident giving him the address of Castle Malwarden, although I still could not work out what had happened to bring about this extraordinary chain of events. Clarence the dragon and I headed west.

It was a cold, clear afternoon when we arrived at the castle. I felt nervous as soon as I saw the massive building. I still expected to face castration or some other penalty. A servant, a woman I did not recognise, approached me when I landed.

"Are you Gethin of Pendroch, once Gethin the Monk?"

"Yes, I am."

"Lord Owen begs to see you immediately. Will you follow me, sir? Someone will take care of your dragon."

I agreed, and she led me to a small room. I noticed how she was careful we were not seen and wondered what was happening now. Had I been lured here on false pretences?

The servant begged me to wait and said she would fetch her lord as quickly as possible. She returned with him within minutes, then left us alone.

I bowed.

"Owen...I don't know what to say. As you can guess, I received your money and the passport, and I came here as soon as I could. But how did you know I would be able to do so?"

He shook his ginger head, tears filling his eyes.

"Gethin, I will never be able to tell you the whole truth. Nor will Ambrose, but he knows little more than you, he merely authorised your passport. All I can say is that I hope I can finally put right what I so foolishly and arrogantly destroyed over seventeen years ago. I apologise. You said you forgave me years ago, but now I can finally bring you and Marjory back together."

"I may stay here then? Stay with her and our children? Marry her even?"

"Of course. Let me take you to her now."

We made our way up a staircase. I tried to ask him more questions about just what he had done, but he would not answer. Eventually we reached where Marjory worked. He put his ear to the door.

"She is with someone. I will knock. Pray move back. She should be alone when you meet."

He knocked, she called out, and he entered. There was a brief conversation and two men left the room, agreeing to return later. They left the door ajar, and I heard Owen speak. He was now crying.

"Marjory. You were kind enough to forgive me for parting you and Gethin so many years ago. I apologise again and can finally put right what I did wrong. He is here, here now in the castle."

The woman I had loved for so long replied in a puzzled voice.

"That is not possible. If he comes here, he risks terrible penalties. Besides, his superiors would never let him. No, this cannot be real."

"It is real, Marjory. This is not a dream. Indeed, your nightmare is over. I am just so sorry that I ever brought it about in the first place."

I opened the door and entered the room. Owen tactfully left us. The colour drained from her face, her eyes widened, and her mouth fell open.

"Gods...Gethin, you are here and here in civilian clothes. Is this real? Are you about to be executed?"

I strode forward and grabbed her cold hands.

"Yes and no, my love. This is no dream, and nobody is going to kill me. I used to tell you that I would come for you one day, as soon as I could, I would. Now that day has come. I will marry you, we will live here, and we will never be parted again."

CHAPTER THIRTY-SEVEN

Narrative closed by Bessy the Nun

Sister Justiniana took over as Abbess of the Convent of the New Moon on 7th December 2017. By this time, I had received many letters.

Percy was happily working on his cousin's farm. Lord Bran's army of animals had attracted considerable attention, and he focused his time on training them, although he was coming to the conclusion that cats do not stir themselves until they absolutely have to. Lady Jane had safely returned to Castle Malwarden and was relatively unaffected by her parents' deaths. She remained devoted to her Aunt Clementia, who was doing well, although she was unlikely to ever fully recover her health. Roisin had made friends and was far from the unpleasant girl I once knew. The investigation into the buying and selling of humans was surpassing everyone's expectations, and many people were being reunited with their loved ones or brought to justice.

Gethin and Lady Marjory married as soon as they could after he returned. Hawise described their wedding in glowing terms. She and Lady Marjory were never going to be close, but she could still cry for joy at her wedding. Lord Owen had clearly had a hand in bringing it about, but he refused to answer any questions. Hawise wrote that King Ambrose knew little more than she did, but they were both content to let matters lie.

Sister Justiniana called every nun and novice in the convent to meet with her alone shortly after her arrival. We now had three new novices, and nobody had left the convent apart from Gethin and Percy. People objected to Sister Agnes and Brother Harold's rule of terror, rather than monastic life itself. I approved of Sister Justiniana already, and I believed I would soon grow to respect her.

Our meeting encouraged this belief. She showed herself to be a wise and humane woman, who was genuinely concerned for those in her charge.

She concluded our meeting by asking me three questions that she said she asked every nun and novice.

"Are you completely sure this is the right place for you? Do you feel this is what the gods intended to be your path in life? One cannot expect uninterrupted joy in a monastic life, but do you generally feel content?"

My reply was sincere but not entirely honest.

"Reverend Mother, I am completely sure this convent is the right place for me. Here, I feel joy and contentment that I know I would never feel anywhere else. Here, I may be useful in the infirmary, praise the gods and love every inhabitant as my conscience and heart dictate."

THE END

About the Author

Ruth Danes has enjoyed both history and fiction since her childhood, and she has lived in four different countries. These interests and experiences inspired her to write the *Life on Another Island* series, which is set in a world where many characters unexpectedly start new lives in foreign, sometimes seemingly hostile, lands.

Ruth has also written a thriller, *The Flower and the Wolf.*

All five books are published by Rogue Phoenix Press.

Her latest work is a new alternate history series called *The Woldsheart Chronicles*, which is published by Next Chapter. The series opens with *The Deadly Favour* and the second book is *Another Green and Pleasant Land*. Ruth has plans for a third book in the series.

Ruth Danes lives in the heart of England. When she is not busy with her imaginary friends, she likes to dance, travel and walk in the countryside with good companions.

———

To learn more about Ruth Danes and discover more Next Chapter authors, visit our website at www.nextchapter.pub.

The Deadly Favour
ISBN: 978-4-82414-461-4

Published by
Next Chapter
2-5-6 SANNO
SANNO BRIDGE
143-0023 Ota-Ku, Tokyo
+818035793528

20th July 2022

Lightning Source UK Ltd.
Milton Keynes UK
UKHW010244090223
416650UK00002B/646

9 784824 144614